Allie McCrae
and the
West Point Half-Blood

Tom J. Abbott

**Roots &
Branches**

Denton, Texas

Roots & Branches
An imprint of AWOC.COM Publishing
P.O. Box 2819
Denton, TX 76202

ISBN: 978-1-62016-149-4 Paperback
ISBN: 978-1-62016-086-2 Ebook

Chapter 1

Ireland 1847

"It should a been me God be takin'."

Allie had slept all night by her side and dreamed she'd be well by morning. But when the sun rose, he sat up in a sick panic. He touched her limp hand, her cold skin.

"It can't be. Bernadette, ye needed me, and I didn't help ye."

He wanted to hold her close, kiss her once more. He brushed back soft brown curls from her forehead and couldn't tear his gaze from her face.

After sitting in a chair for untold hours, Allie was vaguely aware of hammer against nail. He turned at a gentle touch on his shoulder.

"Come, Allie, it is time. I will fetch a shovel and help ye."

He glanced up at his father. "No. I'll be burying me own wife. Thank ye all the same."

"Then I will make the cross. There is more wood in the shed."

"Allie," his mother said, "I have prepared Bernadette. Let me know when you're ready."

Allie drifted outside and noted the early morning sun hiding behind the clouds, leaving the world in shadow. He noted two large elm trees that spread their branches to cast shade over the grave on a sunny day.

"Aye, this is the spot." He reached for the shovel and talked as he lifted the earth. "She helped nurse the sick. The Byrnes, the O'Flahertys, until she became ill herself. But why her? 'Tis not fair."

Almost finished, Allie plunged the shovel once more into the soil until it struck a large rock, snapping the handle. He tossed it aside and dropped to his knees. He gasped air as he scraped out the dirt with his hands. "She was so young. Never had a chance to live a life. I wanted to give her so much more. We would've found it, together." Wiping his sleeve across his eyes, he determined not to cry.

His father returned with the coffin he had made. He laid the cross by Allie's side. "This will be fine."

"Father, what are we to do now?"

The man's broad shoulders sagged. "The blight is already widespread. We can wait until all the plants die and then replant, but only if we're still living. But we wouldn't have seed potatoes." He gazed across the sad bare land, once part of the green shamrock hills of Ireland. "I hoped it would not spread from the west, but..." He shrugged. "We can't grow back any more than the broken limb on that tree over there."

Allie refused to think of the futility of it all—he always believed their lives would be beautiful. "I am ready. I will bring Bernadette." He went into the house and lifted her from the bed. How light she is, he thought. No more than a feather. He carried her outside in a sheet his mother had draped around her and placed her in the coffin, then lowered it into the ground.

With the broken shovelhead, he scooped the dirt into the grave. As each piece fell, his heart wept. When finished, he smoothed the surface, imagining flowers surrounding it.

"But why should God-fearing people of Irish soil have to abide such a famine? Can anyone tell me that?"

His mother, her blue eyes glistening, said, "Son, there is no answer. We must do the best we can."

Allie found a flat stone from the yard. With a nail, he etched her name as deep as he could into its porous surface: *Bernadette McCrae, me heart, 1830-1847.*

During the next few weeks, his mother and father joined Bernadette under the earth. Allie wondered if he might soon be next. *Who will bury me? Who would care?*

The potato crops melted away. Allie heard of the thousands succumbing to malnutrition, scurvy, and even suicide, which would be between them and their God.

Allie survived with the storage of dried potato tubers and potato flour his mother had deposited in small sacks. He ate the stale tubers day after day and grew tired of the bitter taste of the remaining turnips he pulled from the ground. Perhaps if Bernadette were here to cook them... How could he survive without food? Without her?

One afternoon while hoeing weeds and wondering why it mattered, he stopped for a rest and a drink of water from the well. As he drank from the dipper, he sighted a rider approaching down the narrow gravel lane. The man sat erect in the saddle, and Allie couldn't help notice the healthy bearing of the horse. All the horses he'd seen the last few months were malnourished with eyes deadened, just like the people riding them.

"Who can that be?" he asked no one, taking a couple steps for a better view.

"Allie? Aloysius McCrae? Is that ye?" the voice called.

As the horseman drew closer, Allie tossed down his hoe and closed the distance. "Mister Nicholl!"

Nicholl, tall and with a short dark beard, was one of the few men in eastern Ireland who still had any money. A long-time friend of the McCraes, he had a livelihood other than potato farming. He lived in Town Wicklow, only two hours from the McCrae farm.

The man dismounted and clasped Allie about the shoulders. "I worried about ye, lad. What of your family?"

Allie couldn't speak.

"Lad, what is it?"

"Th-they're dead. Me wife... me parents. All dead, sir." He twisted his cap in his hands.

"I guess God has his reasons," Mr. Nicholl said.

"I've tried to think, but I just don't know what they are." Allie looked away.

The two walked down the dirt path toward the whitewashed cottage, the older man's arm on Allie's.

"I'm sorry, sir. I have no proper food to offer ye, unless ye'd like some water?"

"No, no. I don't need a thing. Just tell me what happened."

"We can sit by the door." Allie picked up a wooden stool for his friend and tapped it to shake off the dust. As they sat, Allie related the tragedy.

"I know it is no comfort to ye now, but no matter how bad it is for us in County Wicklow, the rest of Ireland has it worse. People lie dead of disease and starvation by the side of the road, no one to look after them."

"I had heard, but I dinna know if it was true."

"Ye can't stay here, lad. Ye must come with me."

Allie stared down at the ground. "I, I don't want your charity, Mr. Nicholl."

"I not be offering it, Allie. The country suffers, that's true, but I raise jumping horses, not potatoes. I need help with their care.

"But don't ye see, this is me home. And me family's buried here."

"Listen to me, lad. Your parents and Bernadette, they would want what's best. There is nothing here for ye. And if ye stay here, ye'll die too. Believe it."

"It's difficult even to think about."

"Allie, I have connections. I will get your property sold for ye. Your father was lucky to have owned it in the first place, but there are English landowners who will want it for when times are better. In the meantime, ye can come with me to Wicklow."

This kind of offer had never occurred to Allie, although he had wondered what his plans would be if he lived. He gazed into space, thinking of how he'd answer.

"Ye see, Allie, I have only meself and one rider, Jeremy. But he accompanied me last jumper to England and some sickness took hold of him. In the meantime, I need a rider to take his place until he returns, and even then, ye could stay. I really do need your help."

Allie searched his dulled mind and accepted the offer. He had nurtured the sickened land as long as he could, for no reason other than sentiment in what it had meant to his father and his father before him.

"Sir, there are a few things I must do first. Please go on, and I will walk. 'Tis not that far."

"Very well, lad. Mrs. Nicholl and I will be expecting ye." He mounted his horse and waved goodbye.

Before Allie left, he dug up his father's gold watch, which he'd buried in a crock for safekeeping. Destitute Irish could make use of such a treasure, and he had heard of how robbers traveled through the county. He gathered up one last bag of potato flour and the bread he had made the day before.

After filling another sack with what was left of the turnips, he started outside then stopped. He knew it wouldn't take long for thieves to strip the house of its furnishings—anything they could sell for food. "But there is one thing they will not take," Allie promised aloud.

He laid his things on the table and opened the cupboard door, glancing at one shelf after another. *But where is it?* Then he spied the little blue cream pitcher, which had belonged to his grandmother. His mother gave it to Bernadette for a wedding present.

Allie wrapped the delicate pitcher in a pillowslip and tucked it into the lower part of his straw satchel, hoping fine luck was with him and it wouldn't get broken.

There was one more thing left to do. He walked to the small graveyard and said a reluctant farewell to his parents. Silent for a moment, he glanced back at the thatch-roofed house for the last time, and then sat by his wife's grave next to an elm tree.

"Where do I begin, Bernadette? It's not that I want to leave ye, ye know that. I guess I thought we'd never part. And I'm a little tired. No, no, I'm not sick—just weary." He sat alone with his thoughts, gazing at the clear, sad sky, and bowed his head on his knees. For the first time since the day he'd buried her, he allowed himself to sob.

When his tears subsided, he stared at her grave, wiping off the stone bearing her name. "Ye have all my tears now. I vow I will never cry again... It's in me heart ye'll forever stay." He leaned over and kissed the stone. "Goodbye, *grá mo chroí.*"

Allie picked up his belongings, left the only home he had ever known and headed for Wicklow Town.

Chapter 2

Allie's heart skipped a beat when he rounded the curved road and spied the Nicholl's house, so much larger than his family's cottage. The neat dwelling, with ivy covering much of the entry wall, stood at the edge of town on the road from Ashford.

He moved at a faster pace, as it was late in the afternoon. When he arrived at the house, he noticed a missing stone from the walkway and weeds that needed cutting. He thought he could help tidy up the place a bit—the least he could do in return for his friend's kindness.

Allie stood on the steps a moment to dust himself off. He removed his cap before rapping on the door.

Mrs. Nicholl opened it and with a sparkle in her eyes, said, "Allie, come in this minute. We were worried ye might not get here today." She fluttered around, took him by the hand. "Let me show ye where ye'll be sleeping, and ye can put your things away. And there's a press for your clothes."

"It's good to be here, Mrs. Nicholl. It's been a long time." Allie didn't have many clothes to put in the press. He emptied his satchel, except for his father's watch and Bernadette's little cream pitcher. He then set the satchel in the corner and went into the kitchen.

Mr. Nicholl entered from the backdoor. With a big grin, he said, "Ah, ye made it, lad. I can see ye have met Sarah. If you're ready, I will show ye the horses."

Allie, full of anticipation, gave the food sacks to Mrs. Nicholl. He hurried on and followed her husband outside. The prospects of working with the horses gave him a goal—a reason for living. Allie could ride, but he knew little about jumping horses.

They strolled down the path to the stables, where Nicholl showed him around. "First, ye must let the horses get used to your scent. Darcy, over there, is well on his way to England, but a couple need more work."

Allie peered into the stalls, completely impressed by the four horses.

"Ye may think faster than they do, me boy, but they're quick learners. That makes them easy to train. After ye get the hang of it, just give them time to think about what ye want."

Allie leaned over a stall gate and stroked the nose of a dark red mare. "This one's a beauty. Must be 16 or so hands, isn't she, sir?"

"A bit more. 16.1. Her name's Starlight. I believe the sky's the limit and she's light on her feet. I call her Star and haven't had her long. A mare hasn't won the Aintree Grand National since 1841." He shook his head and smiled. "It would be so fine to have Star win."

Allie liked the origin of her name. "I can already tell I'm going to like this. But I guess I'm ready to be trained meself, sir."

We'll get to it first thing in the morning. I'll show ye the others then. For now, let us eat. It's too late to start today. There's a nice room waiting for ye, lad, so after supper get a good night's sleep."

Allie ate well and slept well. He longed for Bernadette to be by his side. His thoughts of her were interrupted only by visions of himself taking horses over hurdles and wondering what the future might bring.

~~~

"That was sure a grand breakfast, Mrs. Nicholl. It started the day off right, it did."

"I'm glad it was to your liking, Allie." She rose, reached for her apron and began clearing the table.

"All right, lad," her husband said, pushing back his chair. "Let's see what we can set up for the rest of the day."

As they headed toward the stables, questions filled Allie's mind, but he hesitated to ask. Finally, "Sir, if ye don't object to telling me, how is it ye can grow crops? And what's more, I even had milk this morning. We gave up our cow a long time ago. I know it's none of me business, but—"

"No, I don't mind your questions. I thank God our circumstances are as they are. Ye see, me mother is English, and me cousin in England actually owns this land. Because of that, I can fish in the sea with no quota and grow grain for the horses. Corn, too, and Sarah makes yellow corn soup for supper a couple times a week. We don't eat like kings."

"Ye aren't Catholic, are ye, sir? Me family is, and I know we're frowned upon."

"No, Protestant, and being English meself, that's the help in it, too."

Allie said no more about it. He knew it had no bearing on anything now.

After a few more steps toward the stable, Nicholl opened the gate. "Now, I'll show ye me pride and joy." He led out a sleek brown stallion. "I like a horse with a sloped shoulder and muscled hindquarters, just like him."

"He's sure a beautiful horse."

"Yes, he is that, just short of 16.4 hands, and he will be the next jumper to leave. I'll hate to give up Darcy. Ye see, I find the horses, give them a start-off, and then me cousin takes them from there." He turned back to Allie. "I remember when ye were a young boy and your father brought ye to watch us train. I wonder if ye recall any of what ye learned?"

"I was only nine, but I have memory pictures."

"Then I'll refresh those pictures a mite." He stroked Darcy's ears. This horse is special. He has all it takes—deep chest and long neck. A superior jumper. No better legs will ye find."

"But are there people who still raise horses, besides you? I'd heard there are very few now."

"Aye, other people were not so blessed. Sometimes I feel a bit guilty, but we accept the advantage. Draught horses have declined, but more than that, people had no means to keep them. They couldn't even register them, couldn't afford doctors. Many fine horses went to the slaughterhouse."

Allie stood on the other side of Darcy and was itching to get started. "Might I sit on him, sir? To get the feel of being on a horse. It's been a while since we had to sell ours."

"I'd say walk around with him a while. Wait a day or two. Get acquainted first." He patted Allie on the shoulder. "The hurdles are behind the stable. Come, we'll walk around back."

Allie's mind was taken for a moment by the water. "I guess I've forgotten how near ye are to the sea. I didn't remember how big it is." He then turned to see hurdles lined up on one side and hedges for jumping spaced apart as the area spread out. "When do I start?"

"Ye can begin with Star, but not to mount for a while yet. Ye must learn the steps, one at a time. Walking her comes first, so she will know ye are a friend, and every day the same, two to four times."

Allie made an effort to conceal his disappointment. "I figured I'd just climb on and the horse would know what to do. I must not have learned much when I was nine."

Nicholl grinned. "There's much more to it, me boy. First, we lay down a pole and the two of ye walk over it together. Everything is slow. And be sure to brag on her. In that way, a horse is like a sheep dog. Let him know he's done a good job, and he'll be for doing it again. Come, let us get the poles."

They returned to the stable where Nicholl reached for four poles in holders on the wall.

"We will put down more as we move along. Simply walk your horse over them but only one pole first. Remember now, never hurry. The horse knows the poles are there, but soon enough they won't bother her."

Allie followed him. "But how long does this go on?"

"Oh, it will take a few days. On the fourth, ye mount her and walk over the poles. Then ye lead her, so she can trot over them alone. Day by day, she will grow into it. Then raise the pole about six inches onto the bar, and with a few days in between, follow the same procedure before ye raise the pole again.

"I can see there can be no short cuts." Allie felt as if he had absorbed a lot in a matter of minutes. "Understanding it and doing it are two different things, but I'll do me best."

"Then it's time the two of ye become friends." He brought out Star, having bridled her. Her eyes shone alert as she looked right at Allie, a stranger.

He planned to change that. He moved close and put out his hand to her muzzle but didn't touch her. Star nosed his fingers and appeared to make a connection. At least, Allie thought she did.

"All right, me boy, she's all yours for now."

Allie reached for the reins and began to walk, aware of a spring in his step.

~~~

Realizing the weeds hadn't stopped growing, Allie decided he'd take care of them right after he finished for the day. "Sir, I was wondering, since I don't get so much exercise with Star, so far...I mean real exercise...and if ye have a mind to let me, I'd be glad to cut down some of that crop out there ye probably didn't invite."

Nicholl laughed. "The weeds, Allie? I know, it's the lacking of time, or I'd have taken care of them meself. You're welcome to it, but only if it suits ye."

Allie found a hoe in the stable and started in on the weeds. He had pride in his work, and he'd also found a replacement for the missing stone in the walkway.

The first week seemed slow to him but midway into the second, Star graduated to the first six inches and was ready for the next height increase. She had given Allie full cooperation, and they each seemed to know the thoughts of the other. He loved the horse and had followed the instructions of never jumping with her when he was alone.

Under the direction of his friend, who was an excellent rider himself, Allie helped train the other two horses, Aherne and Dazzler. They were coming along, but he had grown very fond of Darcy.

"I knew ye'd take to Darcy, Allie."

One evening when they had finished the day, Mr. Nicholl said, "After supper, I have something for us." Later, he brought out a chessboard. "I tell ye, chess I learned when I was about your age. It was the prime interest of those who had the time."

"Time is what I need to get the catch of it, but thinking never did me harm."

After spending the better part of the evening playing, Mr. Nicholl stretched back a bit. "Does it suit ye to call it a night, Allie? We can have another go at it tomorrow."

"Suits me, sir, but I did enjoy learning the game. I hope I get better at it."

~~~

Allie crawled into bed and soon fell asleep. He awoke when rain struck the window, followed by a clash of thunder roaring across the sky. His first thought was of the horses, and he didn't know how they would react to the sounds. He jumped out of bed and threw on his clothes, not wanting to wake the Nicholls if all was well.

Lighting a lantern, Allie headed for the stables. The outer gate was ajar. He couldn't remember if he was the last one to leave the evening before. He'd be certain next time.

He entered the stable and a noticed a barrel turned over, its grain spilled. Of a sudden, his nerve endings tingled. He hurried toward the first stall, which was Star's. The gate stood open. She was gone.

Allie could scarcely get to the house fast enough. "Mr. Nicholl," Allie shouted. "Star isn't here!" He reached the back porch as Nicholl stepped out the door.

"What is it, Allie? What about Star?"

Allie gasped. "I don't know, sir. She isn't in her stall. It was open and the outside gate was undone. I didn't see her anywhere, but the others are there."

"I'll be right with ye." He half-dressed and buttoned his shirt on the way to the stable. "Did ye fasten the stall as well as the outside gate when ye came in last night?"

"I'm sure I did. I remember, because I caught me finger in the strap." Allie wiped the sweat from his brow. *Saints above. She can't be gone. She can't.*

Nicholl glanced toward the other horses. "All right, if the gate was locked...if you're sure, Allie...someone must have taken her. If anything bothers the horses, I can always hear them, but I admit I was a mite tired last night and slept soundly. I was barely aware of the thunder."

Allie glanced at the ground just outside the gate, where a clearing opened toward the trees. The shoreline was over a hundred yards away as the land slanted down to the sea.

"I don't know if Star's been with me long enough to know this is her home, but it surely looks like she dinna want to leave out of it. Her hoof prints are all scuffled."

"What do ye make of it, sir? Is there more than one takin' her away?"

"I think two took part in it. The prints do show that. I'll get me rifle back at the house."

Almost in an instant, Allie heard the door close shut, with Sarah's cautioning voice following her husband. "Aidan, take care with ye. I will worry!"

By the time Nicholl returned with the rifle, Allie had grabbed a rope from a hook and wrapped it three times around his waist, for tying up the thieves. He then reached for the hoe leaning against the wall. *When we catch the thieves, this might very well come in handy.*

Chapter 3

Allie studied the tracks. "Ye know, sir, these tracks came after it rained."

"Which means what, Allie?"

"That's just it. It didn't rain long, and that's what woke me up, that and the thunder. So if they took Star after the rain, they mightna be too far gone. We have a chance at finding them."

"Then we best have a try at it, me boy. The traces lead toward the trees to the north. If ye will, carry the light." Already, slender fingers of dawn pierced the clouds.

Allie carried the lantern in one hand and his makeshift weapon in the other. Not being familiar with the area, he stayed close to his companion as they advanced. Would Star sense they were following her, Allie wondered.

They moved in silence.

"There's barely enough room for a riderless horse and two men to pass through," Nicholl whispered. "Robbers wouldna walk along a public road during the day, let alone at night."

A breeze blew from the south. "With that breeze behind us, Star might pick up our scent. Do ye think so?"

"That she might. We can hope she doesn't stumble on this rough path. We must be quick. If we close the space between us, we'll have a chance."

They had progressed over an hour, not losing the tracks, when Allie grasped Nicholl's arm. "Wait, sir, did ye hear that? Maybe thirty yards distant. Listen, there it is again."

"I hear," Nicholl said. "Come along. We don't need the light, Allie. It's less dim now."

Allie blew out the lantern and set it on the ground, holding the hoe with a determined grip. It was a good enough weapon for him, and he knew he'd use it if necessary.

They continued a few more feet when Nicholl stopped. "There...two men, one holding Star's reins."

Allie stepped alongside him. "Sounds like they're arguing."

One of the men said, "I say we should take her to Dublin."

"Are ye daft? We'd never get her there without drawing suspicion."

"Then where ye suggest we sell her?" the other man retorted in a loud voice.

"This whole thing was your idea, and now ye don't even have an answer that fits." His voice showed clear agitation.

By now, the two searchers were within 30 feet of the thieves. Allie could see Star's outline, hooves stomping and head jerking. The first man kept pulling on her reins.

"'Tis time," Nicholl said. "They have no idea we're here."

"And we have no idea if they have pistols."

"I guess we'll just have to take that chance." Nicholl stepped a few yards in their direction, aiming his rifle. "Stay right where ye are! Or I'll shoot ye both, ye bloody horse thieves."

Allie wondered if his friend would really shoot, and somehow, he thought he would. He raised his hoe and was ready to move in.

Nicholl edged forward, menacing with the weapon. "Stand still, or ye can bet on it, I'll shoot!" He turned back to Allie. "Take off that rope from around ye."

When he took his eyes off the men for those two seconds, one of them jumped on Star. The other leapt behind him, but when they took out, the second man fell to the ground. He was up as soon as he hit the earth and raced away like a hare, through the trees and out of sight.

It was obvious Star wasn't letting the uninvited rider stay on.

Allie and Nicholl were in pursuit when Star snorted, bucked, and threw the thief. He picked himself up and ran limping in the same direction as his cohort.

Nicholl aimed at the moving shadow and fired. The shadow moved on.

"Star!" Allie called. "Here, girl! Look, she's turning around. She's headed to the stables."

By then, early light slanted through the trees. Allie grabbed the lantern and again, the two men gave chase, but this time, after the horse.

Allie was right. Star headed for the stable, reins dragging. When the men arrived, she was standing at the closed gate.

Nicholl grabbed for the reins, and Allie put his arm around Star's neck. "Girl, are ye all right?"

"Let me have a look," Nicholl said. He examined her, checking her eyes and running his hands down her neck and flanks. "Ah, she seems t' be all—begorrah, here's a cut on her foreleg. Bled, it has. Allie, bring some fresh water."

Allie ran to the well while Nicholl led Star inside the gate. When he returned, he watched as Nicholl washed back the hair and let the water run over the wound. "I'm cleansing it best I can, and it doesn't seem so bad. See that chest over there, me boy? Reach in and bring me the bottle of liniment."

Allie flung open the lid and hurried back with the bottle.

"We won't know if the cut pains her until I use this. It'll sting. Stand back a bit, Allie."

He poured the liquid on the wound.

Star shifted her legs and snorted, but Nicholl caught her reins and stroked her neck, calming her. "I will wrap it so flies will stay away and treat it again this evening. We'll see how she is and not work her for a couple days." Nicholl finished bandaging her leg. "I think she will be all right now. We don't want an infection to set in."

Allie heaved a sigh of relief as he settled her down. "Don't worry, girl, I'll stay with ye tonight. He looked her over once more, and satisfied, led her to her stall.

"Let us go, lad. I expect we can both find room for me wife's cooking."

When they reached the house, the door burst open and Sarah stood there, beaming. "Come in, come in. I'm so glad you're back. I was worried ye'd find trouble instead of Star. I don't know which of me prayers was answered, but I guess they overlapped."

Mrs. Nicholl moved around, reaching for forks, cups, then spooned out breakfast on each of their plates. "I've been so flustered, I don't even know what I made ye to eat."

After Allie had seconds, he said, "Whatever it was, it was grand." He was out the door and back at the stables in no time. Nicholl was right behind him.

Star was calm and looked comfortable. "I see no problem. She'll be good as new," Nicholl said.

Allie began taking Darcy through his paces. He felt secure in the saddle, and Darcy responded to everything he asked.

Mr. Nicholl watched it all. "Ye know, Allie, ye are the best thing that could've happened to me. Ye seem t'be a natural with the horses."

"I don't know about that, sir, but I'm the one who's received the benefit."

Allie slept in the stable that night and for two nights after.

~~~

As the months passed, Allie often strolled down to the shoreline when he waked early or had free time. He sat on a rock and gazed out at the sea, morning vapor hovering over its surface. There must be more, he thought. *I haven't seen enough to know what it is. Thing is, I wanted Bernadette to find it with me. And even if I find it alone, she'll still be with me.* "Well," he said with a sigh. "Dreaming me dreams can't hurt."

On one occasion, he wondered why Mr. Nicholl hadn't come down to the stables. Since it was about time for the mid-day meal, he hurried up to the slope. When he entered, he was surprised to see that Mr. Nicholl wasn't there.

"Here ye are, Allie," Mrs. Nicholl said, always with a smile. "Hot 'n ready." She set the plate on the table, covered with a flowered cloth. "Aidan's been called into town. He should be back soon."

"That's good. I was afraid he'd taken sick." After Allie finished, he carried his plate to the wash table. "Thank ye, Mrs. Nicholl. Now, let me know if ye need anything. Ye know where to find me."

"I will. I'll just ring the bell."

Allie liked the idea of a signal bell hanging at the back door in case Mrs. Nicholl ever needed anyone. He knew safety was a priority when she was alone in the house.

No sooner had he returned to his work, the bell sounded over and over. Allie rushed Darcy back into the fenced area and ran to the house.

"Mrs. Nicholl, what is it? Are ye all right?"

There stood her husband and a young man he'd not seen before.

"Allie, I want ye to meet Jeremy. He's back with us, alive and well from the fever." They both flashed big grins, Mr. Nicholl's arm around Jeremy's shoulder.

"Glad t'meet ye, Jeremy."

"The same, Allie."

They shook hands, and the three men headed for the stables.

Jeremy perused the horses, going straight to Darcy. "Hello there, boy, ye remember me? I would think he's about ready for the races, is that right?"

Mr. Nicholl stepped over to Darcy. "That he is. Ye got him off to a grand start, and Allie here finished him up. They will be coming for him in a couple weeks."

The two younger men took turns working the remaining horses, Allie still favoring Starlight. But he thought they ought to have a farewell party for Darcy. The best thing would be for him to win the Grand National. *It might be possible. Yes, it might.*

~~~

Just before Darcy left to find his glory at Aintree, Allie told him goodbye. "I'll be expecting great things of ye, boy. And just think, I never fell off ye, not once! Remember, ye can win The National. Horses dream, too, don't ye know?"

Allie was aware Mr. Nicholl had not yet brought in another horse. Aherne had come a long way and might be ready to go away soon, although he didn't have the spirit Darcy had. As time progressed, he thought he might not be needed as much as before. He reminisced about his past and could accept it, hard as it was, but he felt the need to start again.

Late one morning after finishing in the stable, Allie and Jeremy returned to the house. Mrs. Nicholl had set the table and was preparing to dish stew into white bowls. "Ye'd best wash up before this gets cold."

The latter didn't take long, and they sat down at their places. Nicholl said his brief blessing, and they ate.

Jeremy was first to finish. "I'll see ye in few minutes. I have an idea that will take Dazzler up a notch. I think he can do better."

Allie held his thoughts long enough. He had to get them out. As soon as Jeremy left, he said, "Sir, can I have a word or two with ye?"

Nicholl tilted his head and looked at him. "Of course, lad, what is it?"

"It's a wee bit hard to say, but...'Tis not that I'm ungrateful for all ye've done, I've learned so much, but I've been thinking. It's time for me to walk in me own steps."

"I had a feeling, Allie. Wanderlust, is it then? Ye look strappin', but do ye feel fine?"

"Yes, sir, I do. And I know I've gained weight since I first came here. Your wife has seen to that, haven't ye, Mrs. Nicholl?"

"We were more fortunate than most, Allie. But ye've been the biggest help."

"I'm not so sure about that, but I will miss ye both...and the horses." He looked up and smiled. "And besides, I learned to play chess."

"That ye did, Allie. It's mighty grand work ye did this last year, but a lad like yourself must see what he can find in life. Where are ye planning to go?"

"I've saved me wages, and I'll be working me way to the city. I may never see County Wicklow again. But now that Jeremy's back...Without him being here, I'd never be thinking of leaving ye."

"There's not that much to do now, but good times will come again. The English will continue to want jumpers. I'll locate more."

Allie felt that with fewer horses, Nicholl really didn't need two riders besides himself.

"Jeremy knows his horses, me boy, but so do ye." He smiled, reaching over to slap Allie on the back.

~~~

Allie stayed another week, and on the morning of his departure, he gathered his things into his satchel. He needed to say goodbye to the horses, and to one, in particular. He approached the stable and went first to Dazzler and then to Aherne. He said his own few words to them.

He brought out Star from her stall, bridled her and cantered down to the shore. He stopped and stared at the ocean and sky for what he felt might be his last visit. Finally, returning the horse to the stable, he climbed off and spoke to her. "Starlight, you're my first jumping horse, a real lady. I hope ye don't forget me." He patted her shoulder and leaned against her head, feeling his eyes mist over. But he had to go.

At the house, Mrs. Nicholl put a sack of food in his hand. "If ye have a mind to, send us word of your whereabouts." She hugged him, her voice beginning to tremble. "Ye have enough food to get to Dublin and maybe more. Now, Allie, there are two wee bags of potato flour."

"Thank ye, Mrs. Nicholl. I'll never forget ye both."

"One more thing. Here's a blanket ye'll need at night on your walk to Dublin." She folded it over his free arm. "Oh, oh, I almost forgot." She scurried over to the table and wrapped something in paper and tied a string around it. "I fixed this baked fish for ye. I'll just put it in top of the sack. That should give ye a meal. Oh, I'm so afraid ye'll be hungry."

Allie smiled at how she bustled around. "Don't worry. I'll be fine." He put his arm around her and kissed her forehead. He shook Jeremy's hand, and then turned to Mr. Nicholl.

"Sir, I can't tell ye—"

"Then don't, me boy. I couldn't have done it without ye. I've looked on ye like a son."

He threw his arms around Allie in a bear hug. "Let us hear from ye, lad."

Allie gathered the rest of his meager possessions, stuffed them into his straw satchel and slung the sack of food over his shoulder.

Chapter 4

Grateful for Mr. Nicholl's help in selling the farm, Allie still had to let it go for next to nothing, scarcely enough money to bother counting. With his savings, he began the long dusty trek through County Wicklow to Dublin. He passed small dwellings with only stumps left of what were once trees, clearly showing someone had either sold the wood or traded it for food. Since Allie had lived in the Nicholls' home, he hadn't fully realized the depth of poverty that blanketed the Ireland he had not seen.

The second day clouded, and he feared rain would come. As he walked by the side of the road, he thought he detected someone following him. He turned to look back and decided it was a small animal skittering through leaves.

He glimpsed a house and decided to inquire if he might exchange menial labor for food. He still had some but didn't know how long it would last. The woman who came to the door slightly opened it. Allie could see she was frail.

A small boy, looking gaunt himself, clung to her skirts.

"What do ye want?" she asked. "I'm afraid ye'd better go away."

Allie noticed the dark circles under her eyes, and he had a fair idea there would be no work here. And certainly no extra food. He would settle for sleeping in the barn for the night, if they would agree to that.

A harsh voice called out from twenty yards away. "Hóigh, there. I'm afraid we have nothing for strangers, but..." He glanced down at the partial string of fish he carried.

"No, no, I'm fine with me sack of food. I was thinking if I might stay the night in your barn. It looks like rain is coming."

The man didn't answer until he was almost face to face with Allie. "Go ahead. You're welcome to sleep there." He changed to a softer tone and held up the fish. "I caught only three wee ones. That was me allowance for the day. Our son's not well, and I try to provide."

"Me thanks to ye. All I need is a place to sleep." As rain started to fall, Allie ran toward the barn. "I'll be leavin' at daylight," he called back over his shoulder.

"Then have a good night. I'll be going into the house now."

Allie opened the barn door and noticed hay on the floor but no signs of a cow. He supposed they had sold it, even though the milk would've been of use to them now. He unfolded the blanket, grateful for Mrs. Nicholl's thoughtfulness. Restless, he thought of the hollow look on the little boy's face and of the woman's sad eyes.

Soon after he drifted to sleep, he awoke to a noise—not from outside but very near. Before he could respond, two forms jumped at him. One man dragged him to his feet. The other grabbed him from behind. "Where's your money? Give it up now, or I'll snap your neck."

"There's no way in Erin ye'll get anything of mine," Allie choked. He twisted enough to jab the ruffian in the ribs with his elbow. When the attacker loosened his grip, Allie let go a swift right at his jaw—so hard, he thought he might've broken his hand.

"Ye'll be sorry ye did that," the ruffian bellowed. He picked up a rake and as he swung, a rifle blast shattered the night.

"Stay right where ye are!"

Allie spied his host standing in the doorway, a crease of moonlight glinting off his rifle. "All right, ye bloody pair. I ought to put holes through ye like that roof there, but I don't want to waste me ammunition." He swung the weapon from one man to the other. "Go and don't stop runnin' till ye get back to where ye came from."

The young culprits stared at each other, blinked, and took off.

Allie's host slumped against the splintery wall.

Allie thought he might fall, but he reached him before finding out. "Are ye all right?" he asked, breathless.

"Aye. It is a good thing I am a light sleeper, or I never would've heard the voices."

"Ye must know how thankful I am. I will be on me guard the rest o' the way to Dublin. By the way, me name is Allie."

"And I am Liam. Ye must understand, Allie, hungry people are desperate and will do anything to fill their stomachs. We are in dire straits, too, but God is on our side. That is, when he isn't too busy to hear our prayers."

"If ye are sure you're all right, I must soon be going." He drew out one of the sacks of potato flour. "Here, ye must take this. It will last a while, at least."

Liam hesitated. "I hate to take it from ye, but me wife and boy...I worry about them."

"'Tis all right. I am strong. I'll be fine." Allie shook Liam's hand. "With a little more sleep, I will be leaving."

Liam gripped the sack of flour. "Thank ye, friend, an' may trouble be a stranger to ye."

He headed for the house.

Allie lay back down on the dirt floor and drew his blanket over him. It even occurred to him the two ruffians bore a resemblance to the horse thieves who stole Star. He closed his eyes but was too rattled to sleep for long. After he awoke, he collected his things and started out before dawn, closing the barn door behind him.

He made as little noise as possible as he drew some water from the well. He mixed a little into a tin cup of flour and ate his meal of mashed potatoes. He was surprised at how much food Mrs. Nicholl had given him. He rationed the dried beef and saved the cinnamon scones—for what occasion, he had no idea.

~~~

Less than two days to Dublin. He didn't stop at houses again, but instead, chose secluded spots at night, with a clear view of the roadway. One morning a flock of small birds flew overhead. What do they find to eat, he wondered. Do they know where they're going?

Allie had never been to Dublin, but at last it loomed in the distance. After arriving, he stared at the town's buildings—some painted yellow, some green. Overall, he didn't find the dismal city to his liking. Streets smelled of garbage. The stench of sewers and the pungency of saloons thickened the air. He had no disposition to partake of liquor, but when he noticed a pub that didn't stink, he thought one glass of ale would do no harm.

Inside the smoke-filled pub he watched a few slovenly people drink more than he thought necessary. Perhaps if they had money to spare, drinking made their worries seem less. Two men who appeared reasonably sober stood next to him at the bar. Allie couldn't help overhear their conversation.

The taller man, who leaned against the bar, said, "All I know is a man can make a living and not have to worry about famine and fear of dying."

The other replied, "Ryan, ye must be daft to think a man could travel the ocean to a place he's never seen, and set hisself up as a bloomin' king."

"Bloomin' king is it! Who mentioned bein' king? What I'm saying is a man can make a place for hisself in America." He slapped his hand down on the bar top. "Me cousin, Gerard, lucky bastard, left before this cursed blight. He's a policeman for the city of New York. Makes a lot of money, he does, if ye can believe what he writes in his letters."

Allie sipped his ale as he eavesdropped. The longer he listened, the more "America" became a magic word. He finished the glass of warm ale in a single gulp and gathered up his satchel. An hour earlier his path had been unclear, but now he knew his destiny.

He headed for the dock.

Allie had heard lots of folks left for America but never dreamed how many. He tried to keep his focus ahead but still looked both ways and behind him as he noticed other emigrants dressed in ragged long-tailed coats and dirty unbuttoned knee breeches. His clothes were almost as tattered, but at least he had better ones in his satchel.

He stared in awe at the square-rigged ship by the dock. The line for passengers stretched for what seemed a mile, with some women and children traveling alone. Allie took his place at the end. Distrusting those around him, he didn't dare pull out his watch to see how long he waited.

He finally reached the front of the line. One thing he hadn't checked on for sure was the fare. He drew out what he thought would be enough and handed it over. "Here's me fare, sir."

The captain, one of the few stout men Allie had noticed, stopped short of laughter. "Lad, ye'll have to come up with more than this, if it's to America you're goin'. The fare is seven pounds."

"But Captain, it's all the funds I can afford. Please let me board." For the second time in his life, Allie tasted fear—it bled into his mind and heart, as if his hope were being wrenched from him.

"Now there's no business tryin' to go if ye have not the fare. How will ye get along in America?" Compassion flickered through the captain's gray eyes. "Tell me, do ye have something to trade for your passage?"

"No, sir, nothing. Well, I do have these cinnamon scones." He dug into his food sack. The thought of his father's gold watch crossed his mind, but only for a moment. Allie knew he would not give it up.

"Scones aren't what I had in mind, but here, give them to me and what money ye can."

Allie gave him more of his funds, along with the cinnamon scones.

"Go on. Get on board," the captain ordered.

Allie began to question his decision to go to America. *Maybe the captain is right. What will I do with so little money? But it's me only choice.*

As he worked his way through the crowd onboard, he couldn't imagine finding a spot to call his own. Squeezing through the passengers, he noticed a young man about his age. He managed to wedge in and, smiling, stood beside him. Feeling at least some humor of the moment, he asked, "Are ye saving this space for anyone?"

The traveler offered a half-hearted laugh. "It's all yours. I'm Robert Perry," he said, straightening his worn collar and standing a little taller. "If we can manage to breathe this stale air, we might get to America alive."

"Well, I'm Aloysius McCrae, but call me Allie. And it's a pleasure to have your company." He pulled out his cotton handkerchief and swiped it over his forehead. "Come to think of it, with the air this stale now, what will it be in eight weeks?"

"Worse before then. They'll be directing us to the steerage any time now. Me uncle Andrew, who set sail one year ago, said a dozen or so of us can take our turn on deck for fresh air and t' wash our clothes, and ourselves, then go back down and others come up."

"I guess I don't know what to say to that. Just a surprise is all. Never dreamed there'd be so many people."

"Me uncle said each passenger is supposed to have a certain amount of space, but we don't seem to have much of that. And food gets scarce. Maggots may even join us in a meal. He also told me to bring aboard as much staples as I could, for if the ship's rations run out."

Allie could almost feel himself turn green. "I never dreamed the ship wouldn't have enough food. But I had no one to tell me any of this."

"And another thing, me uncle wrote he had part of his worldly goods stolen on board ship. Later, someone bilked him of his savings in New York. So if we can avoid that, the rest should be milk and honey." Robert laughed. "And that's why we're going to America, is that not right?"

Allie nodded. "I'll keep a tight hold on me belongings. But where do we sleep, I wonder. We don't have pallets?"

"Me friend, we sleep on the floor in steerage. Lucky ones could buy a bunk. It'd be nice to sleep on deck, if there's room to lie down."

"I never slept standing up before but guess there's always a first time."

~~~

Four weeks out from port, Allie noticed Robert seemed listless, his skin gray. With the crowded conditions and poor hygiene, they half expected illness. But no one had prepared them for ship fever. Several passengers were ill. So miserable himself, Allie began to wonder if his prayers would be answered.

It was their turn on deck when Robert said, "I haven't been feeling so well, Allie." He sank down and leaned against a barrel.

Allie washed his friend's face with water from his own small allotment.

"Seems like more people now than when we started...so crowded. Does it seem the same to you?" Robert asked, his voice thin.

Allie didn't answer. "With a decent water supply, maybe this wouldn't have happened."

"They were supposed to give us at least six pounds of food each week. And we haven't had..." He caught hold of Allie's hand. "Thanks, Allie. Ye are a good man."

"Quiet, now. Ye'll be all right." Allie didn't believe the lie he just uttered.

Robert tightened his grip. "Take me sack of food for yourself. Ration it even if it's only five bites a day."

"But—"

"Listen to me, Allie." He drew out a slip of paper from his pocket. "I won't make it, but if ye do, will ye write to me mother? She never wanted me to go, but I had to see America for meself."

Allie took the paper. "But Robert, we're on our way to America now. Milk and honey. Don't ye recall?"

Robert let go Allie's hand. Within hours he succumbed to rampant typhus.

"No! Ye can't be dead," Allie yelled, crossing himself *God, where are ye?* He had never felt so alone.

Allie faced the truth when crew members quickly gathered Robert up and prepared him for the sea. They placed him in canvas, sewn together and weighted with stones. Allie listened to the captain's prayer committing his friend to the deep. He instructed the crew to tilt the board upon which Robert lay on the gangplank.

Allie wondered if there would be enough canvas for the dozens who would die and join Robert in a watery grave—a grave one could never visit, never pray over. Each night, with his eyes clinched shut, he wondered if he prayed to a non-existing God.

Chapter 5

The last days of the voyage, Allie strained to sight land. Would he really ever see America, he wondered. Two months after leaving Dublin, his dream came true. Even though he learned the ship would be under quarantine for a month and the ill remanded to the quarantine station on Staten Island, he felt he would gain release. Still, anxiety grabbed at him until the officials checked him out.

At last he was free to leave. *I don't know how it ever happened, but God, if ye had a hand in it, I thank ye.* Grateful for the chance to clean up before disembarking, he then boarded a towboat to Manhattan, which was only five miles from Staten Island.

He drew deep breaths of fresh air—not the same as the Irish countryside but far cleaner than on the ship. He walked to what he considered the heart of the city. Never had he seen so many people rush about: women with parasols, men with business written on their faces. Of course, there were others, too, poor people much like on the streets of Dublin, although without the forlorn appearance of abject poverty.

He stared in amazement at all the buildings in this new land.

Two young boys ran close to him, one spinning him around.

"Hey, watch it there, laddies!"

They pushed him into a lamppost, his satchel falling from his hand. After righting himself, he straightened his coat and picked up the bag. He grinned to see a bakeshop just in front of him. The smell of fresh pastry soothed his senses, removing the last remnants of the ship's smell. He entered and perused every item in the case.

A pleasant rosy-cheeked woman behind the counter seemed impatient until Allie finally said, "I'll have one of those little sugar cakes, please."

He reached into his satchel for his money. Then realization struck. "No! Oh no," he exclaimed. "It can't be. Me money's gone. Someone stole me money!"

Allie bolted from the store, remembering when the boys had pushed him. But he knew it was too late. *Now I have nothing— only me father's watch.*

Numbed by his loss, he wandered up and down, passing teams of horses with wagons full of vegetables, vinegar, and beer.

"Look where you're going," one of the drivers yelled.

Allie jumped away from the wagons. Then he recognized a familiar brogue of Northern Ireland. "It's an argument I'm hearing, is it?"

A robust policeman was delivering the message of law and order to a wayward teamster who tried to force his way into oncoming traffic.

"I'm wise to ye, ye little weasel. Now haul that wagon down the proper street and go around the block like you're supposed to." The policeman twirled his club in a circle and pointed it north. "Get to it."

Allie figured he had to be a policeman, even though he didn't wear a uniform. If not, how could he be issuing such official orders? Intent on asking him for help, Allie pushed toward the gesturing Irishman, dodging horse-drawn carts and wagons as he went.

"Watch out!"

Allie heard only the warning before the wagon hit him a glancing blow. The road proved an inadequate cushion. He opened his eyes and tried to focus on the faces and bodies hovering over him. As double vision again blended into one, the first face he saw clearly was that of the big policeman.

"Ye're lucky to be livin', son. That beer wagon tried its damnedest to make ye a piece of the road. Can ye be movin' all your parts?"

Sensing his limbs still attached, Allie wheezed, "Aye, but I feel like those wheels rolled over me."

The policeman reached down to Allie and helped him stand. "Ye just fell off the boat, didn't ye now?"

"It shows, does it?"

"I'm afraid it does. Let us get ye to that bench over there. I'll get your satchel."

Allie took the policeman's arm and sat on the bench. "I was on the way to ask ye for help when me lights went out. Some kids pinched me money, and that makes a little bit of a quandary, it does."

"Well, I'm Brian Clancy, and I have all the help me young friend from the old country needs. I'm finished for the day. You're comin' home with me."

"No, I can't be doing that. Ye don't even know me," Allie insisted.

A friendly gleam lit the policeman's eyes. "Now, don't be making it difficult. I'm the law, and I say you're coming with me."

And again, Allie realized someone had come to his rescue. "I hate to put ye to trouble but guess I don't know what else to do." Feeling dazed, he allowed the policeman to lead him down the street. Barking dogs and bellowing vendors did nothing to ward off his headache. "I'm Allie McCrae, so that means we're no longer strangers."

"All right, Allie McCrae, come along now. But are ye needing a doctor to check ye over?"

"No, no, I'll get meself together soon enough," he said, as he rubbed his shoulder.

Brian didn't argue, and they walked three more blocks before stopping. "Ah, here we are, this red building here."

A cobbler's shop and haberdashery occupied the ground floor, with a single door over to the side. Brian unlocked the door that led to a flight of wooden stairs. "Any noise ye hear is apt to be our wee ones."

His prediction was right. The sound of small feet echoed down the stairway. "Papa. Papa!" exclaimed two little girls as they ran to meet him and grasped the big Irishman's legs.

"Here, here, ye scalawags. Have ye no respect for your poor tired father?" Brian lifted both giggling children high in his arms. "The smaller one is Katie and this one is Emma."

Both girls giggled some more and hugged their father around his neck.

A lump formed in Allie's throat over the tenderness displayed between father and daughters. Moisture formed in his eyes, but he'd left all his tears in Ireland.

At the top of the stairs, Brian said, "Come in, me boy." He ushered Allie in before him. "Woman of the house," he called, "it's a visitor we have from home, and 'tis injured he is."

A petite woman walked in with light brown hair tied in a braid draped over her shoulder. She pursed a lovely smile—a perfect example of the colleens of whom the Irish gentlemen were so proud.

"Allie McCrae, this is me wife, Doreen."

"How do ye do, ma'am. I'm sorry to put ye out like this."

"No trouble at all, Allie. It is welcome ye are," Doreen Clancy said. "But how come ye to be injured?"

Allie started to speak, but Brian took over the conversation and explained about the beer wagon.

"Well, ye can stay with us until ye feel like yourself again."

"I'm a little sore is all. I do have a headache." Allie figured that could be from lack of food.

Brian pulled up a chair for him while the children stared wide-eyed at their visitor.

"There, sit down," Doreen said. "And I see ye have a bad scrape on that hand. Let me have a look."

"Mrs. Clancy, I appreciate your concern but, I wonder, might I have the time to shave me face?" Allie scratched his chin. "I expect I'm a wee bit overgrown. And...and I do have a change of clothes." He looked down at the clothes he had on. "I washed these meself the day before the ship docked."

Doreen smiled. "Brian, while I'm getting supper together, will ye show Allie where he can freshen up?"

When Allie returned, he smelled the aroma of ham and cabbage, leaving him faint from hunger. Mounds of mashed potatoes, gravy, and biscuits added to the fare.

Doreen and Brian shared nodding approval. Katie and Emma blinked at each other as if Allie had turned into an entirely different person.

Allie grinned and pulled at his shirt. "I believe I used to fit these clothes before I left Ireland."

"Ye look grand. Now just a minute more," Doreen said. "Let me put a little Iodine on your hand. Ye don't want it infected."

Allie flinched at the sting. "I'm grateful, Mrs. Clancy."

The girls were perched at the table, ready to eat.

"Allie," Brian said. "Ye must be starving. Here, sit."

Allie knew they had no idea how starved he was. He hadn't eaten a real meal in weeks and hoped he didn't appear rude as he shoveled food into his mouth. After cherry pie to top it off, he praised the cook and conversed with his new friends about their homeland.

Allie told them about Bernadette, his parents, and how he happened to come to America.

"And here I've just met ye and ye seem like family."

"That's good to hear," Brian said, "but now, we must let this boy get some rest."

Doreen prepared a cot in the parlor. "Now sleep well, Allie McCrae."

He noticed the tidiness of the room, certainly not costly furnishings, although obviously cared for. He lay on the cot and stared at the ceiling, wondering what his second day in America would be like, after all that had happened on the first. His thoughts waned, and he plunged into an abyss of hard sleep.

During the middle of the night, his own voice awakened him. "No, no! Robert, ye can't go like this!" All he could see was the vision of his friend floating in the water, sinking beneath the surface, bobbing in the murky waves, although he knew that could not be. The image transformed into Bernadette, smiling, arms outstretched to him. Allie reached for her, but she vanished. Dark waters rolled on.

Allie struggled to erase the dream from his mind.

The light of dawn crept through the window, and he arose from the cot, rubbing the sleep from his eyes. He pulled up his suspenders as Brian walked into the room.

"Ah, and how was your night, Allie?"

"It must've been fine. Last thing I remember is going to bed and waking up."

"Breakfast is almost ready," Doreen called from the kitchen. "Allie, come let me have another look at your hand this morning."

"'Tis a little swollen, but it feels better."

Doreen opened the Iodine bottle and blotted a bit more on the scrape. "Now be sure to keep it clean."

"That I will. Ye'd make a fine nurse." Sitting at the table, he asked, "Brian, could ye maybe let me go on your beat-walk and learn a bit more of where things are? Then I must be on me way, whatever that way may be."

"Certainly ye can. But I need to tell ye, lad. Ye'll find it out soon enough; however, it's better ye know now. Jobs are not easy to come by."

"But I thought this was a country of plenty."

"There's plenty all right, but everybody doesn't have it. I meself came over two years ago, so that's the only reason I got a little ahead."

"But I would do anything. Help at the docks, sweep the walks—"

"Well, we will see what we can do."

After a filling breakfast, Allie said, "Again, a fine meal. I won't forget it. And now I need a moment to repack me satchel," He pulled out his father's watch to make sure it was safe. In the depths of his satchel his fingers ran across something sharp. He felt a thud in his heart and knew. He wondered why he hadn't discovered it the night before. The little blue pitcher. Broken.

"Allie? What is it?" Doreen asked.

His brow furrowed. "I...It's...It's all right." Allie pulled out three pieces of porcelain.

"This was Bernadette's. It must've broken when I fell on the street."

"Oh, no! Let me see." Doreen looked at it a moment. "I know of a place that might be able to glue it back."

Allie tried not to let his disappointment show, but after all, the pitcher was Bernadette's. "Even if it could be repaired, not knowing where I'm going or what I'm to do, it would just get broken again."

Doreen rose and placed the delicate pieces on the sideboard. "Never mind. I want to at least find out if it can be mended."

Brian returned, his billy club in hand and ready to go.

Allie watched as he kissed his wife and said goodbye to the girls. *I can almost see me own children, but we never...*

"Allie?"

"Huh? Oh, aye. I'm coming."

Brian walked down the front steps and turned to the outside of the walkway.

Allie grinned. He figured Brian didn't trust him next to the unpredictable traffic. "I wish ye would look at all the commotion already. This is the first time in me life I ever saw a city this big wake up to the mornin', or any city wake up for that matter." New York wasn't as clean as he expected. *Too many people cluttering the streets.* "Oh, me!"

"What is it, Allie? Are ye all right?"

"I came to America to find milk and honey, but that sure wasn't honey I stepped in."

Brian almost rolled with laughter. "I'm sorry, Allie, I should've cautioned ye."

Allie scraped his shoe on the curb, and since Brian thought it was worth laughing about, he laughed, too.

Street peddlers had either already set up their carts or were in the process. Brian nonchalantly swung his club when Allie noticed a woman walking toward them.

Brian touched his cap. "Ah, a bright sunny day to ye, Mrs. Nolan. And is your husband on good behavior? Just ye let me know, and I'll give him a whack on the shins with me club."

"It is a bright day, Mr. Clancy. Mr. Nolan's turned himself around completely. Thank ye for asking." She smiled and continued walking.

Brian volunteered an answer to Allie's unasked question. "Mr. Nolan took a liking to the bottle, and they've had a difficult time. I gave him a firm talking to before he became hopeless."

A large poster on a storefront window another block down attracted Allie's attention. A cartoon of sorts, it depicted a bearded man in a stars and stripes uniform with the name "Uncle Sam."

"Brian, who is this Uncle Sam?"

"Uncle Sam's the country. It's been needing more soldiers for longer than I've been on this soil. Even I can smell war in the air, coming certain and sure." He gazed upward, as if he could actually smell it. "The 'when' is the question. Likely it will be the northern states fighting the southern ones."

"But how do ye know?"

This land had slavery long before I came. And one day it'll come to a boil. The Union is short on troops, and this here on the right is a recruiting office. Will ye be seeing what they have to offer?"

Allie thought a moment before he nodded. They stepped inside to see a desk stacked with papers. Behind the desk sat a slightly gray-haired man in a blue uniform. He greeted them with a wide smile.

"Come right in. Have you come to join the best fighting army in the world?"

"Enough of all the smoke blowing," Brian said. "This young lad is fresh off the boat from the old sod and doesn't know ye like I do, so tell him a little bit about the Union Army."

"All right, Clancy, you got me. My friend, right now we need men who can sit a fine horse and shoot at the same time. You know much about either?"

"Well, sir, next to potato fields, me second home was on the backs of the best jumpers in Ireland, but I haven't had much experience shooting. I learn quick, so where would they be sending me to learn the army way of doing things?"

"You'd like as not wind up on the frontier."

The word frontier was enough to sell Allie on the idea. He knew that much about America from the little schooling he'd had. Besides, he knew he had limited choices, and this might be the only way to find that milk and honey Robert spoke of—and be paid for it.

Allie stood in silence for a minute, glancing at Brian. "Very well, I think I'll join."

"Then I need to fill out this paper," the man said. "What's your name and how old are you?"

"Me name is Aloysius McCrae, but I go by Allie. And I'm nineteen, sir."

"Well, you'll be Private McCrae from now on." The recruiter looked Allie up and down. "Let's see here. Medium build, a little weight wouldn't hurt. Clear complexion, eyes—blue, hair...I guess I'd say corn color. Do you know how tall you are?"

"No, sir, but I'm taller than me father was," Allie said, with a sparkle in his voice.

"Then stand over here and we'll find out for sure."

Allie moved to the side wall and pulled himself to full height, in spite of a still-aching shoulder. He stood on a white square painted on the floor.

"Five-feet-eleven-inches it is," the recruiter announced. He returned to his desk and finished filling out the form. "Just sign this on the bottom line, soldier."

Without more thought, Allie signed his name on the army's official papers, stood straight and heaved a satisfied sigh.

"You're in luck. You'll be moving out tomorrow, so be here at eight o'clock sharp." He turned his attention to Brian. "Now, Clancy my friend, how about you? We can always use another fighting Irishman. Seems like you've been waving your arms around here long enough."

"None of your wily ways, ye black-hearted divil," Brian replied, winking. "There's not enough gold in all the western states to sign me up, so good day. We be finished here. Let us go, Allie."

They stepped outside into the flood of sidewalk traffic and paused when something in a store window caught Allie's eye.

"Forget about any clothes in the shops," Brian said. "The army will provide your needs."

"But they don't know me size or me best colors," Allie protested.

"Ha! Private McCrae, your best color is blue from now on."

It took him only a couple seconds to reply. "Oh, that's fine. I like blue, but I hope the uniform fits."

"Ye can lose or gain weight to fit it." Clancy chuckled.

"I guess I will at that."

"And Allie, don't forget, we Irish aren't accepted with open arms here in this America. But ye get used to it. That's one reason I think joining up is good for ye. I'll be going about me work now and will see ye about suppertime. Think ye can find your way back in one piece?"

"I can do that all right," Allie replied, giving his friend a handshake.

Before he returned to the Clancy dwelling, Allie strolled the streets, watching people as they moved along in their daily activities. For the first time, he felt better about the future in his new world. He spent most of the day taking in the sights and wondering where all the people came from and where they were going in such a hurry.

~~~

The next morning after breakfast, the family gathered amidst hugs and goodbyes, including hugs for Katie and Emma.

"Mrs. Clancy, if ye can get the little pitcher repaired, will ye keep it yourself, as a reminder of me?"

"Of course I will, Allie, but we hope to see ye again one day."

"Remember," Brian said, "ye've been through a lot, but ye're young and full of hope. Write to us when ye can, Allie McCrae."

"I couldn't have made it without the Clancys. I don't write so well, but I'll try, ye can be sure."

Chapter 6

Allie made his way to the recruiting office where several others also waited—young men like himself, some several years older. He was the last one to climb into the third army wagon, taking a seat on a length of bench on one side. The fourth wagon belonged to the cook.

The sergeant leaned in and said, "Soldier, I'm entrusting this roster to you. Give it to Lieutenant Cummings. He'll be taking your wagons."

"Yes, sir, Sergeant." Allie took the folded papers.

An older recruit spoke up, "Friend, my name's Jeb Speck. You seem to be the only one on this here wagon who can tell us exactly where we're bound. Why not take a gander at that roster there, so we'll all know."

Allie, surprised at his temporary importance, was hesitant to read an official document.

After a quick glance, he announced, "It says here we're going to Jefferson Barracks in Missouri. Do any of ye know anything about this Jefferson place? And where's Missouri?"

One of the men replied, "I know it takes a while to get there."

"So are ye saying it's on the western frontier?"

"No. Didn't say that, but at least we know where we're headed."

"Well, I don't know much about America, but I've read a little about the west."

Allie learned more as the soldiers traveled. He became friends with the tall rangy Jeb Speck. Allie figured since his new acquaintance liked to talk, he could learn a lot from him. In the evenings when it came time to make camp, they formed a semi-circle with the wagons. The cook wagon tried to make a circle of it.

Allie and Jeb climbed down and stretched their legs. They strolled around until cook announced supper was ready.

"C'mon, Jeb. Let's eat."

Jeb filled his tin plate and made room for his coffee. "Let's go over there by those rocks." He took a bite of supper on the way. "These vittles ain't all that good."

"Vittles? Now, I don't mean to be making fun of your talk, but aren't they mainly beans?"

Jeb reciprocated with, "I forget you're a foreigner, with all yore 'ye's' an' 'me's'. There's some that'd say Kentucky's a foreign country, too. That's where I'm from. I come up east for a kin's funeral and just stayed."

Allie mulled over Jeb's manner of speaking. "I'll let ye know first time I can't understand ye, but if Indians are coming ye sure better say 'Indians are coming,' loud and clear."

Trudging a few extra yards, Jeb sat down on a boulder and motioned for Allie to sit.

"Not me," he said. "I'm tired of sitting." He set his tin cup of coffee on the rock and began to eat. "I tell ye, though. Rutty encampments and eating beans and hard bread is nothing like a picnic in the Irish countryside."

"Well, be glad we got what we got. I notice you're eatin' it all."

"I know. Food's food. I just hope Missouri will have better than what's before us here."

"Once we're there, we're there. Not much we can do about it."

Allie took another bite "Say, Jeb, if Indians do come along, what will happen?"

"If the lieutenant has the chance, he'll give 'em food and blankets, and they might leave us in peace. I hear it works sometimes."

"Sometimes? Well, it still..." Allie turned so fast, he knocked over his coffee. "Jeb, do ye hear that?

Jeb stopped his fork between his plate and his mouth. "Hear what? I don't hear anythin'."

"It sounds like a rumble. Ye think it might be Indians?"

"Maybe thunder. Or your imagination."

"So maybe it *is* thunder." Allie pulled his collar closer around his neck. "And it's getting cold, too."

"It was fair warm when we left New York. But we've been seein' America for 'bout two weeks now. Weather's different."

"About these Indians," Allie said. "It seems t' me if they're hungry, they'd take our food no matter what kind of deal the lieutenant makes. How large is a band of Indians, anyway?"

"Some get pretty big and pushy from what I hear. You can be sure we'll accommodate them with a fight if we hafta."

"Lieutenant Cummings says we won't shoot them just because they come in firing range. They have to shoot first."

"Sometimes they take a look and go their way, from what I know about it. What happens next depends on the temper of the officer in charge. Dang, some people think an Indian's behind the death of every white man. So even if they shoot a redskin for no reason, they figure it's payment for a white man the redskins kilt earlier."

Allie thought that over, furrowing his brow. "But ye have to think maybe the white man shot first." He paused, reflecting on such a possibility and gazed into the sky. "I sure hope a snow isn't coming on."

"That may be the least of our worries."

A distant shot rang out. Allie twisted around and looked toward the sound. "Jaykers! Indians for sure." Then a couple more shots.

The two grabbed their rifles and raced from the large rock to where the others had scrambled.

"Men," Lieutenant Cummings called. "I don't know what's out there, but be ready in case of trouble. Take your stations behind the wagons. Nobody get itchy fingers till I give the order. We don't want a fight. Let's see what they want."

The moon cast away straggling clouds. "Jeb! I'm thinking they're coming straight at us."

Allie thought his heart would pound a hole through his shirt.

"Dang it. Them's not Indians. Them's buffaloes."

The drumming hooves drew nearer across the flatlands north of the encampment. "My Jesus," Allie said under his breath. "Would ye just look at the size of 'em." He raised his rifle then remembered he wasn't to fire without orders.

Suddenly the buffalo herd swerved to the east. Allie relaxed his trigger finger but didn't let go his weapon. "Jeb, I don't know anything about that kind of animal, but wouldn't they be sleeping this time of night?"

"Yeah, but someone musta wanted buffalo steak, and those shots woke 'em all up. I hear they can cover more miles in an hour than a horse."

"At ease, men." Lieutenant Cummings rested his rifle. "The Indians are more interested in that herd than us. We'll have to do without buffalo meat ourselves. With a herd in the area, the Indians'll be happy. Leastways, they won't need our supplies. Let's just hope they don't want our scalps."

"Allie," Jeb wheezed through clinched teeth. "You can let go your rifle now. They're gone."

Allie heaved a sigh of relief and realized he was almost frozen to his weapon—not from snow, which never came, but from apprehension. "I'm still planning to sleep with one eye open and maybe an ear."

~~~

Sunrise brought an all clear.

The previous night was the closest Allie had felt peril on the entire journey, except for broken axles and wagon wheels. Once after an axle broke, they had to pry off a sideboard from the wagon to fashion a new one.

As the wagons approached the Mississippi, Allie, now in the lead wagon, was first to hear the lieutenant's order to halt. He peered out to see why they stopped. He blinked, with a wary shake of his head. "Jeb, am I seeing what I think?"

Jeb caught hold of the wagon rim and swung out. "Dang. Look at the flies. Or don't. Looks like somebody tried giving him an Indian burial by tryin' to set fire to him, an' not on a pyre, either."

Lieutenant Cummings ordered the men from the wagons. Closer inspection showed the Indian was shot full of holes. "Here, two of you men get a shovel. Cut this man down and bury him. He's been here a while. The stench doesn't lie. Be alert, but my guess is, whoever did this is long gone."

Allie whistled low and put his hand on his weapon. "That's the first Indian I've ever seen, alive or dead."

"Dang it, most men would leave him hang there. Let the buzzards pick his bones, but not the lieutenant. Must have a different soul than most."

"What's an Indian doing out here alone?" Allie asked, glancing around, just in case they weren't alone themselves. "We haven't heard of any since the buffalo stampede."

"Well, civilians hired as territorial soldiers could've tracked him. Their only mission is to exterminate Indians, friendly or not. Peculiar, he still has his scalp. Most of the time those so-called soldiers take it, just because."

Back on the trail, by the time they got to the Mississippi, Allie couldn't imagine crossing it in a wagon. "That's too big. Too big and too wide. How will we be getting to the other side?"

"It's wide all right," Jeb said. "We'll jest git these wagons on a boat and take off."

Cross they did, with Jefferson Barracks looming before them on the other side.

Out of the wagons for the last time, Lieutenant Cummings ordered the troops to form two ranks.

A sergeant greeted him, saluted, and after a few words with the lieutenant, directed the men to the entrance of a building, where he read the roster. When finished, he announced, "You'll do most of your fighting from the back of a horse. At the first light of morning we'll have a manual of arms demonstration for those who haven't learned by now. You must know something to get here in one piece. For now, go inside and check the board for your quarters assignments."

Tired as he was, Allie still found it difficult to drift off to sleep the first night in Jefferson Barracks. His thoughts shifted to Brian Clancy. *I have to get some paper and write the Clancys and Nicholls.* Smiling, he wondered if Brian earned a lot of money as a policeman, like the Irishman in the pub said. Somehow, he doubted it. *But I must write Robert's mother first.*

Those tasks completed, he left them for mailing and spent otherwise unoccupied time drifting by the stables, looking over the horses. He offered to help brush them down and check for injuries that might have gone unnoticed.

The army cut short their stay in Missouri, which suited Allie just fine. After hearing they'd missed a cholera epidemic that had just swept through, he was ready to leave.

"Jeb, do ye suppose they really cleaned up this place before we got here? I mean really cleaned it?"

"I reckon they did. Haven't heard of any of us gettin' sick, unless it was a bad case of catarrh, an' that's jes' an annoyance."

Allie and most of the same group who came to Jefferson Barracks, including Jeb Speck, received orders for Oklahoma Territory. It took extra troops to put a stranglehold on the marauders—white men robbing the Indians. Allie wondered why in the world whites would be robbing Indians.

The sergeant gave the men a last report concerning their orders. "You will be going to Fort Guardian on the outskirts of Indian Territory, near the Choctaw Nation."

Allie listened closely, not altogether confident he was ready for this.

"Outlaws are rampaging throughout the country down there," the sergeant continued, "holding up and murdering the well-t' do Indians every mile of the way. Now there's a report this outlaw, Lewis Dekker, and his gang have veered from their usual stomping grounds. They ventured into the Cherokee and Choctaw Nations, doing more than their share of damage. Anyway, they need more help running down Dekker, and you're it."

"I never thought of Indians being rich," Allie whispered to Jeb.

"What's that you say, McCrae?" The sergeant snapped.

"Uh, nothing, sir."

"Then get ready. You leave in the morning."

Allie and Jeb headed for their quarters. They bunked in a long room with two rows of cots the length of the building. Allie arranged his gear and plopped down on his cot. "But about those rich Indians—"

"McCrae, Indians were here first. Maybe they had time to get rich. I haven't been west before, but I do know something about Indians." Jeb shifted his long frame on the cot. "Dang, this here cot's sure short. Anyway, from the time these five tribes, the ones they call civilized, were forced to come to Indian Territory, they expected at least some protection from the government, since that's who made them come."

"Are ye saying they didn't get it?"

"That's what I'm sayin'. The local authorities didn't follow through. Sometimes they'd call in Federal troops. No sooner'd they arrived, the area got peaceful again. The troops retreated, only to have the outlaws come back."

"I guess I'll learn as I go, but it can wait till I have a good night's sleep."

Allie did sleep well, but by morning he was ready to leave, not holding back his enthusiasm for the long journey to Fort Guardian. Moving farther west was still uppermost in his mind.

As they jostled along, Allie asked, "Jeb, how many wagons would you say we've passed since we started out?"

"I think this is what they call a kind of massive migration. Some may be just adventurous."

"What I'd like to know is, where are these people going and do they know why?"

"Allie, don't you know there's always somethin' better on the other side of the mountain? Well, that's what these folks are lookin' for."

"Makes sense, I guess. That's what I was looking for...something better."

~~~

During the days, Allie took it all in. One evening while camped near a creek, he trekked back from gathering firewood. "I've learned how to build a fire with the best of them. Good thing, it does get chilled at night."

Jeb sat against a tree. "I'll tell you, this is sure fine land. Water an' trees—not what I expected. 'Course, I did expect those dang crickets to be hollerin' all night."

Allie set about arranging the wood for the fire while the cook pulled out a skillet, cans of beans, a slab of bacon and biscuit makings. "Me eyes have sure filled up with the middle of America. I've added five years of education to me life already, and I haven't even seen a war dance."

"Jes' hope you don't." Jeb grinned. "I'd hate to see one of them Apaches flailing your curly yellow hair on his belt. 'Course, ain't no Apaches around here."

The cook soon rang the supper bell. "It's ready! Better get your share!"

Jeb laughed. "I'm for sharin'."

While sitting around the camp after supper, someone decided to start up a little singing, which became an almost nightly ritual. Allie liked to sing but didn't know any of the words to what the soldiers came up with. They sang the same ones over and over. "Poor Dog Tray," "The Girl I Left Behind Me," and some they made up.

"C'mon, McCrae," one of the men called, "what about one of them Irish ditties I've always heard about?"

Jeb guffawed. "Allie, he's talkin' to you! Step out there so's they can see you."

"Aye, I guess I could get a few notes out." He patted his sleeves and held back his shoulders. "Let's see, what'll it be? How about 'The Last Rose of Summer'? But I haven't opened me mouth to sing in some time."

"He's opened it enough to talk, that's for sure," Jeb said. "Let's hear it, Allie."

Allie cleared his throat and started to sing. By the time he finished the second line, the men were silent. Even the crickets grew still. When he finished, he couldn't believe they liked it, even wanted more.

"Hey, Mick," a voice called. "You didn't tell us you could really sing. Can you do one of those, what do you call them, a slip jig song?"

Allie didn't even mind the slur. He knew "The Rocky Road to Dublin," maybe could make up some lyrics of his own. He got into it, even added a slip jig as he went, although he knew he wasn't graceful enough.

Lieutenant Cummings interrupted the fun. "Enough jocularity for one night, men. Stoke up the fire. We've got a long day ahead of us."

~~~

The rest of the trip passed with little incident, the most being early chills before the sun broke through. An occasional buzzard or two circled as if they'd spotted a treasured meal. The troops arrived safely and on schedule at Fort Guardian.

The men settled in, and Allie was pleased with the arrangements—even the food. He turned to Jeb after their first meal. "Let me say this plate of food is the best since New York."

"Glad to hear it," his friend said. "An' even if it wasn't, you'd be stuck with it."

The end of the second day, a sergeant named Bentley ordered Allie's unit to attention.

"We haven't had enough men up till now to track down this Dekker, so you know what you're here for. We'll find him, roust him out, kill him—whatever it takes, then maybe our Indian friends won't have so much to worry about. We have a patrol scheduled for tomorrow morning."

Allie listened intently. *Back to Indians again. At least he says they're friends.*

The sergeant continued. "You'll be issued a mount. Go check on that now. Be sure you have all your gear so you won't have to attend to it before we leave tomorrow."

When tomorrow came, Allie and Jeb rushed over to mess and finished eating before the rest of the men ever got there. While waiting, Jeb pulled out tobacco and papers, rolled a cigarette and lit up.

Allie wrinkled his brow. "Ye know, I never took to smoking, but since I've been in America, me thoughts have gone to a pipe. Maybe I'll get meself one first time I have a chance."

"Can't hurt. Smells, though. Cigarettes are easier. An' cheroots cost more—"

Lieutenant Cummings, having returned from officers' mess, said, "Pick up what you need from your quarters, men. We'll be on our way."

"There's enough of us, with Sergeant Bentley and his men," Allie said. "If that Dekker's around, we sure ought to find him."

The hours moved on until dusk closed out the day. Allie slapped the reins on his saddle.

"We've spent twelve hours looking for Dekker. Where could he be?"

"Mebbe in Wyoming by now. They must have some kind of hidey hole."

When the patrol returned to the fort, Allie was annoyed at what he considered failure. "I studied the drab grasses...noticed horse traces. We were right on him. How could we miss?"

The lieutenant glanced at him. "I know, Private, we caught up where he'd been, but he and his men seem to have made a complete turn-around."

"I don't like to fail, sir."

"That's what'll make you a good soldier, McCrae. Don't be impatient. We already knew Dekker's slippery. At times I think he's some kind of shape-shifter." Cummings stroked his jaw.

"We'll get him next time. Dismissed."

Allie felt better, now that the lieutenant more or less credited him and the men, rather than blamed them.

"Jeb, what's a shape-shifter?"

"Oh, it's a thing I hear Indians can do. You know, like changing from an Indian to a wolf or cactus or somethin'."

Chapter 7

June 1853

Allie McCrae received his sergeant's stripes, and he wore them proudly. He picked up a smattering of Choctaw from some friendly Indian scouts who hung around Fort Guardian. He and his men managed to do away with a major part of the robbing and turned several of the perpetrators over to the law.

When a new report came in that renegades had again been spotted in the area, Allie gathered a patrol and gave the command to move out. "All right men, we don't know exactly what we're expecting to find. Could be hostiles or whites. Or whites dressed like Indians. We want to see trouble before it sees us."

"We'll flush 'em out," Jeb said. "Ain't that many places they could be we don't already know about. Leastways, not close. Don't suppose it's Dekker again. Do you?"

"I couldn't guess the answer, but rumors have to be followed up."

By noon, in sun's heat, a private wiped his forehead with a bandana. "Sergeant McCrae, you think we're wasting time?"

"That may be, but I'm thinking ambush. All I've seen so far are red-tailed hawks and one skinny deer drinking from that creek pool over there."

After filling their canteens, they proceeded from the meandering creek bed. Drab grasses grew all around, almost to stirrup height.

The patrol moved on near some brush and rock. Allie heard movement in the tall grass. He knew a small animal would have skittered away by now. "Halt, men. There's something up there. I better check." He drew his weapon and with caution, approached the sound. "Move out easy, or I'm shooting."

"Don't...please..."

"A woman's voice it is." Allie jumped from his horse. He moved toward the sound and spread away some of the grass. "One of you men keep a lookout." He hesitated for only a moment, trying to grasp what he saw—a young woman with tangled dark hair, tawny skin, but with a beauty that showed through the scratches on her face.

"Well, begorrah, 'tis an Indian ye are. What's happened? Have ye been thrown from your horse?" He knelt by the woman's side. "Let's have a look at this arm—a right bit of blood ye've lost." Allie shoved back his cap and inspected the wound, fearful of causing more pain.

A soldier had followed him, weapon drawn. "What is it, Sergeant? You all right?"

"I'm all right, but not this one. Hand me a canteen." He took the water and offered the injured girl some of the cool liquid. "Not too much now. Ye can have more later. Can ye talk English?"

She nodded.

"This blood's coming from a bullet wound, and a lot more is dried. It's fair ruined her arm. We're taking her to the fort." He turned back to the men. "Somebody have whiskey?"

Jeb dismounted and pulled out a small flask.

Allie washed the wound first with water. The girl gasped as he poured the whiskey on her arm. "I know it stings, but we need to clean it up best we can. We're here to help. Can ye tell me your name?"

With a faint smile, the girl answered, "Yvonne Graham. My father is Judge Graham, in Red Oak. I don't know where he is now."

Allie's brow furrowed. "Lordy, Lord. If I take ye to your village it may be too late, and I don't know what kind of care ye would get there."

Jeb whispered over Allie's shoulder. "Are you sure you know what you're thinking?"

"We'll take her to the fort and hope our doc's better than hers." Allie wasn't quite sure why, but he stuck to his decision.

"White men ambushed our party and took me for ransom." Yvonne sucked in a deep breath and winced. "I slipped away...got a horse...A white man in dirty buckskin shot me. I fell off the horse, and it bolted."

"Hush, now. Save your strength."

"The man must have thought I was dead." Her voice grew softer. "He did not follow." She turned away and closed her eyes.

Allie leaned over and said, "Miss Graham, we're going to the fort. Our doctor will soon fix ye up like new." He wasn't entirely certain about that.

"You are not taking me to Red Oak, to my people?" It was almost a statement instead of a question. "We have a doctor there," she murmured.

Allie, still shocked at finding the woman, wondered what kind of doctor they would have. "We want ye to have the best and soon. It would take too long to ride to Red Oak, and ye need help straight away. And may I say, it's very brave ye are."

Yvonne swallowed dryly. "My father will reward you...if he is safe."

While watching the scene, one of the men snickered. "Hey, Jeb, I think the sergeant's smitten all right. Maybe he ought to ask her how many ponies he'd have to tie in front of her pa's tipi before he can claim her."

"You nibnob." Jeb shook his head. "Heck, they're more educated than us, and most of 'em have more money."

Allie mused the same thing about the ponies. He'd read about it. Feeling a rush of discomfort, he was mindful of the gawking troopers. "I need some help here." He climbed on his horse, and one of the soldiers lifted Yvonne to him.

They angled away from the creek bottom and traveled some hundred yards over a rough terrain before the sergeant gave the order to halt. "And how are ye now, Miss Graham? I know ye must be feelin' a lot of pain."

"It's all right. A Choctaw can take pain." A slight smile appeared on her face.

The small patrol turned in the direction of the fort. About a half mile from where they rescued the girl, Jeb, riding at the rear, trotted to the front of the group. "Sarge, hold up...I swear there's something over at that ledge yonder. Either it's human or a prairie dog's learned how to whinny."

"Let's pretend ye didn't hear anything. Men, keep facing straight ahead, but turn your eyes that direction. And stay quiet."

In the silence, a snap of a stick confirmed their suspicions.

"Yep, there it is again. Somebody's out there for sure," Jeb said.

Allie turned to the soldier who had pulled up beside him. "Private, lend a hand here."

The private dismounted, lifted the girl from Allie's arms and laid her on the ground in the protection of tall grass.

Allie slid off his horse and aimed his rifle. "Over there behind the ledge," he yelled.

"Come out from there with your arms raised."

A shot pierced the air. Allie ducked. "Take cover, men," Another shot followed, this time coming from the far left of the rocks.

Jeb crouched behind a barrel cactus. "Dang, there ain't that much cover to take."

"Well, find some."

The men leapt from their horses and scrambled into the brush.

At least one figure on the rocks showed himself for a split second. Shots came from two other sources along the ledge. The soldiers returned fire.

"I guess there's just three of them up there." Allie squinted against the sun. Then, one rifle fell silent.

"Make that two. Somebody musta got one of 'em." Shots fired in rapid succession. "Dang! That one plucked my sleeve."

"You hit?"

"Nah. Nothin' serious. They didn't get my shootin' arm." He grabbed at his shoulder, still gripping his rifle with the other hand.

"Jeb! You are too hit!"

"I tell ya, I'm all right. Let's move over three, four yards so's the sun won't blind us."

"I'm not sure I believe you, but let's go."

Staying low, the men snaked over to a choicer spot.

Jeb put one elbow on the ground, bracing his rifle. "I'll fire next to where I think he is. If we can get one of 'em to put hisself out there again... then you shoot 'im." Jeb fired.

A man poked his shoulders and head above the rocks. Allie let go a shot right on target. A white man in dirty buckskin cried out and fell off the ledge, bringing crumbled rocks with him.

The only other sounds from the ledge were horse hooves going in the opposite direction.

"They must've been here all morning, waiting for us to finish our business. Two of you go up there and see what we have. Jeb, check for the ransom money, then load them up."

Allie raced to where the private left Yvonne. Sound asleep, she couldn't have known what just transpired.

Jeb and two of the soldiers arranged the dead men over the back of one of their horses.

"I guess the one that got away figured his life was more important than the money." Jeb swung the moneybag above his head. "Here it is, Sergeant!"

"So far, so good. It's time to be moving now." Again, with Yvonne in front of him, the sergeant set the patrol in motion at a faster pace. They arrived at the post hospital in late afternoon. The pungent smell of ether and disinfectant cleared Allie's head. After the clean air and fresh smell of the trees, the odors were overwhelming. Allie found the post surgeon, Dr. Barnes, peering through a lens glass.

He turned when the door opened. "Ah, Sergeant. What can I do for you?"

"We're bringing you a patient, Dr. Barnes. She really needs your help." He stepped to the door and yelled, "In here, men."

As they brought the girl inside, the doctor protested. "Sergeant, you've brought me an Indian. I'm not sure what the colonel will say, even if she is an injured female." He briefly examined her arm. "Get me permission from the colonel before I treat her. In the meantime, I'll check her out and give her laudanum to ease the pain."

"We had no time to find her people, sir, and she's lost a lot of blood. She can speak English, so ye'll know."

Allie left for the colonel's office. On the way, he told Jeb, still sitting on the steps, "Get in there and let Dr. Barnes fix up your shoulder!"

~~~

Allie related the events to the colonel. "And, sir, good treatment by us might aid in relations with her tribe."

"Sergeant, any help we can get to keep peaceful connections with the Indians will be most welcome, but you must understand, the Choctaws will give no problems. And indeed I hate that a white man did this, but it's nothing new. I'll telegraph the judge we have his daughter, assuming we can find him."

Taking the directive for Yvonne Graham's treatment, Allie returned to the hospital. "Ah," the doctor nodded. "You had success, although I can't see the colonel not agreeing. But let me tell you, the young lady's wound is serious. It could still have complications. She might lose her arm."

Some of his concerns came true. Yvonne's fever soared. Cold compresses and alcohol rubs would not bring it down. Allie found himself worrying about the young woman. He had never thought he would even notice another woman after Bernadette, but something about Yvonne Graham seemed to promise a new life for him.

When she slept, Allie couldn't take his eyes off her. When she awoke, they talked. He wondered how they could've been an ocean apart all their lives, yet it seemed to him they had always known each other. Unless on duty, Allie remained every waking hour by her side. When he first found her, he felt a gentle warmth shining through when she smiled at him.

Then one day, after Yvonne's fever broke, Dr. Barnes announced to Allie that she was out of danger. "I recommend Miss Graham stay here for another week or so. Certainly in her favor, there's no infection, but she's not ready to travel. As I understand it, her father cannot be located?"

"That's right, sir. I want to go find him, but I have patrol duty beginning tomorrow. You'll take the best care of her, won't you, Doctor?"

"Of course I will, Sergeant."

The two days Allie was gone, he thought of nothing but Yvonne. He came to an important decision. After reporting to headquarters late the second day, he headed straight for the hospital, where he found her bright and smiling, color back in her face.

He took her hand. "Ye were just as pretty the day I found ye, even with dirt on your face and tangled hair."

Yvonne laughed. "You're painting a not-so-pretty picture of me, Allie McCrae."

"Dr. Barnes says you're not ready to travel, but I'm going to Red Oak to see if your father is there." Allie hoped for her sake, the judge was alive. "He may still be searching for ye."

"Thank you, Allie. Please find my father... and be careful."

He returned to headquarters and gave a smart salute to the colonel sitting behind the large oak desk.

"At ease, Sergeant. What can I do for you?"

Nervous, he finally came out with, "Sir, I have a request. I'd like permission to marry."

Colonel Sherman nearly lost his balance in his tipped-back chair. "Well, well. What have I been missing, Sergeant? Who's the lucky girl?"

"We have discussed her before, sir. Yvonne Graham."

"What?" He scarcely paused. "Absolutely not! I thought you were joking." The colonel leaned forward from his chair. "Sergeant, it isn't allowed. You may be old enough to know your own mind, but right now you're completely out of it."

"But, sir, other wives are here—Mrs. Dickens and..."

"Sergeant, those were extenuating circumstances."

"Please, Colonel, can't you extenuate me, too?"

"You don't even know this woman." He tapped his pencil on the desk. "No, Sergeant, I can't go along with you on this."

"Sir, I think I know all that's necessary to know. If she will have me, I want to marry her."

Colonel Sherman's eyebrows raised. "You mean you haven't even asked her?"

"No, sir. I thought if she said 'yes,' and I couldn't get permission, then what would I tell her?"

"Sergeant, marrying an Indian woman isn't that simple. You must think of the consequences."

"Sir, I'm aware of the problems, but I have feelings for her. These are still me plans."

The colonel huffed a sigh. "All right... All right, if your mind is made up, I'll permit it. I will write a directive that there will be severe punishment for anyone who allows harassment of you or your wife. But be prepared, because I won't stand for any more trouble than we already encounter on this post."

Allie managed to conceal his excitement.

"And Sergeant, you need to know the Choctaw Nation has its own laws by which you will be bound. However, the next thing is to make sure we can locate her father. I guess you'd better see if she wants to marry you. Anything more, McCrae?"

"No, thank ye, sir. And I may say, sir, ye have been more than understanding and generous in this matter. I'd like to ride to Red Oak tomorrow."

"Very well. If I didn't know you as I do, I would never permit it. I have to keep my men happy, or I might have to run this command by myself. Sergeant, give it one more night's thought, will you?"

As if Allie would think of anything else.

Chapter 8

Early the next day, Allie wrote to the Nicholls and Clancys. Letters to them were long over-due, but he thought they would be pleased at his news. As soon as he finished, he reported to headquarters. He spied a corporal already there. "Corporal, I have some personal business to attend to. I'll be back late day at best, but most likely not till morning. I want ye to take me duties until I return."

"Be glad to, Sergeant."

Allie departed from the main gate, and giving his big mare a tap with his spurs, he headed her toward town. Blossom responded with a burst of speed for about thirty yards, and then settled into a slower pace.

Allie had developed a liking for pipes and took this opportunity to light one. All the while, he thought if the remaining part of his plan went as well as the first, everything would be good in his world. He might even get drunk later, but the thought of an ensuing headache gave him pause. He picked up a little speed when he saw the church spire of the town in the distance.

Riding at once to the bank, he asked for a withdrawal from his account.

The banker strode to the safe. "You sure you aren't leaving the army or maybe going into business?"

"No, I wouldn't be after doing either one."

"All right then. Here's your money, Sergeant. Sign here."

"Thank ye for the trouble." He turned and was out the door, leaving the banker without an answer. Allie kept his savings in the bank rather than in the fort. It wasn't much, but he figured money, like love, was a private matter.

He took Blossom's reins and walked down the street to the livery stable. The sign read, "Horses traded, sold, and boarded—Race Adams, Prop." Allie guided Blossom alongside the corral fence, eyeing the horses then dismounted and went into the weathered barn. He spied Adams on the far side, hanging up some bridles. He recognized him because he was the only man Allie knew who wore red suspenders.

"Mr. Adams?"

The proprietor turned at the sound of his name. "Hello there, Sergeant. Haven't seen you in a while."

"I hadn't had need to come into town till now. Mr. Adams, I need to make a purchase of two or three mares. And maybe that big roan stud out there."

"You planning to start a ranch?"

"Nothing that grand. I merely want a few horses to keep Blossom company. I'll take the stallion and look over the others before I choose. We'll get serious about the price once I finish."

"No hurry, Sergeant. Take time to tend your mount."

After giving his horse oats and water, he made his selection. He wondered if Yvonne's father would take three horses, or maybe he'd better offer four. Reaching over the fence, he removed a coil of rope from the pommel and measured the appropriate lengths. When finished, he returned to the stable office to complete the transaction. He laid his money on Mr. Adams's desk.

The proprietor glanced at it and drummed his fingers for a moment. He cocked his head. "Whoa now." He frowned and stroked his jaw. "That's not what the sign on the barn says."

"That may be your price, but I'm giving ye mine. Don't forget, I know me horses. Since I'm making a purchase of four here, I figure the offer's fair enough."

Adams stepped to the door and surveyed the sergeant's choices. "You're a tough one, McCrae." He hesitated. "So be it. I'll take your money. You did me out of some of the best horseflesh I had. Now, if you'll excuse the nosiness of an old horse trader, what are you planning to do with them?"

"I intend to start a family, but first, I plan to have a wife. These horses will be the price."

Adams grinned. "You buying an Indian bride?"

"Ye bet your saddle. And she's special. Her name's Yvonne Graham."

A momentary surprised expression crossed the horse trader's face. "You mean Judge Graham's daughter? Over in Red Oak? Well, I doubt he'll be taking any ponies for his daughter." Adams chuckled as Allie left.

Leading the string out of town, he turned due south, still curious over what Adams meant by his last remark and especially the chuckle. He noticed Blossom seemed nervous with the stallion behind her. He reached over to rub her ears. "Now, don't worry, girl. You'll be fine."

He soon passed the creek and small grove of trees where he and his men had stayed earlier. Ten miles or so farther on, he ran into a group of mounted Choctaws a few miles outside of Red Oak. Allie slowed, but the Choctaws continued toward him, locking eyes.

Armed with four horses and a little nerve, Allie wondered what he had to lose—besides four horses. "Afternoon to ye. Do ye happen to know where I can find Judge Ellis Graham?"

One of them nodded. "Yes." After lighting up a cheroot, he gave directions. "He may be back now. He seeks his daughter."

"Thank ye for the information." With a sigh of relief, Allie rode away, clearly hearing, "Ye, ye, ye," then subdued laughter. *Are they making fun of the way I talk? I might could change that to American... and I might be king of the leprechauns, too.*

He continued riding, glad to know the judge was safe. By afternoon, he arrived in Red Oak and had no trouble locating the Graham's house. The judge had not returned, so he wouldn't have received the message about Yvonne's safety.

Allie took a drink from his canteen and sat in a chair on the porch, propping his feet on the railing. He started to doze when a horse came into view. The rider wore a dark and dusty suit, his long, graying braids showing beneath a black-brimmed hat. The man slowly dismounted and rail-hitched his sleek palomino before stopping at the well for a dipper of water.

Allie stood. "Judge Gra—"

The judge was obviously unaware of Allie's presence. "Oh, you startled me. I'm sorry."

"Judge Graham, are you all right?"

The judge removed his hat. "Please excuse my appearance. I am very tired, and I have injured my ribs. It is painful to ride."

"Sir, I'm glad to know you are safe. I am Sergeant McCrae from Fort Guardian. I have news—"

"I am sick with worry over my daughter." The judge pulled the bandana from around his neck. "She's been taken from me."

"Sir, your daughter's safe. That's why I'm here."

A broad smile flushed away the shadows that had clung to Graham's cheekbones.

"Where is she? Is she all right?"

"The doctor is treating your daughter at Fort Guardian, sir. She was shot, but—"

"Yvonne shot?" The judge caught his balance on the porch banister. "I must go to her."

"That won't be necessary. She is much better now. You need to rest. I'll see that she gets home when she's well enough to travel."

The judge's tension visibly eased. "Come, sit down. I'm indebted to you. Those men sent word for us to place money in a grove of trees fifteen miles out... and they would return my daughter. I placed the bag of money there, but I have not found her."

"It was by accident we caught sight of your daughter. A few more yards either way, we wouldn't have."

Graham stopped and gazed into the distance. "I did not know if I would find her, but still... I had to try. My men and I have searched for many miles. This is a kindness I will not forget, Sergeant. I will be anxious to have Yvonne home."

"Judge Graham, I must tell you, me men and I shot two of the three men who ambushed you, including the one who shot your daughter. The money he had on him is at the fort. I suspect it would be the ransom money. I chose not to bring it with me, but it will be returned to you."

"My thanks, Sergeant. Do you have an idea who the outlaws were?"

"No, sir, I hoped you might. One of them got away. The other two didn't have names on their possessions."

"It makes no difference now, as long as my daughter is safe. Her mother died three years ago, and Yvonne is all I have. Yes, as you can imagine, I am overjoyed you found her."

The judge looked out at the string of horses. He studied them a moment. "How did you acquire such fine animals, my friend?"

Allie felt embarrassment coming on. "Well, sir, I thought when a white man sees an Indian woman he wants for a wife, he asks her father if ponies are enough payment... And I do want to marry your daughter—with your permission—and hers."

The judge's face was one of astonished amusement. "Sergeant McCrae, I would not sell my daughter into marriage for any price. If there were a price, though, you have already met it by rescuing her. However, I would like to purchase these animals to add to my herd, that is, if you have no other plans."

"I have to tell you, sir. I was getting a strange feeling that bringing these horses here might not be the right thing to do."

"Perhaps it still is for some," the judge explained, smiling. "In my father's day, it was expected. However, I insist on purchasing these mounts if you are willing. I was planning to add to my herd but had not found time. We've had marauders lately in the area, and after all, being a judge takes priority over my personal business." Judge Graham stood. "One moment, Sergeant." He went into the house and returned with coins and handed them to Allie. "This should cover the cost and save me time in purchasing more."

"I don't want to be disrespectful, but... if you really want the horses, I cannot accept more than I paid. This is too much." He handed part of the money back and stuffed the remainder into a small leather sack.

"Sergeant, as for marrying my daughter, it seems a little soon. But I cannot answer for her. She is a sensible girl, and if she says she will marry you, you have my permission. Mind you though, Yvonne will not say 'yes' only because you saved her life. She will decide with her head, as well as her heart."

Allie nodded his understanding. "I rather thought so, sir."

"If she consents, however, after you marry according to your religion, you will return to Red Oak for a Choctaw ceremony conforming to our ways. I will not attend your first ceremony but will wait for your return. Agreed?"

"Agreed. Thank you, Judge Graham. I'll be most disappointed if she doesn't accept." A feeling of disquiet engulfed him when he thought of that possibility.

The judge invited him to stay for a meal, and even the night, but Allie was anxious to get back to Yvonne. They exchanged farewells, and Allie made one last stop before leaving the town. Reining his horse in front of the General Store, he entered, took a deep breath and asked for the prettiest dress they had.

When the storekeeper asked the size, Allie replied, "On the small side of medium, I'd say."

From three choices, he selected a light blue dress with embroidered collar and cuffs. And if she wouldn't marry him? he wondered. Well, she would have a new blue dress.

A few miles out, overtaken by darkness, he regretted not accepting the judge's invitation.

He spent a hungry night under the stars, while Blossom grazed on the grass near him.

"I say, girl, about now, eating grass almost sounds tasty to me."

At first light, he headed for the town near Fort Guardian to deposit most of the money the judge had given him. He stopped for coffee and biscuits, thinking he had to eat something to quell the hungry rumbling in his stomach.

After Allie arrived at the fort, he checked in at headquarters then hastened to see Yvonne.

He saw at once that she was sitting on the front porch of the fort's hospital. "I came back as soon as I could. My, ye look so well."

"I missed you, Allie McCrae. I'm happy you're here."

Even though he had stayed with her as much as possible during the last few weeks, he was a little surprised, although gratified, at her response to his return.

"Did you find my father?"

"Yes, that I did. He will be fine and is anxious for your return." The smile that covered Yvonne's face seemed to Allie to be one of relief.

"That helps me get well faster. I knew he would be worried, as I was about him." She paused. "Allie, what I'd really like right now is to walk in the sunshine. I haven't been outside much, but I feel like going for a walk. Do you have time?"

"I do." He held her hand as they walked into the warmth of midday. Allie felt a quiver in his insides. He steeled himself to the question he was about to ask. "Yvonne, I have something important on me mind."

"Yes, what is it?"

"Uh... we've never even talked about what color ye like or even your favorite food."

"Oh, now, that's important!" She laughed.

"Well, of course I care about your choice in colors and your favorite food, but that's not me real question. What I want to know is, Yvonne... will ye marry me?"

Yvonne stopped short. Turning toward him, she asked, "Marry you? Allie, are you sure? You haven't known me long."

"Ye haven't known me longer. Besides, I've known ye long enough. Do ye have thoughts in that direction toward me?"

Yvonne's pause made Allie certain she would turn him down. *I'm thinking it's sure to be a "no."*

She turned quickly. "Allie McCrae. I will be happy to marry ye."

"'Ye'? And I'm trying to say '*you.*'"

"Don't try. It's your connection to Ireland."

"It's a happy man ye've made me, darlin'." Careful to protect her injured arm, he half-twirled her around.

He was surprised at how soon the ceremony was arranged, once the commandant issued orders to set it into motion. One of the army wives was reluctant at first, but she took care of details. She even found flowers for Yvonne to carry. The dress Allie bought for her in Red Oak fit perfectly.

The fort's priest married the couple, with many of Allie's friends as witnesses. Jeb stood up for his friend and seemed totally embarrassed, shifting from one foot to the other.

The priest's words were impressive, although Allie wasn't sure he heard any of them, except the man and wife part. He gazed at the loveliness of his bride and wondered if this was really happening to him.

As soon as he made arrangements for the trip to Red Oak, he packed the wagon. He made sure Yvonne was comfortable and then climbed aboard. Reins in hand, he was ready. "Oh, oh, I forgot!"

"What, Allie? Is it important?"

"It is that. I won't be long." He rushed back inside. *Where is it? I thought I had it right on me table!* "There. begorrah!" he said aloud. He grabbed the paper and hurried back to the wagon.

"Allie! What is it?"

He heaved a sigh of relief. "It's me letter of reference from the colonel."

Yvonne laughed. "Yes, I guess that *is* important."

"Your father told me that before a white man could marry into the tribe, Choctaw law required him to be of respectable character, and the colonel wrote that I am that."

"And my father will also write for you."

Chapter 9

When Allie and Yvonne moved closer to the Graham home in Red Oak, they could see the judge pacing on his porch. As they pulled up in front of the house, the judge was there before their spring carriage came to a halt.

"Sergeant, you have brought her. Yvonne, come." He helped her out, then grasped her hands and stood back. "You look beautiful. And to think, I feared I would never see you again."

"You might not have, except for Allie."

"And for that, I thank him." Judge Graham put his arms around his daughter. "Let us go inside and we will talk. Oh, but you must feel the need to rest or change clothes from your journey."

"I will lie down for only a moment," Yvonne said. "I am anxious to talk, as I imagine Allie is also."

When all were ready, the three sat at a table, and the judge spoke. "First, my daughter, I want you to know I gave Sergeant McCrae my consent when he first came to tell me of your safety. But after he left, I gave it my best thought and wondered if my mind should change."

Allie looked at Yvonne with apprehension.

The judge continued, "And you know, my mind did not change!"

Immediate relief spread on the young couple's faces.

"Sergeant, you will be interested to know that lengthy Choctaw ceremonies were changed recently. Yours will be more brief than they used to be."

Allie didn't know how long that meant and thought papers he filled out and questions he answered seemed lengthy enough. The documents formed a major part of a Choctaw wedding between an Indian and a white. After all were completed, attention turned to the ceremony and the festivities.

As soon as family friends and various cousins heard the news, they went to work. Since Allie needed to return to the fort, they moved fast. The simple wedding came to life with Yvonne colorfully dressed with ribbons in her hair and a family necklace belonging to her mother.

Large tables under shade trees almost succumbed to the weight of food arranged on top.

The line of guests was long, and it would take some time for everyone to be served. All came dressed in reds and blues, yellows—all bright. After they finished eating and shaking hands with everyone, the festivities at last came to an end.

The couple stayed one more day. "And now we must go. I am expected back to me duties." Sergeant McCrae, with his new bride, made ready for the long ride back to Fort Guardian.

Yvonne and her father said their goodbyes, but before leaving, Allie had one last thing to say to the judge. "Sir, I want to thank ye."

"You mean for permission to marry my daughter?"

"No, sir. I heard the Choctaw Nation sent money to help Ireland during the potato famine. I never thought I'd have a chance to give ye thanks in person."

"Now that's been a while. Let us hope such a need does not arise again. And Sergeant, let me know if you ever come across any more fine horses."

~~~

Allie's marriage to Yvonne did not create as much stir within the fort as he had anticipated. He learned that his wife knew how to quilt and was adept at sewing and tatting. She also told him she feared the women would think she felt herself superior. But it was not long before they began asking questions concerning other matters. She had gained their trust.

By fall, Yvonne told Allie she would be having their child.

Not that he never expected to hear such news, but his jaw dropped just the same. "That's grand. Just think. Me, Allie McCrae, a father. Ye will have it in the fort hospital under Doc Barnes's care."

"No, my husband, our child will be half Choctaw. The great grandchild of a Choctaw leader must be born in the home of its family."

Allie thought only a moment and smiled. "Yes, of course he must." He knew before that day came, a winter would be upon them. And it came with a vengeance. The first norther swept the Territory with a raw veracity that blew dust into every crack of every building at the fort. Each dry norther that followed made life unbearable for the soldiers. A bucket of water from the well had to be covered on the way to their quarters. Sand even flew into a dipperful before a person could take the first sip.

Christmas came and went. The snow stayed. Lines were down, and no word could get to or from Red Oak. With Yvonne concerned about her father, Allie knew the judge would have the same worry about her.

It was a long winter. But when the curtain of brown covering the sun dissipated, a prayed-for brightness shown through. Snow melted, and the fort came to life.

With the arrival of early spring, Yvonne announced, "I do not know when our child will be born, but soon."

The next month, Allie secured a light spring carriage, and they rode the distance to Red Oak. "The time is near for the birth of your grandchild," Allie told the judge, "but I can't stay. I ask ye to please send for me when the babe is born, or if there is any trouble at all."

"It will be done," answered Judge Graham. "You need not worry. We will have plenty of help, and Yvonne will get the best of care."

"Then I will leave, with my thanks."

He kissed Yvonne. "I love you, Yvonne. Be safe."

~~~

As soon as Allie got word from Judge Graham that his son had been born, he made arrangements to return to Red Oak. He hated not being able to leave immediately, but once he did, the carriage jolted him until his muscles ached.

The judge greeted him at the door with the words that the child was healthy and strong of voice. "The midwives did their work well. Come, Yvonne is waiting."

"That's the best news of all, Judge, and I can hear the lad bellow from here." Allie rushed into the bedroom to see Yvonne, beautiful to him as always, holding their son.

"You are here, Allie, and even sooner than I expected. See what I have for you."

Allie started for his son, then stopped. "Maybe I'd better wash me hands first."

"Once won't hurt. Hold him, Allie."

"Well, all right, if you think..." He reached for his son, while leaning to kiss Yvonne on the forehead. "I've not had a good night's sleep since in I don't know when, for worrying about ye."

"Isn't he handsome?"

"If ye say so. He's a bonny little thing, but I do feel a bit awkward holding him like this. Am I doing it right?"

"Perfectly."

"But a name. What about a name?"

"Well, I've been thinking. What do you think of Marcus Graham McCrae, after his Irish and Choctaw grandfathers."

"No name could be better," Allie replied, beaming. "Now, are ye sure ye feel up to traveling?"

"Oh, yes, I think so. Our things are there on the bench." Yvonne held out their son so her father could have one more proud moment before they left.

"Goodbye, Judge," Allie said. "I hope it won't be long before we see ye again."

"Take care of my grandson, Sergeant... and my daughter."

"I will, ye can be sure. And Marcus, m'boy, ye will grow up to be the biggest, strongest, and smartest man in the west. But until ye do, we must be on our way."

Chapter 10

1863

As Brian Clancy predicted when Allie first arrived in America, the "certain and sure" war had indeed occurred. In both North and South, people heard the strong words of a man named Lincoln. Settlers flooded westward, many not knowing their destination, nor caring, as long as they left the hostilities behind.

Allie's regiment was called to protect riverboats on the Mississippi. He said a reluctant goodbye to his wife and son, who returned to Red Oak to stay with her family.

He had told Yvonne, "I feel torn within. I hate the thought of slavery and want none of it. This Choctaw Nation is part of the Confederacy, with its own regiments. Some of your father's friends own slaves. The judge could have them, too, but he is as much against it as I am."

"I want you to be safe, my husband. You must stay alive for me... and for your son."

~~~

Allie wrote often to Yvonne during the years he was away but never mentioned his wound of the last battle. After recuperating at the end of the fighting, he received his release but had no intention of leaving the army. It was all he knew.

After Allie returned to Fort Guardian, Judge Graham drove his daughter and grandson to the fort to join him. When they arrived, the judge helped Yvonne from the carriage. She stood at a distance for one brief moment, then took their son by the hand and they both ran to Allie.

He reached to put his arms around her, but quickly brought one away.

"Oh, Allie, you hold your arm. What has happened?"

"I'll have this sling off in no time. A bullet got off its course, that's all. I wouldn't want to miss this homecoming."

Allie grinned when he saw his son. He leaned over for a big hug. "Marcus, ye have grown twice the size you were. I kept thinking how you would change while I was gone."

"Mother calls me Mark. Father, I was afraid you might not come home." The little boy grabbed onto his hand.

"I had to come back to see you. And it's Mark, is it? And have you learned more of your Mother's language while I was away?"

Mark nodded vigorously. "Waw kay."

"Ah, and I believe that's a 'yes.'"

"Allie, your son can sit a horse as well as any cavalryman. Now that the government is re-opening the schools, he will gain more knowledge."

"Ye have raised our son well. I am pleased, I am."

1870

The army was Allie's life, but he wanted a change. He hoped they wouldn't remain at Guardian much longer. Soon after he had these thoughts, rumors of a transfer arrived. Allie wired Judge Graham to come to Fort Guardian. Moving could mean hundreds of miles away, and they might never know when they would meet again.

One morning, wagons lined up at the fort, and Allie knew that for some of them, their time had come.

"McCrae, wait up," Jeb yelled. "Did you get orders for Fort Hellsgate?"

"Yes, me name's on the list. Are ye going, too?"

"Why, sure as hell I am. I'm about ready to see some new scenery."

Allie anticipated the troops' main adversaries in Arizona would be Apaches—chiefs such as Victorio and Geronimo, all dangerous. Since Jeb would serve with the protective patrol, he felt secure that the few family members would arrive safely the following week.

~~~

"I know we've used up all the miles in America," Allie vowed to anyone in earshot. "Will we ever see green again?"

No Indians had crossed their paths, although a range war or two erupted through New Mexico Territory. It was not in their military jurisdiction, so the troops moved on. Little arid land confronted them, and water and trees were home to deer and elk. The wagons soon crossed the border, and only scrubby trees stood alongside the trail.

After crossing into Arizona Territory close to a hundred miles from the New Mexico border, one trooper voiced, "That must be the fort yonder. I can sure see why they call this place 'Hellsgate.' May be right close to hell itself."

At noon, they passed through the double-gated entrance of Fort Hellsgate, a name befitting its reputation of holding forth in an area of destruction, desert, and oftentimes the unexpected.

"I thought going from New York to Jefferson Barracks was something," Allie said. "From there to Fort Guardian was nothing, but this time..."

A soldier from Jefferson Barracks agreed. "How could the beauty of New Mexico turn to such barren land?"

Allie thought a moment. "It still has its own beauty, and maybe more, once we've seen it all."

A voice broke out. "Men, into that building with the lantern on the door." The owner of the voice introduced himself as Sergeant Elliot. "But hand over your papers to me first."

They did so in exchange for their assignments. "Take your gear and report back for mess."

Allie heard the early sounds of pans banging in the kitchen, and he knew he would hurry back. By the time the men returned, the hall smelled of coffee, fresh bread, and whatever kind of meat they ate in Arizona. Allie found out after his first meal in Hellsgate and decided it wasn't too bad. He knew Yvonne could give the cooks a few pointers.

The wagons carrying the soldiers' families arrived two weeks later. Allie had their quarters ready, not the same as for officers, but since he had a family before the transfer, he was eligible for family quarters.

Allie helped his wife and son from the wagon then hugged them both. "I was beginning to worry, but I knew Jeb would've taken care of ye if trouble came about."

"It wasn't bad at all," she replied. "But I'm glad we're here now. It's a bright day. The sun seems larger here than in Fort Guardian."

"It may be, at that. And Mark, Is it possible that ye've grown in the last two weeks?"

"I'll soon be as tall as Mother," Mark bragged.

"I do believe so," Allie said. "Now, let's get your belongings, and I'll take ye home. I guess that's not exactly the right word, but it's where we'll be living."

~~~

For the next several days, Yvonne put together as much as she could toward making their quarters comfortable. She had brought curtains from Fort Guardian, and personal possessions, including two quilts that had traveled all the way from Red Oak to Arizona Territory.

Allie beamed to see his wife transform their living arrangement into a place of comfort.

"Allie, this chest needs to be over on the west wall. Do you have time to do it now?"

"Aye, that I do."

"And don't you think it would be good to move the bed over here, so when we wake in the morning, we can see the morning sun?"

"Aye, that I do."

Yvonne tugged on one side, until they placed it just right. "There now, that's perfect." She placed her prized hand mirror, brush and comb on the dresser. Of course, the crocheted dresser scarf also helped. Without upholstered chairs, the antimacassars would have to wait much longer to find use.

"Mark's room is small, like an annex to ours, but there isn't much we can do about that. You know, Allie, the land seems peaceful and serene, but we have left behind much beauty."

"That last part is true. The Indians here are far different from those in the Territory, so I'll question the peaceful part. I hope I haven't done wrong, bringing ye here."

"But Allie, where else would we be? One thing, though. There are a few women and what if they won't accept me?"

"Don't ye worry a bit. Ye'll have them come calling in no time."

Mark spoke up. "There are some boys here about my age. They might be friendly."

Allie was right. He took pride in Yvonne's not being presumptuous concerning her own talents or education, and she could offer help. The women were stand-offish, but they soon began asking her advice ranging from child rearing, especially after seeing how polite Mark was, to Indian folk-remedies.

The McCraes saw to it that Mark started in the small school at the fort. His education in Indian Territory put him ahead of the local curriculum. His teacher suggested he should enroll in the school run by the church in Clear Springs. Again, he couldn't attend every day, but could take a week's worth of homework back to the fort and complete it for the next trip into town.

~~~

By the time Mark was fifteen, he'd already decided he would be a military man like his father. He was adept at the rifle and had the eye of a hawk. Mark and his friends often went out on hunting trips but always within safe boundaries.

In the coming months, he heard rumors that Colonel Hardin, commanding officer of Fort Hellsgate, had received a bulletin from the War Department. If he thought it relevant, he was to post a notice for army dependents to take tests for appointments to West Point.

When the rumors proved true, Mark's head spun for a week. *But will they ever accept an Indian?*

Colonel Hardin called Mark and two of his friends into his office. All three attended the fort's school. "I'll tell you now. The test will be in one month. Until then, review your math studies and military tactics you have learned in school.

"Each of you has a chance, but only one, if any, will win an appointment. Concentrate on your work and try to think it through rather than merely memorizing it."

The boys left the colonel's office with smiles on their faces, jostling each other as to who had the best chance of being accepted.

Mark saw more of his study books than of his parents. After taking the tests, the next few weeks were the longest he ever spent, until the colonel finally called him into his office. He thought the colonel's face appeared grim.

"Well, Son, I must tell you of the report. You see, I also sent in my recommendation."

"Sir, it's all right. I didn't really expect to win, but thank—"

"You didn't? Well, that's interesting, because this paper right here says, you, Marcus Graham McCrae, have received an appointment to West Point."

"Sir, are you sure?"

"Here it is. See for yourself." The colonel leaned back in his chair and smiled broadly.

"Have you told my parents?"

"No, I thought I'd let you do that."

~~~

A few weeks remained before Mark left for West Point. Even though his friends were glad for him, he knew they were disappointed in not going. One of the boys said, "Okay, Mark, you learn all about that place and let us know. Maybe we can go one day soon, and if not, we'll know somebody who did."

Prior to Mark's leaving Hellsgate for the east, Colonel Hardin called him in to give last-minute advice. "Mark, you must remember what I tell you. Everyone in West Point will be a stranger to you. You'll feel alone. Because of your heritage, you will be the object of many jokes—more than normal hazing given by upperclassmen on all freshmen, or plebes, as they call them. There is no doubt in my mind they will make it difficult for you."

"Yes, sir. I think I would expect that."

"As far as I know, you will be the first half-blood to enter the Academy. The Point has one student of color, and I have learned of his trials. Don't let it get the best of you."

"Yes, sir."

"Study and do as instructed. Expect difficulties. That will make it easier for you, and you won't be blindsided. Later, you will be an upperclassman yourself. I wish you the best of luck."

"Thank you, sir. I'll remember."

"When you graduate, I will write the superintendent and another personal friend who has some say to see if you can return here to serve under me. You have many friends who want you to do well. Be sure to write to your parents often and perhaps an occasional letter to me."

"Yes, sir. I plan to, and I appreciate all you've done, sir."

Mark went back to their quarters. He thought his mother was more concerned about what he should take with him than he was, but he let her pack what she wanted.

"Son, I guess I forgot to notice you're a young man now and so handsome. The New York girls won't leave you alone."

Mark laughed. "You think so because you're my mother."

"Here, now let me look at you." She brushed off imaginary lint from his shoulder.

"I doubt there will be girls at West Point."

"Well, you never know. They may have some kind of party. Anyway, here is a tin of cookies, and I've put together necessary clothes for your journey."

"I will have uniforms at West Point."

"I know. I know..." Her voice broke off. "Oh, I hear your father now." She reached over and kissed him on the cheek.

Mark opened the door, and then put his arms around his mother for one last hug. And, after a tearful goodbye from her, he said, "Don't worry, Mother. I'll be fine." He might have thought to shed a tear but would never actually do so.

"Come on, Mark. Time to go!" Allie called.

~~~

Mark climbed into the wagon, and off they went to catch the stage in Clear Springs. After the two-hour trip, they arrived early and went inside.

Allie said a few words to the stationmaster, and then turned to Mark. "Son, I brought a directive from Colonel Hardin to make sure the driver knows how important it is for you to be on the stage and to make all the changes."

"He didn't have to do that. I can handle it."

"Nevertheless, the driver is to pass it on to the next way station. Colonel Hardin doesn't want anything to stand in your way of getting to West Point on schedule. He feels responsible."

"Well, he may have a good idea at that."

"Son, I wish I could stay to see ye off, but the stage is late—always is, and I have to get back to the fort... but... I don't know what else to say, except do the best ye can. That's all we ask. Mind your temper, and don't let it get in the way of solving a situation. Ye already know you're going to have problems, but ye can handle them by staying on the right side of proper."

Mark stood silent a moment. They shook hands then broke into a father-son embrace.

Allie climbed into the wagon, and with a final wave, rode away.

Chapter 11

When Mark attempted to board the stage, a surly man stepped in front of him and pushed him aside. "Outta my way, kid. You don't belong here."

Mark righted himself, prepared for a fight, until he remembered what his father had told him less than an hour earlier.

To his surprise, the driver, a large man about the same size as the man who pushed him, climbed down and shoved the ruffian aside. "As long as I have this letter from the commandant, we'll have no further grief." Arming Mark into the stagecoach, he returned to the driver's seat. He reached around for the man's luggage and threw it off with such force, the lid flew open, slinging contents into the would-be traveler's face.

"Now get yoreself outta here. You ain't gettin' on my stage." He pulled away, leaving the reprobate rattling off a slew of cuss words as he shook his fist at the swirling dust.

"We've seen the last of that one," the driver yelled.

Mark felt his eyes grow wide at the incident, and then noticed a passenger sitting across from him dressed in a trim black suit and a flattop black hat.

The man stared at him from the time the stage departed. "Where you bound, kid?"

"I'm going to a school for soldiers, called West Point. Do you know where the school is, sir?"

"Of course. In New York State. Sits on a high plain overlooking a great river. They hire you as a servant?"

"Oh no. Colonel Hardin at Fort Hellsgate arranged tests for sons of army men. My father's a sergeant there. My scores were highest, and I won an appointment.

"Well, I'll be. That's hard to believe." With that, the man fell silent and turned his interest toward the arid plains.

Mark thought if he touched the man, his skin would be cold. He noticed him stealing occasional glances, as if to see reason for an Indian to be enrolled at West Point.

The children at Fort Hellsgate had played with Mark, and even when he became a teenager, no one had ever given him cause to believe he was so different. He was his parents' only child, and he meant everything to them. But the bad-tempered traveler and the unfriendly passenger plagued his thoughts the entire day. Colonel Hardin had warned him it would be like this. He thought he was prepared for the next time.

After a dust storm and a lame horse had shut them down for part of the way, the last stage made it to Mark's final stop in New York, almost on schedule. The driver directed him to the shuttle wagon. It would carry him and other newly arrived students to register their presence and obtain barracks assignments.

"Good luck, Son," the driver said. "You'll need it."

"Thank you, sir." Mark gathered his belongings and walked to the wagon. He'd tried to grab all the luck he could, because at this point, uncertainty began creeping into his nerve endings.

Mark and the rest of the group reported to the grounds where the cadet captain admonished them. "Plebes, speed it up. It's time to start work, so form three ranks. Now! A rank, for those who don't know, is a line."

The cadet officer stared at Mark. "Well, what have we here? A real redskin among us. Does the superintendent know you're here, or did you sneak in?" The other students snickered. Mark had a gut feeling his formal education had formally begun.

"All right, you nothings. West Point is a military school where you'll get a fine education, but you better pay attention to instructions and remember what you learn. Now! This building on the right is for plebes and is known as Beast Barracks. All of you are beasts, and we will train you—some more than others." He glared at Mark.

"Upperclassmen must be treated as superiors, so when a superior tells you to stand at attention, it's done like this." The speaker stood tall, with his chin in, in an exaggerated manner. "And bring your shoulder blades back until they touch!"

Mark gave it a try. *This is impossible.*

The cadet continued. "When asked your name and who has more authority than you, you will say, 'Sir,' and give your name. Then you'll answer, 'Those having more authority than I have are any upperclassman, the commandant's dog and the cat belonging to the commandant's wife.'"

"And one more thing. You never salute while smoking or with a chaw in your mouth. Don't dare do it, or you will wish you'd swallowed the whole wad."

After the cadet had given all the information for the first day, he directed the men to collect their bedding and go to their assigned quarters.

The young men avoided Mark on the way to the barracks. His stomach churned as he contemplated his immediate future.

Mark was pleasantly surprised when he entered his room. Metal beds were placed against the wall on each side. Spacious bookshelves stood at the end of the room with a gun rack, and each man had a desk, seemingly large enough for an open book, paper, and inkwell. He noticed his name was framed and hung on the wall above his bed. While Mark neatly rolled his blanket and sheets on his cot, another plebe walked in with his own bedding. Extending his hand, he said, "Hello, my name's Daniel Thatcher."

Mark turned around to introduce himself.

The new arrival took one look at Mark. "Not me! I'm not bunking next to any Indian." He made a quick exit.

Mark didn't spend time worrying about it. He covered the short distance to the classroom for instructions in military courtesy, wondering who such courtesy was for. Not that it came as a surprise to him, because he already knew that sometimes a man was unworthy of his uniform, but as long as he wore it, the uniform got the courtesy, not necessarily the man. He thought that might be hard to remember.

The following morning, Mark rose early for marksmanship testing. A hike on a narrow dirt road led to the practice field. He and the other men arrived at a clearing with a hillock blocking one end. A long trench rimmed the base of the embankment. Mark guessed it to be for the target crewmen to work in, elevating the six-foot paper targets.

One of the plebes called out, "Hey, Injun. Are you going to fire a rifle or did you bring your bow and arrows?"

This brought chuckles from the group. Mark showed a half-smile, but chose to remain quiet, thinking no reaction might lessen remarks.

A short, heavy-set lieutenant bawled out, "All right, everyone form three ranks in front of me! I'm Lieutenant Dailey, your weapons instructor. I grade each of you as either marksman, sharpshooter, or expert. Keep in mind these scores become part of your permanent file."

"Today you will qualify with the main weapon of the U.S. Army, the Spencer rifle. You will qualify at distances of a hundred, three-hundred, and five-hundred yards, all in the prone position, except the one hundred." The instructor paced back and forth in front of them then spun to face the first ranks.

"Starting on my left, count off in twenty-fives. The group will assume a prone position from the left on the line closest to the target. The second twenty-five will take up a standing position at the feet of the prone shooter. Each man will lay his hat in front of his position so the ammunition carrier can put your cartridges in same. Now! Count off!"

Big Jeff, a plebe designated as ammo bearer for the day, walked the ranks and dropped shells for each man. Nearing Mark, he slowed down. "Here, half-breed. Or can you count?"

Mark made no response. Each time it came his turn to fire, he held steady—just as his grandfather had taught him. He concentrated on the target and squeezed the trigger.

After class, the instructor called out, "Plebes, your qualifying day is over. Your classification based on hits will be posted on the bulletin board."

When Mark returned to his quarters, he found a new student in Thatcher's place. The sandy-haired young man introduced himself. "I'm Andrew Thompson from Stafford County, Virginia."

They exchanged small talk, and Mark thought Andrew seemed a bit too nice.

Andrew chuckled and leaned back in his chair. "I hope you can handle the hazing you got today. It's only the beginning. We'll all have our turns, but you, uh..."

"My background never bothered me."

"Friend, you may be in for more than you expect. I think you need to stay calm."

Mark continued to arrange his possessions in the small trunk by his bed. "My feeling is that a person can make of himself what he wants. If it takes studying by the light of burning coals, then that's how it will be. If it takes being courteous and a gentleman, even when I don't feel like it, I'll be courteous and a gentleman. I plan to graduate from this school on the hill. And then I'll go back to Arizona Territory with a commission."

~~~

"Expert!" Andrew said. "Did you see your score, Mark?"

"I see my marksmanship score all right, but where did these demerits come from?" *Who can I complain to? No one.*

Mark glanced up to see Daniel Thatcher searching for his own name. "Ah, Andrew, I see you have a new barracks-mate. I guess you're satisfied though. I paid you enough."

The glare Andrew gave Daniel could have melted a saber. "Daniel! You sorry... You'll get it back... all of it."

Mark didn't want any part of this conversation. He turned on his heel and strode toward the barracks.

"Wait, Mark." Andrew ran to catch up. "I'm sorry. Really. It was a lousy thing to do."

"It's nothing. Forget it." Mark accepted Andrew's apology, although he wouldn't forget.

Back in their quarters, Andrew didn't mention it. He pulled out his desk chair and changed the subject. "How did you get so good with the rifle?"

"We hunt where I come from. Firing at a piece of paper tacked on a board is easy. My great-grandfather was a Choctaw leader, and Grandfather has a cattle ranch in Indian Territory. He taught me to hunt and shoot."

"An Indian with a cattle ranch? I don't understand that at all."

"That's the way in the Territory. My mother went to school in New York City."

"That doesn't sound Indian. Nobody'd believe it. Besides, you don't look all Indian."

"I'm half. My father came from Ireland. He met my mother in the Territory."

Andrew shook his head. "Well, even part Indian is the same as all to most people. Anyway, we need to head for the stables. Let's get out of here."

"You go ahead. I need to finish this letter to my parents. I'll be right there."

"Don't take too long," Andrew called back. Mark finished writing and sealed the envelope. He rushed out the door and down the hall, making a quick turn to the left at the stairs.

"Plebe!" a cadet shouted. "Where do you think you're going? You almost knocked me down."

"Yes, sir. I'm sorry. I didn't come close to you, sir."

The cadet took a step forward. "Don't contradict me, plebe. If I say you knocked me down, that's what you did. Since you're so set on getting your exercise, why don't you try some eaglings? And flap those arms!"

"But sir, I have to get to—"

"Bend those knees, redskin. Here and now! So let's you get started until I tell you to stop."

After ten eaglings, Mark thought he'd done enough, but the cadet ordered him to continue. Sweat drenched his jacket.

"All right, plebe, that's it. Now, when you go to class, tell your instructor you couldn't get your lazy carcass there on time."

"Yes, sir." Mark took off at top speed, breathless before he started.

Captain Hawes, the instructor, came straight to Mark. He brought out his pocket watch. "You earned yourself a demerit. No need to ask your name. I think I already know it."

"Yes, sir."

Hawes climbed up the corral fence to make himself heard. "Attention," he bellowed.

"We'll parade the mounts inside the corral and see how good you know your horseflesh. Those who scored expert with the rifle will draw first. Sharpshooters next. Then the remaining qualifiers."

Mark could understand his father's Irish brogue. He'd grown up with it, but Hawes talked like he had a chaw in both sides of his mouth.

"After selecting your mounts," Hawes continued, "get a lead rope off the fence. Take your choice around to the stable. From the tack room, secure a curry brush and burlap bag and give your horse a rubdown."

The night before, Mark had thought of his grandfather's instructions on how to choose a pony. Choose one with good lines. And the eyes... the horse needs soft eyes.

Big Jeff drew lot number one.

Mark had third choice. He climbed the fence for a better view and surveyed the group of horses. *No, not that one. Legs too short.* Then one stood out among the rest—about sixteen hands high, with well-muscled hind legs. Mark held his breath for fear another plebe would choose the mare. No one did. The horse's eyes were soft and bright to Mark. *She's intelligent. I've found my horse.* He raised his hand, indicating his choice.

"All right, McCrae. Claim your mount," Captain Hawes barked.

Taking the lead rope, Mark headed toward the bay and led her to the barn. While he gave her a rubdown, Big Jeff became interested.

"How did I miss that one? And I had first choice."

"Well, I put an Indian spell on her to make her invisible."

"Listen, I'm supposed to be the funny man around here."

Mark patted the mare's nose. "Well now, we're going to be just fine, but you need a name. Hmm, how does 'Belle' sound?" It was the first name that came to mind. He stroked her long sleek neck. She nuzzled his shoulder in response.

After everyone finished, Captain Hawes announced, "Attention! When you report tomorrow, bring your sabers. Make sure they're in condition. Dismissed!"

Mark was anxious for saber practice. As boys, he and his friends had played with limbs cut from young saplings and pretended they were sabers like the soldiers carried.

He, Jeff, and Andrew set off hiking to the barracks.

"Hey, McCrae," Cadet Captain Webster yelled. "Did you ever find an Indian pony?... Say, redskin, I'm talking to you. Don't ignore me. That's a demerit for sure."

"A demerit? For what?" Too late, but he knew he should have kept quiet.

"Make that two demerits, plebe! One for ignoring an upperclassman who addressed you and another for talking back. You'll see this on the board tomorrow morning."

Andrew and Big Jeff slowed their pace and Mark caught up. "C'mon, Mark, don't worry about him," Andrew said. "It'll be all right."

Upperclassmen ridiculed Mark as Colonel Hardin had warned. Instructors seldom interceded. One morning he arrived at the stables to find Belle with bright stripes painted on her side. Even though uppers deviled other plebes too, Mark made a better target for insults. He tried not to let the remarks get to him, but his patience wore thin. After scrubbing off the paint, he knew not to report the incident to higher-ups. He didn't intend to become a crybaby—never had been—never would be.

~~~

Ward Hill, from Pennsylvania, pulled Andrew off to the side. "How can you be civil to this Injun? You know yourself when we get out of this place, we may be killing some of them."

"We might, but Choctaws are civilized."

"What difference does it make? He's still an Indian."

"He's a half-blood," Andrew answered. "It's him being at the Point that really bothers you, isn't it?"

Ward ignored the question and stalked away.

~~~

After mess, the wisk-wisk of honing stones on sabers echoed on each floor. Mark sighted down the cutting edge, inspecting it for nicks. He found none. With a light touch, he ran the stone down the length to make sure, and then returned the blade to the scabbard. "It's smooth now."

"Yeah, well, this one seems first-rate to me too," Andrew said, "but it probably won't be. And even if it is, it won't be."

"That's enough for tonight. Think I'll go for a walk. I'll be back before lights out."

"Okay, but you better get started on your French. It sounds more like Italian to me."

Mark threw a pillow at him and went out the door, heading toward a path to the river.

Suddenly, he heard a flock of geese soaring overhead—a sound unfamiliar to him. Their beauty impressed him, as well as the scenery. He wondered if his father once knew its equal in Ireland.

The trees had begun to change, green turning to orange, but they in no way compared to the vivid yellows of aspen leaves. Arizona had its own beauty in the sunset and colored desert.

Mark continued toward the Hudson but couldn't stay long. It would soon be dark.

He noticed stillness took over, except for a slight rustling of the first crisp leaves of fall.

His instinct told him it was more than a squirrel. He turned, but a swift blow sent him sprawling. Catching his breath, he glanced up to see three cadets staring down on him.

Mark recognized Clint Webster, a smirk on his face. Another, he'd seen around and thought his name was Bolling. He couldn't see the third, who remained in the shadows.

"C'mon," Webster said, "let's see how much of a man you really are."

He and Bolling yanked Mark to his feet, and the third pinned his arms behind his back.

The first two took turns clouting him in the ribs.

"Don't mangle his face, Clint. Aim where it won't show."

"What's the difference? We can always say he started it."

Clint hit him again in the mid-section. Harder this time.

Mark gasped for air. He felt as if one of his ribs might be cracked. His father's words stuck in his mind—"Mind your temper...solve a situation...this side of proper." But for Mark, turning the other cheek wasn't his style. He struggled to free himself and jerking an arm loose, punched the cadet in front of him. He then back-kicked into the knee of the assailant behind. The man let go, and Mark lashed out at Bolling.

"He puts up a pretty good fight for a squaw," Bolling jeered.

Mark, quick on his feet, let go a terrific blow at the tallest upperclassman.

Clint squealed, "You could have broken my nose, you filthy redskin." He pulled out a handkerchief to his bloody face.

The last thing Mark remembered was the word, bloody, before he collapsed on the leafy ground.

~~~

Andrew darted out of his quarters and spied Ward. "Have you seen Jeff? Mark isn't back yet, and it's ten minutes to curfew."

Ward hesitated. "Mark can find his own way back. And I don't know where Jeff is."

Andrew turned to see his friend in the hallway and hurried to meet him. "We gotta find Mark, or he'll be in real trouble."

Jeff hesitated, but Andrew pressed. "C'mon! I think he'd go toward the river, and it's already dark." They set out at a dead run.

About thirty yards down the path, Andrew shouted, "There he is. He's hurt!"

Mark attempted to stand, but buckled, holding his side.

Jeff bent over to help him. "Here, we'll carry you."

"Don't need help." Mark tried to pull away from them but had trouble getting to his feet.

"Yeah, sure, you don't need help," Andrew said. "Let's get a move on, or we'll all be expelled."

Half-carrying Mark, they managed to reach their third floor quarters two minutes before curfew. Andrew moved the lamp closer. "Not good. Not good at all. What did you connect with?"

"I walked too close to a ledge and lost my footing. Thanks, Jeff. You took a risk."

"Yeah, well, okay," Jeff replied, leaving the room.

~~~

"Andrew, thanks. Go to bed, I'll be all right. And don't say anything about this, not to anyone."

"If you say so, but it won't just go away."

Mark tried to be careful breathing and didn't dare go to the infirmary. Early morning, the men on Mark's floor hiked to the stable. Mark's ribs ached, but he suspected Clint's nose hurt worse.

Captain Hawes gave them the command to form three ranks. "All right, men, pay attention. First rank will secure its mounts. Take your place on my right. Second rank repeats that command to the left. In the center, you'll see the obstacle for you to jump, then the straw dummies. Keep your blade covered until you're about twenty yards away. After your jump, the dummy will be your target."

Mark strained to understand the captain, but he already thought the rest of the procedure was self-explanatory.

"If you're right-handed and make your charge to the right of your opponent, your cut will be from left to right. The spot you will aim for is where the right shoulder connects the neck. The reverse if you're left-handed. Your grade depends on the cleanness of your cut, and of course whether or not you touch the top rail of the jump fence.

"Now, if everybody..." He stopped in front of Mark. "By what I see, you've been in a scuffle of some kind. Report to Major , On the double!"

Mark knew he had bruises on his face, in spite of what Clint Webster had said. He took off, hoping he didn't miss all of saber practice.

Chapter 12

"That was quick," Andrew whispered. "Did you tell the major about the guys who beat you up?"

"I told him I fell out of a tree, but he knew different. I'm confined to quarters for a week except for classes and meals. And I think he threw in some demerits."

"All right, McCrae, I see you've rejoined us and none too soon," Captain Hawes said. "Take your position. Get even with the jump fence and begin."

Mark, still sore, mounted his horse. After a quick check of his blade, he leaned over and stroked Belle's neck. "All right big lady. Make us both look good." Belle's ears perked up when Mark set her into position. He lightly touched her. The bay left the ground, giving a feel of grace and power to her rider. He was sure she cleared the fence with a foot to spare.

As he neared the dummy, Mark raised the blade. With the saber slicing through the air, the dummy's head fell to one side, making a crunching sound when it hit the ground.

Afterward, Hawes said, "Clean as a whistle, McCrae. Where'd you learn to ride?"

"My grandfather taught me, sir. In Indian Territory."

"Hmm, well, choosing the right horse is part of your grade."

"Yes, sir. Thank you, sir." He took the compliment as a glimmer of hope.

When everyone finished, Mark, Jeff, and Andrew left the grounds together. As they neared the barracks, an upperclassman, standing in the middle of the narrow road, called them to a halt. "Okay, plebes, who's the leader of this lowly bunch?"

Before any of them answered, the upper took a step toward Mark. "Well, well, what have we here—appears to me I've seen this redskin before. How about it, Injun? You ever face a fully armed, charging cavalry unit? Or do you sit in a wigwam all day? Yeah, that's it, maybe just shoot fish with an arrow?"

Mark recognized him as Bolling, and without thinking, went for the cadet. He didn't give him time to see the punch that put him on the ground. At once, Mark was on his knees astride the bully. The small knife he drew from his uniform was so close to Bolling's eyes, the cadet didn't dare move.

"Now, *sir*, let me ask you. Have you ever seen a band of Apaches, fully armed, when they've been insulted? I'll take just so much of your childish game you call hazing, because that's the way it is. Sooner or later, though, I'll take it personally. Understand?"

Bolling, his mouth apparently too dry to talk, nodded. When released, he scampered off, running like a frightened rabbit.

"McCrae, are you crazy? Where'd you get that knife?" Andrew asked.

"My grandfather gave it to me. It's small, but serves a purpose. My Bowie's back in Arizona. Bolling's lucky I didn't have it."

"You'll be up on charges before the day's over," Jeff added. "You'll get booted out of the Point."

Nothing happened that day, the next, or the next. Mark could only wait, in case Bolling was planning some kind of revenge. But for a reason he never understood, the incident didn't come up.

~~~

Reaching the second year at West Point made Mark more comfortable. At least he had made it this far. He still chalked up a fair listing of undeserved demerits, being culpable for only a few. He instinctively thought upperclassmen and most plebes still resented him.

Mark maintained top grades. Although he liked engineering and enjoyed the four hours of mathematics a day, he favored the classics. He obliged if anyone asked for tutoring. He didn't know what the students said afterward, but they were courteous so long as they needed his help.

One evening, Ward came by Mark's quarters. Visibly shaken, he said, "Mark, if you can't help me, I'll be forced to resign. There's no way I can pass this mathematics exam tomorrow. I'd rather resign than fail."

Surprised at the admission, Mark said, "You waited a little late to start studying, don't you think?"

"Well, listen to this. Some of the others, including Webster, have figured a way to break in and get examination papers. They asked me to go with them. That's the only way I can make a passing grade. I've got to try."

Mark laid down his quill and leaned back in his chair. "Now think about the Honor Code. That's supposed to mean something to us. Besides, they'll be caught and you with them. Then you'll be tossed out, and that's worse than failing."

Ward threw his book on the bed. "But what else can I do?"

"You can do what I tell you. First, don't mention a word about the break-in to anybody. If you knew and didn't report it, you'd be just as guilty, so get your books. We'll have a short lesson on a long course."

"I just kept thinking I'd catch on. If you can help me understand it, I'll be indebted."

Mark helped him all night, stopping twice to stoke the fire. He went over and over the same problems. Andrew slept through it all.

Ward hadn't been friendly and might never be. But at least for the present, he'd changed.

~~~

Near noon the following day, Ward knocked on the door. "Time to eat!"

"Door's open," Mark answered.

Ward stepped inside. "I'm so nervous over this test, I want to get it over with before I forget what you taught me."

"Don't worry, you won't forget."

Andrew reached for his books. "I'm ready. You, Mark?"

Mark rolled his bedding. "Don't want a room inspection to turn up another demerit while we're gone. Let's go."

In the dining room, Ward picked at his meal. "That's all for me. Probably won't keep it down anyway."

At that moment, a brusque voice cut the air. "McCrae, come with me." Captain Loggins clasped his hand on Mark's shoulder.

"Sir?"

"I said come with me, McCrae."

As they left, Ward shoved aside his chair.

Looking puzzled, Andrew asked, "What's that all about?"

"There's no doubt in my mind what it's about."

~~~

The captain said nothing more. Mark thought it had to be serious and knew for sure when He entered Colonel Turner's office.

"Have a chair. The colonel will be right in." Loggins turned and left.

Mark glanced around the room and was startled to see Clint Webster, a sly smirk on his face.

"So, redskin. I'm in trouble and you're going with me."

"What do you mean? I didn't do—"

They stopped and saluted the colonel when he entered the office.

Mark felt a chill coming, which he interpreted as almost fright. He didn't like whatever it was.

Turner pulled out a chair and sat at his desk. He paused a moment before he spoke. "Men, in my opinion, anyone who steals examination questions is the lowest kind and certainly not officer material."

"Sir, may I—?"

"You may have your say later, McCrae. Webster here says he's a witness. You both are an embarrassment to this school." Leaning forward, he continued, "Personally, if I ever had the slightest inclination of doing such a thing, I'd not be stupid enough to leave behind the incriminating evidence you did."

Mark knew Webster had framed him, but for now, it was only Webster's accusation.

The colonel picked up an item from his desk. "Webster, I believe this belongs to you? Your name's carved on the holder."

Webster squirmed. "Why, yes sir. It's... it's my key. I must have dropped it somewhere, but that doesn't mean I stole the tests."

"I believe it does. We found it in plain sight inside the room where you stole the papers. You both deserve severe discipline, if not expulsion." His stern expression could not be mistaken for anything other than a preformed judgment. "I believe more than two people were involved in this break-in, and I intend to know the names of the others. What do you have to say?" Mark tried to assemble the right words to defend his innocence.

"Sir," Webster interrupted, "McCrae here started the whole thing. It was his idea. I didn't want to, but he insisted. Said he'd use his knife on me if I didn't help him."

Mark flew out of his chair, lunging at Clint.

"McCrae! Sit down." Turner ordered.

Mark pulled back from the upperclassman.

"If that were the case, Webster," the colonel said, "why were the papers stolen for your class and not McCrae's?"

As Webster began stammering some kind of answer, there was a sudden commotion outside the room.

"But please, sir, please let me in. It's important."

Colonel Turner arose from his desk and opened the door. "What's going on out here?"

"I'm sorry, sir," Loggins said. "But Hill insists on seeing you."

"All right. Be quick about it."

Ward hurried into the office, and if he didn't tell what he knew, Mark would be out of West Point. "Sir, McCrae had nothing to do with the break-in. He helped me with my mathematics all night. Why, if it weren't for him, I'd fail, and I don't plan to fail, sir."

Mark heaved a sigh of relief and hoped this was the end of it.

After the colonel had a private talk with Ward, he released Mark. "I see no reason for further discussion on your involvement in this matter. You may go."

All week the break-in was the talk of the school. On the way to mess one evening, Ward hurried to walk with Mark and Andrew. "Well, the truth is out. Clint Webster led the bunch of 'em! He ratted on the rest. And the reason Bolling didn't tell about the knife incident is Webster told him to wait. He'd frame you for something bigger."

Mark couldn't help smiling. "Thanks for coming to my rescue. I wonder if we should expect demerits for burning the lamps past curfew last night?"

Laughing, Ward reminded everyone, "Clint and one more upper were expelled flat out, and another man was allowed to resign."

Jeff added, "The last one is the son of an influential friend of the superintendent. If he hasn't already gotten off, I think he will."

"Very unfair," added Ward.

Mark said, "A stupid idea for anyone even to consider a break-in, wouldn't you say, Ward?"

"Absolutely. Anyone would be a fool to try."

During rare minutes in the upcoming weeks, away from classes and study, Mark often sat by himself either in his barracks or at a special spot overlooking the Hudson. He was the only Indian to attend the Point. Who knew if there would be another? When he had time for meditation, his few close friends never bothered him, as they liked this half-blood from the west. He wanted to be true to his heritage—but which heritage—white or Indian? Both? How could he be a soldier, knowing what the future might hold?

~~~

December of Mark's last year brought June graduation nearer. He even enjoyed the Christmas Eve Hop. Associating with young ladies of the east made him uncomfortable, although they flirted wildly with him at the dances. One girl in particular caught his attention—a saucy blonde from a military family. He danced with her twice and brought her a cup of punch. But she had too many admirers waiting. *Besides, what can she see in a half-blood, and one who doesn't dance very well at that?*

Mark yearned for home. Winter came strong to the high plains of the Point. The next change would be green shoots decorating plants already lining the banks of the Hudson. Eons ago, deep gorges formed the high mesas where the academy stood. His mother always called attention to the beauty of nature, and Mark anticipated its changes.

The mantle of white, which had draped the academy, melted away. Mark grew impatient for graduation. He was surprised that more than a third of his class did not finish, mainly because of their grades or character, although a few had family reasons for dropping out.

He wished his parents could have been there for this event, but they would soon see proof of his studies. What will Grandfather think of his grandson now, he wondered. Letters from home spelled out what Mark already sensed—Apaches rebelled against being remanded to the reservation. He wondered about the welfare of his parents, as he couldn't tell what might be unwritten in their letters.

Mark was third in his class and could have been commissioned into the Corps of Engineers or to any favorable area he chose. Graduates with lesser accomplishments were more often sent to far away moldering fortifications. Not many would choose Arizona, but Mark never considered any other place. He wanted to return to Hellsgate and serve with his father.

Ward and Big Jeff were the first to approach Mark after receiving diplomas. Ward swallowed, as if trying to clear a lump in his throat. Pumping Mark's hand, he said, "I owe you, friend. I couldn't have faced going home a failure from here, and that one exam could have been the end for me."

"You owe me nothing. If you recall, you came to my rescue, and I thank you again for it."

Ward started to leave, then turned back. "There's one more thing. I can't go without telling you. It happened a long time ago, but our first year, the night of the fight by the river—"

"I know. I figured it was you all along."

"But I want you to understand. My father worked with Webster's father in the same bank, and—"

"Forget it, Ward. I have."

Big Jeff's eyes glistened. "We had some great times, Mark. 'Course, some of those times were pretty bleak, but everything worked out. And by the way, as long as we're confessing, I wasn't the one who painted those stripes on your horse."

"Never thought you did. You like horses too much to embarrass Belle."

The three stacked hands and agreed that someday they would meet again. Ward and Jeff left, and Mark searched the crowd for Andrew. He saw him running down the walk toward him.

"Wait, Mark! I've been looking for you. You don't know how I wanted them to send me to Arizona. I requested, but they've got me going somewhere else. I don't even know where."

"Your friendship has meant the world, Andrew. I wish you could go, too. You were the first one on my side and never gave up on me. I hope you have many reasons to smile during your career and your whole life after."

"Thanks, friend. You know where my Virginia home is, if you ever have the chance. Until then, good luck. Oh, and Mark... keep watch over that little knife. Beats me how nobody ever spotted it."

Mark pulled the knife from under his waistband. "Here, Andrew. Take it."

"I can't do that. Your grandfather gave it to you."

"He'd be glad for you to have it. Besides, he gave me a Bowie knife my father's keeping for me. I expect I'll be using it from now on."

Chapter 13

Mark knew he was home when he smelled the dust of Arizona. After leaving West Point, he traveled with several of the men who were headed west toward Jefferson Barracks. He joined a supply train going to Fort Verde in northern Arizona. There, he and Belle left the train, branching off south to Hellsgate.

Arriving at the fort, he bound straight for headquarters. He took the four steps in a single leap and immediately recognized the man who stood with his back toward the door.

It was all he could do to keep from calling out to his father. Instead, he announced, "Second Lieutenant Marcus Graham McCrae reporting for duty."

Allie quickly turned. After a swift salute, he threw his arms about the new young lieutenant.

"Hey, you could break some ribs," Mark joked. "I see you're promoted, Top. That's great."

"I guess I hadn't told ye. One more promotion and I'll be that 'Top' you're always calling me. Mark, ye look fine. See here now, you're taller than your own father." He stepped away and appraised his son.

Mark stood over six feet, unusual for a Choctaw. His dark hair came from his mother, but he figured that hint of a wave was surely from his curly-haired Irish father.

"I've missed you both more than you know."

"Your mother couldn't sleep last night, waiting for today."

"I can hardly wait to see her, but first, I have to check in. How's Colonel Hardin?"

"Aye, that's the question I was dreading. Last month when the payroll came in, the colonel chose the wrong time to be at the paymaster's. A couple of worthless noncoms, Waddell and Simmons, got into the office and stole the payroll."

"But what about Colonel Hardin?"

"That's just it, Mark. The scoundrels killed him and the paymaster. They got away, but the paymaster identified them before he died. It was Waddell that pulled the trigger."

Mark's eyes misted. He knew he would never have gone to West Point if not for the colonel. "This is some kind of homecoming. But who could replace him?"

"The man's name is John Blair. He's a green twig to these western ways and is under the impression that Apaches do what they're told. Blair may make a grand blunder of everything we've managed to do so far. We know Hardin had Victorio's confidence, but I don't know about this one."

Allie gave him instructions and barracks assignment. "The colonel will be back in a few minutes, Son, so go ahead and take your things to your quarters. You'll have to wait to see your mother."

Mark could scarcely think of waiting. But he deposited his gear, glad not to worry about demerits. After washing his face and combing his hair, he returned to headquarters and rapped on the commandant's door.

"Come in," Blair said. "At ease, Lieutenant. Take a seat."

Mark knew right away the colonel didn't mince words. Straight to the point.

"What I am about to do breaks with army procedure, but circumstances require it. Effective this date, I am promoting you to first lieutenant. Frankly, because of your heritage, I believe you, more than anyone else, would be accepted by our foes. You know, be able to communicate with them. That is, if they have the ability to communicate."

"Foes, sir?"

"Indians, McCrae."

"Well, please remember, sir. I'm Choctaw, not Apache. I'll do my best to fulfill your confidence in me."

"I take it the sergeant has briefed you. I know it's rough to hand you this assignment as soon as you're back, but we received word someone spotted Waddell in and around Prescott. That's not an easy ride. I want Waddell and Simmons first, the payroll second, but I do want what's left of that money."

Mark thought the colonel rattled off his words as if reading from a book.

"We'll be concerned with Victorio when you return from this mission. First thing in the morning I'll fill in details. We don't want the trail to get any colder. That's all. You're dismissed, and, Lieutenant, send in the sergeant."

"Yes, sir." Mark exited with a tinge of disquiet.

"Well, I'll say one thing for ye Point boys," Allie said, admiring his son. "Ye don't waste any time getting promotions. The colonel told me earlier. I have the paperwork ready for his signature."

"Thanks. You're the best Top I've met in this man's army."

"That sounds like Irish blarney, and I've heard it all before. Now, ye better get some rest. We leave early."

As Mark left for his parents' quarters, his reaction to the colonel was as his father said. This man does not understand. Mark already knew the vast differences between Arizona Indians and those in Indian Territory. Still, he knew the Apaches respected honor, no matter these differences.

~~~

Mark could see his mother standing in the doorway, straightening her skirt, then with her arms outstretched. He hurried toward her, sweeping her up in a twirl, her long black hair flying.

"Mark! Just let me catch my breath. You have grown so big. I can't believe it's you."

Yvonne's expression showed her happiness as she gazed at him.

Mark let her down and stood back. "You're beautiful, Mother."

She almost blushed. "Oh, I have surely changed. I didn't have my son to keep me young.

Come inside and tell me all about West Point. Don't leave out anything," she pleaded. "I felt I could read between the lines of your letters. I read some of them through tears, but I always had faith."

"If you read between the lines, then you knew I would make it." He began telling his mother only the enjoyable things that happened at West Point. *Why tell her the unpleasant?*

He then told her about his orders for the following day.

"Take caution with you, my son," his mother warned. "You face a dangerous mission as soon as you have come home."

"Don't worry," he said with a wink. "Top will take care of me."

He returned to his quarters and gave serious thought to the conversation with his commandant. *Blair's using me, and I'm not sure I like it. But for now... it's been too long since I heard a desert wolf's howl. I'll sleep well tonight.*

~~~

The next morning, Allie and Mark reported to the colonel's office.

"Men," Colonel Blair said, "we telegraphed towns within a two-hundred mile radius to be on the lookout for big money being flashed. Only one reply came in, from Marshal Creel in Prescott. Two men, still wearing remnants of uniforms, came through, spending money like they had a private mint. That may give you a starting point."

Colonel Blair cleared his throat and reached for a small box on his desk. He pulled out a cigar and lit it. After a couple of strong pulls, he said, "If you find them, you have my permission to bring them back alive or leave them dead. At this point, Waddell and his companion don't know anybody identified them, so your buckskins won't attract their attention. A company of troopers will leave tomorrow for Prescott to help safeguard the payroll, assuming you find it. Otherwise, you'll have company on the way back, which may not be a bad idea in itself."

"I understand, sir," Mark said.

"If you have no questions, that's all. And good luck."

"Thank you, sir. We'll take care of it."

Mark and Allie left at once.

"I had Lafferty make us up some nourishment," Allie said. "Ye never know what he might come up with, but he says it won't hurt us. I put yours in your saddlebag."

"That Lafferty. Sounds like he does enjoy his work."

As they moved from the fort's gates, a cool breeze fanned across the desert. Sand blown in by strong gales of previous days had formed riffs. By afternoon, the day turned overcast and brought in a sweeping chill from the north. Stopping to rest the horses, as well as themselves, slowed traveling.

"Nobody says we have to get to Prescott in one day," Mark said, 'but I'm what you'd call just a little eager to find those killers."

"That makes two of us."

Near sunset, Prescott, the territory's capital, became visible in the distance. As the wind grew colder, both men pulled their greatcoats close and picked up pace.

The marshal's office was easy to find on the main street of the small town. It was next to the General Store, which was next to the town doctor's office, with the Cold Stone Café next.

They tied their horses and entered the open door. A grizzled lawman, feet on his desk, was cleaning his fingernails with a knife.

"Marshal Creel?" Allie said, "we're—"

"You must be from Hellsgate. I've been expecting you. Close the door, will you? Afraid we're gonna get snow before dark. Unseasonable." The marshal stopped short at seeing the tall man in buckskin.

Mark's complexion was that of a suntanned cavalryman, unless one noticed the high cheekbones, dark eyes, and rim of dark hair from beneath his hat. Then no one could doubt his Indian heritage.

Addressing Allie, the marshal said, "And now, Lieutenant—?"

Allie raised his shoulders, took a quick breath and glanced at Mark. "This is Lieutenant McCrae."

The lawman registered a slight reaction, which Mark didn't miss.

Allie leaned onto Creel's desk and in his brusque Irish brogue, asked, "Is there anything wrong, Marshal?"

Creel squirmed in his chair. "No, no. Like I say, I've been expecting you."

"We're hoping more information is available on our quarry," Mark said.

"Must be your lucky day. I saw them this morning, headed northwest, I expect to their hideout. That's the direction they've come from the last week or so. One rode a gray mare and the other, a sorrel. Seems they're the ones you'd be after. Trail don't go much of anywhere ever since a landslide cut off what road there was."

"Thanks for your help, Marshal. There's one other thing. Colonel Blair is sending troopers to keep the money in army hands, assuming our hunt is successful. We think it will be. I hope you don't mind us using your office as a meeting place?"

"Not at all. Glad to help. You sure you don't want me to go along?"

"Like as not they'd recognize ye, and we couldn't take them by surprise. But thanks."

After leaving, Mark said, "Those two won't be going anywhere tonight."

"We better get our mounts to the livery. It's a hard day they've had."

The stables had plenty of hay and water. The proprietor had no objections to their rubbing down their own horses, but the price remained the same.

Allie spoke up. "I was wondering if ye mind if we bed down here. It's mighty miserable outside."

The proprietor didn't seem surprised. "Ain't the first time that's happened. Sure, go ahead, but I don't want t' see anything missing tomorrow. I'm turning in."

Mark nodded and grinned at his father.

"Well, we're looking just like we want to—a couple drovers," Allie said. "Can't afford for anyone to think different. Besides, it's not miserable out there. It's just hay's more comfortable."

"Before we see just how comfortable it is, I could stand something to eat. How about trying the food down at that place by the marshal's?"

"Fine idea ye have there. The sign in the window said they had good food. We'll just be seeing for ourselves."

Chapter 14

A light blanket of snow had fallen over the town during the night. Mark gazed at steam rising from the rooftops. "Waddell would have bedded down before snowfall. I don't know, Top. It seems you ought to be chief of this mission."

"Not on your life. You're in charge here. Once this snow realizes it's July, it won't stay."

Lingering over an early breakfast of eggs, hot biscuits and coffee at the Cold Stone, they decided the sun might rise sooner or later.

After eating, Allie looked over at the proprietor. "Say, is there some way ye can wrap up a couple pieces of that cream cake there?"

Mark knew his father had a sweet tooth and wasn't surprised at the request. He paid for their meals, plus a bundle of ham strips and biscuits.

They tended their horses and headed the direction the marshal had indicated the day before.

"I don't see how we can miss them. According to Creel, it's the only way in or out," Mark said.

The narrow trace slanted upward into a small forest. Mark led the way. "If we follow the stream, we might run across their campfire, or at least something to tell us if they're still around.

Both men prodded their horses over broken brush, stopping twice for rest. After the second stop, Allie said, "We've been tracking all day. And it may be an all-day waste of time at that. I suggest we make camp. It'll be dark before we know it."

"The marshal strikes me as a man who knows what he's talking about, but our luck's pretty slim so far."

Mark dismounted and reined his horse. "I'll see if I can find some wood. There's no shortage if it's dry."

"No, you stay put. I'll get it."

The snow had brought a clean freshness, and chilled as he was, Mark savored breathing in the clear mountain air. He returned with enough wood for a good fire. More pieces were within stepping distance. "This will see us through till morning.

Seems dry enough. Waddell and Simmons won't detect our fire, not with one of their own."

Allie unsaddled the horses and poured water to make coffee while Mark arranged the logs and started the fire.

Allie wedged cold ham slices in the biscuits. "Nothing filters through the woods like the aroma of ham once it starts to warm. Besides, this is good enough cold. Come to think of it, that cake's all we've had since breakfast."

After they ate, their saddles formed pillows, and even though the ground was a cold mattress, the fire was warm.

"You sleep, Son. I'll keep one ear open."

Before dawn, the fire had burned itself low, leaving only the orange glow of remaining embers. Mark stirred, wondering if that was his own deep breathing he just heard. He awakened fully when his father leaned over and patted his shoulder, letting him know to be quiet at the same time. "Listen, Son... It doesn't sound human, but it doesn't sound like a bird either."

Mark sat up and reached for his rifle. "What do you think?"

"Better lower your voice. Lordy if I don't think it's a grizzly. Smells like one."

"But a grizzly'd still be in a cave somewhere."

"This snow coming now probably confuses his seasons. I expect he senses food and wants to root out his breakfast." He pointed toward a shadowy shape. "Over there. Doesn't appear to be coming this way—just snuffing around." At that moment the morning moon emerged from the clouds.

The head and shoulders of an enormous grizzly loomed into view over the rocks.

"If we hafta shoot, we'll sure catch Waddell's attention if they're camped close."

The bear must have sensed something. He hunched, sniffing as if to distinguish what he thought was edible and turned toward their camp.

Allie reached for his rifle. "A bear can't see any better than a man. I'll just—"

"Wait, let me try something. Keep your finger on the trigger and don't lose sight of where you're aiming." Mark pulled off his blanket and reached for a broken limb. He wrapped the blanket tightly around the end and placed it on the burning embers. When it ignited, he gripped the limb and ran toward the grizzly.

The bear turned in time to get a snout full of smoke.

Mark expected him to run, but instead, it started toward him. Mark moved back, almost tripping into the fire. The blanket began to unwind.

"Son, I sure don't want to let go a shot unless I have to." He picked up a broken tree limb and frantically waved it in front of the animal, stopping it momentarily.

Mark managed to twist the limb back into the burning blanket. He started for the bear and jabbed it toward him. This time it worked. The bear spun, shaking the ground as he lumbered off.

"Now that's what I call well done. Son, you notice that limp? He might not've put up such a big fight at that." Allie laid down his rifle. "It's almost dawn, not that ye could go back to sleep anyhow. I'll toss the last bit of wood on the fire."

"Shh... This time I don't think it's the grizzly... a scraping noise, maybe metal, like a coffeepot or a skillet."

Mark already had his rifle in hand. "Let's go. If it's them, our visitor may've waked them."

"Angle over to the side here. Watch your step."

Mark caught a blurred movement off to his right. He waited for a better view. What little light came through the trees slanted on a man as he filled a coffee pot with water from the stream. He fit the description of either Waddell or his cohort, so Mark decided to find out.

For cover, he chose a fallen tree, partly draped by foliage. "Waddell! Simmons!" he called. "This is Lieutenant McCrae from Fort Hellsgate. You don't stand a chance, so come on out now. The whole army's coming after you!"

A bullet sprayed splinters of rotted wood over Mark's head and shoulders. *I guess he didn't believe me.* Peering over the shelter, he tried to locate the man's position. "We don't want to kill you. The longer you stay hidden and we shoot at each other, the slimmer your chances get."

Another shot whined above the tree trunk and was lost in the expanse of woods.

Mark ducked. He thought he was prepared for his first gunfight, but he didn't expect the anxiety that coursed through his veins.

"Top, he's way over on the right, where that big tree's fallen." He turned toward Allie, not about to have his father take the chance. "I'll see if I can flush him out. You cover."

"Right. Let 'er rip!"

Shifting his position, Mark pointed the Springfield over his barricade. He found a target in the dimness and squeezed the trigger, then dodged. A rifle answered, its heavy slug making the rotting log shake against him.

Allie threw himself flat behind some small boulders. He signaled Mark first and opened fire on the target.

Mark stared at where the first shot came. Pulling himself up, he bolted over the brush, running low and using the protective cover of thick pines.

Halfway there, still low, he stopped and fired. A sharp cry, followed by silence. Standing sidewise to a broad pine, he shouted, "Waddell!" The acrid stench of lingering gunpowder was strong in his nostrils. He heard no answer, so he darted out, running around the deadfall that had hidden the man.

"Okay, Top. It's all over for him."

"Watch out, Mark! There's the other one."

They weren't finished yet. Allie fired and dropped Simmons in his tracks, then bounded out from his shelter. "You all right, Son?"

"Yes, and thanks. That was close." He knew death was nothing new to his father. His somber expression didn't change at the sight of their handiwork.

"So 'tis the end of the line for them, dead in their own blood."

"Too bad they wouldn't give themselves up."

"They'd wind up hung anyway."

After finding most of the payroll in Simmons and Waddell's saddlebags, Allie and Mark hoisted the two men onto their horses. "From the weight of these two bags, I'd say they hadn't wasted away as much money as I'd thought."

As they wound their way down and across the gentle slope back into town, Mark knew his father wouldn't be having the same intense feelings he had. *He's used to it by now. But this is the first man I've killed.* He didn't look forward to the second.

The day was more than half gone by the time they rode in from the woods, and the sun had taken its place in the azure sky. Shopkeepers waved to one another from across the narrow main street as they swept snow off the boardwalk. A couple of stray mongrel dogs nosed about in garbage boxes and then sauntered off on some mysterious errand.

With the blanket-covered figures strapped over the horses, Mark and Allie rode up to Marshal Creel's office. The passengers draped across the horses created interest among the passersby, who stopped to stare. Mark figured this wasn't the first time such a scene had occurred.

Allie knocked on the door, and the lawman admitted them. "I was wondering about you. Did you get 'em?"

"Marshal, Waddell and Simmons are out there under a blanket," Mark said. Without turning his head, he jerked his thumb over his shoulder toward the tethered horses. "They didn't see it our way to surrender."

Obviously relieved, the marshal glanced out the window. "I'll take care of 'em. You done a fair piece of man huntin'. Sure wish you'd let me tag along."

"You gave us enough help in letting us know they were in the neighborhood."

"Glad to oblige, Lieutenant." He extended his callused hand in a firm shake.

Allie shifted his interest to a stack of wanted posters on the corner of Creel's desk.

"Sergeant, if you ever have any spare time, you might come back and help scare up some of them characters you were studying on those dodgers."

"Doesn't seem likely I will, but I'll keep me eyes open."

"By the way," Mark said, "If our escort's here, do you know who's in command?"

"A Lieutenant Whitfield. Young feller. Seems kinda uppity to me," snorted the marshal. He shifted in his battered chair.

"Do you know where the detail's camped?"

"Well, I don't know about the detail, but the lieutenant's doing his camping in the Town House." He pointed out the window. "Kinda fancy for the army, if you ask me. Oh, I almost forgot." He handed Mark a piece of paper. "This wire came in from your Colonel Blair. He says for you to get back there soon's you can... something to do with Indians."

"Thanks, Marshal, and thanks again for your help."

Allie dropped the dodgers in a pile, bid goodbye to the lawman and accompanied Mark onto the bustling street. "So he's in the hotel, is he? I expected all the men to be bedded down on leaves."

"The rest of them will be. Top, would you mind taking the money across to the bank until we're ready for it? I'll stop in and see Whitfield, then be right with you. We'll leave first thing in the morning."

"That I'll do. As long as Whitfield has a room, might be a smart idea to find one yourself. Ye know, get your thoughts on him. He's been at Hellsgate less than a year."

Mark questioned the idea but agreed. "I'll get that room, but you come on up when you're finished."

"I'll do that, too. But another thing... back there when Simmons shot at ye?"

"Yeah, Top?"

"Well, in the future, when ye have two targets, make sure where your second one is before ye shoot at your first." Clearly embarrassed at offering advice, he headed for the bank.

"You're absolutely right. I'll remember that in the future." Mark grinned as he watched the departing trooper. He suspected his father's feelings for him matched his own admiration for his father. Mark led his horse to the livery, then strode back across the muddy street to the porch of Prescott's finest. He edged his way through the clustered groups of townspeople. If he heard any of the sly remarks, he gave no indication.

He stepped inside the hotel, and first thing he heard was, "Huh, an Indian, a damn breed in the hotel, big as life," said one.

"Yeah, they got lotsa gall."

Mark stopped at the desk. "Excuse me," he said, attempting to get the clerk's attention.

The clerk turned, stiffening at the sight of the individual before him. He raised his chin a trifle and said in a matter-of-fact tone, "We don't have any vacancies, and we do not expect any." He went back to sorting mail.

Mark let out a long breath. "Is Lieutenant Whitfield in his room?"

The pompous little man stopped cold.

"Yes, but—"

"Room number, please." Not a question but a command.

The clerk glanced at the register. "201," came the clipped reply.

Mark took note of the clerk eyeing him as he headed for the stairs. He walked down the narrow hall to 201 and rapped on the varnished door. He heard the curt answer of, "Hold on."

Several seconds later the door swung open. A young man leaned on the facing, his hand still on the doorknob.

Mark took in his appearance with an experienced eye—polished boots, clean uniform, tunic open at the neck. The well-scrubbed, almost boyish face was topped by a shock of thick, curly hair. He could tell Whitfield appraised him as he glanced at his trail clothes—close-fitting trousers worn inside rawhide boots. "You want to speak to me?" Whitfield asked.

"Yes, I'm Lieutenant McCrae. I believe I'm expected?" He noted Whitfield's eyes widen as he snapped to attention.

"May I come in?"

Whitfield stammered. "Why, yes, come in. Excuse me, sir. I didn't expect you back till this evening. Your dress... and... Whitfield flushed to the roots of his yellow hair, and his jaw muscles tightened.

Not again. "You see, Whitfield, my mother is Choctaw."

"I'm sorry, sir."

"That my mother is Choctaw?"

"No, not at all, sir. I meant I was sorry I didn't realize, you not being in uniform."

Mark glanced over the small room with its oiled pine floor. "May I sit?" Not waiting for an answer, he eased himself into a padded chair.

Whitfield remained standing a moment then sat on the edge of the bed. He glanced at the long figure of this different officer. "Was your mission a successful one, Lieutenant?"

Mark thumbed back his Stetson. "Matter of fact, yes. I'm sorry to say we didn't take them alive. While I doubt those two shared information about the payroll with anyone, I'm glad you're here—just in case."

Mark knew the word around Hellsgate had been the sergeant's son was at West Point. Whitfield couldn't have known much about him. He also figured the second lieutenant didn't take to the idea of serving with a half-blood, and certainly not one ranked above him.

"I guess you'll be wanting to leave soon after first light in the morning, Lieutenant?"

"Soon as we get the money from the bank. I guess that'll be later than first light."

"The detail will be ready when you are, sir."

"Good, Whitfield. Goodnight."

Mark walked into the hall and took the first few steps down the stairs.

A woman dressed in green satin approached, escorted by a well-dressed man. He stood aside so they could pass and touched the brim of his hat.

The woman smiled, just short of winking. Her gentleman friend seemed put out at her flirtation and half-pushed her up the stairs.

Mark shook his head and descended the stairs to the lobby. Once more he approached the desk clerk. "Nice room Lieutenant Whitfield has."

"Gentlemen and officers are always welcome in this hotel," the clerk retorted.

Mark felt his expression smolder. "Then I'll sign the register, if the rank of first lieutenant suits for a recommendation. Sergeant McCrae will be here soon. And I would appreciate it if you send up a couple of meals."

The clerk hesitated only a moment. "Room 203... sir." He sighed and placed the keys on the desk.

"Thank you again," Mark said dryly.

He entered his room and lay on the bed in his dusty trail clothes. He wanted a hot bath but was too tired. Besides, he kept thinking about Colonel Blair's wire—and the Apaches.

Chapter 15

Allie picked up the money from the bank and secured it in the wagon. As the soldiers headed for Hellsgate, it didn't take the brassy sun long to dry the ground.

While he drank in the splendor, Mark suddenly became aware of Jerry Whitfield riding up beside him.

"Right pretty land, isn't it, Lieutenant McCrae?"

"Funny you feel that way. Most men don't think about it."

"On the way up here, I couldn't help notice. If Lafferty hadn't led us, we would've ended up in Canada."

Mark smiled. *A man could live here the rest of his days and be content.*

A voice called out from behind them. "Lieutenant, the sergeant says you two might better change direction, or you'll not get to the fort this year."

"I do believe he's right," Mark said, "and the sun's supposed to be our compass. We might not get to Hellsgate today either, since we started late," he yelled back.

Allie rode next to another of his Irish cohorts, Ian Lafferty, who was also the cook. Allie had known him since arriving at Hellsgate, although Lafferty had come there two years earlier. The two pugnacious Irishmen carried on a continuing friendly feud.

Allie, having been on similar missions, was well acquainted with bivouac spots, running water and ample grazing for the horses. Finding all at the same time didn't come easy, but somehow he put it together. A picture of robust health and regimented discipline as he carried out orders, he occasionally added something of his own creation, if it made the situation better.

"Tell me now, Lafferty, how did ye manage to bring these fine boys all the way to Prescott?" Allie inquired of his stocky countryman. "Ye can't find the outhouse by yourself half the time."

"Can't find the... why ye damn Mick! Many's the time I've held your blasted head for ye after leadin' ye half blind away from a barrel of pinther juice."

"I don't drink more than's necessary. Never will," Allie retorted.

Mark couldn't but help grin at the conversation alongside him.

By mid-afternoon, a sweltering sun blazed across the clear sky. Mark gave orders for the men to stop and rest and water their horses. After a break, he rechecked his canteen, and they moved on.

It soon became apparent they would have to spend one night under the stars. And again, Allie found a suitable spot in the shade of a large rock face.

~~~

Mark began rubbing down his rifle barrel. It didn't need it, but he cleaned it anyway. He glanced over at the second lieutenant.

Whitfield stretched out on his blanket, hands locked behind his head and gazed at the sky.

"What's your first name, Whitfield?"

"Jeremiah, sir, but I go by Jerry."

"My name's Mark. You seem to be miles away."

"Huh? Oh, guess I was at that."

Mark took a wild guess. "A girl?"

"How'd you know? And a very lovely girl. She's Colonel Blair's niece...long golden hair and eyes so blue a fella could almost drown in them. Skin like pure cream."

"Sounds like a girl I once met."

Mark knew Jerry couldn't be any older than he was, but the look in his eyes reminded Mark of a moon-eyed kid recognizing that girls differed from boys. "Now that's downright poetic. She sounds like a goddess."

"You could say so. Of course she noticed me, but she treated every officer with the same courtesy. I plan to change all that. Think how my promotions would pile up if I was in with the colonel's niece."

"Just a minute," Mark broke in. He put his cleaning rag down and faced the reclining officer. "You mean this young lady's at the fort now?"

"Not now. She visited Blair once, but he sent her back east. Didn't think she should be in a place like this when she could live in a big city. But I'm hoping she'll make a return visit."

Mark lay down his weapon and inquired, without facing Whitfield, "What kind of officer do you think Blair is?"

"Real spit and polish. Military all the way. You know the kind."

"Yes, I know the kind." Mark couldn't help thinking of the closeness between Colonel Hardin and his family. Now he must face the intangible attitude of his new commander toward an Indian in a white world. *Still, Colonel Blair had enough confidence to send me after Waddell.*

"Say, Lieutenant, I was wondering. Why do you suppose the colonel sent you on this mission? I mean I've been here close to a year. Still, he let you go."

"I can't answer that one. Why don't you ask him?"

"Probably shouldn't do that... It's getting dark. Guess I'll go to sleep for now."

The next morning, Allie moved over to Mark. "Son, the wagon's ready. All we got left is coffee, so the men are a wee bit hungry."

"I'll just grab a cup," Mark said. "Then we're on our way."

Mark estimated it would take about four hours to get to Hellsgate, plus stopping to tend the horses. The outpost was an under-manned and aptly named fort on the Arizona desert. It answered needs of the men, but the desolate expanse of land provided its name. As Mark rode, he pondered the richness existing in some places. In other areas, the scorching Arizona sun and little water formed the undesired forced domain of the Apaches.

He felt a gnawing pang of apprehension as they approached the rough barricade surrounding the compact outpost. *Here I am, an officer returning after a successful mission. Why worry?* Mark stopped, hitched himself around in the saddle and reviewed the small column.

Satisfied with its formation, he urged Belle forward.

On sentry duty, Corporal Jeb Speck hollered down to have the wide log gates thrown open.

Mark wheeled his mount to one side, while his detachment filed past.

"Dee-tail, halt!" Mark bellowed. "Lieutenant Whitfield? Deliver the payroll to the paymaster."

The officer reined his horse to a stop, and snapped, "Yes, sir." He dismounted and strode to the wagon to collect the moneybags.

"Sergeant McCrae, dismiss the men."

A private reached for the reins of the big mare as Mark dismounted in front of headquarters. He removed his wide-cuffed gauntlets and slapped them against his breeches, a thin cloud of dust enveloping him.

When Mark and Allie entered headquarters, Sergeant Pearce was sitting behind the desk.

"Good hunting, Lieutenant? Sergeant?"

"The entire post can get drunk this payday," replied Allie, smiling broadly. "We got your money, Pearce."

"Never a doubt in my mind."

Mark asked, "Is the colonel in?"

"No one's with him now, sir. I'll tell him you're here."

Mark peered out the window. He hadn't noticed the revitalized appearance of the post before he set off to find Waddell. He expected the colonel ordered the large rocks whitewashed. Everything spoke of sharp discipline and demanding neatness.

Rows of stables behind the enlisted men's barracks were out of sight from the colonel's window. Unless the wind blew from the east, he couldn't smell the sweetish odor of hay and manure. Mark suspected Blair would have it no other way.

The door opened and Pearce returned. "The colonel will see you both now, sir."

The lieutenant sucked in a deep breath. With his hat under his arm, he entered the colonel's office, with Allie joining him.

The commandant was studying a document, making notes.

Mark drew to a halt three paces in front of his desk. "Sir, Lieutenant McCrae and Sergeant McCrae reporting the recovery of the stolen payroll."

"I trust you will have a full report promptly on my desk." Colonel Blair continued to write. Interminable seconds clicked off, with only the scratch of a quill breaking the silence. Blair finally stood and returned the salute. "At ease, gentlemen. Have a chair." He eyed Mark from behind thick, tufted eyebrows. "And Waddell?"

"Sir, both men are dead. They're underground in Prescott."

The colonel sat and leaned back, tenting his fingertips. Only his expression showed hardness. Graying hair at his temples emphasized the narrow face and caustic blue eyes.

"You are both to be congratulated. Well done."

"Thank you, sir."

"Did you encounter any trouble on your way back?"

Puzzled, Mark said, "Trouble, sir?"

"Indians, Lieutenant. Did you see any?" snapped the colonel.

"None at all, sir. If they were there, we didn't see them."

"Sergeant, did you notice anything unusual?"

"No, sir. I dinna."

"Very well. That's all. And remember, the report first thing tomorrow."

"Yes, sir," replied Mark. After sharp salutes, they withdrew from the room. Mark stopped by Sergeant Pearce's desk and inquired, "What's this about Indians?"

"Didn't he tell you, Lieutenant? Victorio led his people off the reservation again. Says he'll die before letting them stay in San Carlos. Something about the government not helping them irrigate their land, among a whole lotta grievances."

Mark stared at Pearce as if he didn't believe the chief's threat. "In a letter from my father, he mentioned they've been leaving the reservation, but I thought they were settled down by now. Has the colonel made arrangements to meet with Victorio?"

Now it was Pearce with the puzzled expression. "Pardon, sir. The colonel didn't explain?"

"Exactly what should he have explained? He sent a wire to Prescott about the Apaches, but he didn't mention it just now, so I didn't ask."

Pearce darted a glance toward the closed door. "Victorio will talk, but he wants to talk to, and I quote, to his 'young Indian friend, Mark McCrae'."

Mark straightened. "Well, I guess that isn't a total surprise, since I do have an acquaintance with him."

"How's that, sir?"

"Before going to West Point I often rode out in the foothills. One time I got lost. When I stopped at a lake for water, Victorio rode up beside me."

"You actually talked with this Apache, sir?"

"Yes, I did. I admit he gave me a start at first. He recognized my heritage—just not which heritage."

"But, sir, if I may ask, what did you talk about?"

"He told me a pathetic tale—the sordid life his people endured away from their native haunts—cheated and exploited by the white agents and traders. I figured something would have to change sooner or later. Then he directed me back to the fort. We met again on one of my later rides into the desert before I left for school. He spoke enough English to get his point across."

"I expect, sir, the colonel is making plans. He will tell you after you've had a night's rest."

"I certainly hope so. I'll look forward to it."

Mark left headquarters and met Allie coming up the steps. He related what Pearce had said. "Why didn't Blair tell me about Victorio when I was in his office a few minutes ago?"

"No thoughts on that one. It's news to me. But right now, I need to let Pearce leave so I can catch up on me work."

On the way to his quarters Mark still questioned the actions of his commandant.

A few children of the noncoms were engaged in a youthful pursuit of playing soldiers and Indians. One of the rompers collided with Mark as he rounded a corner.

"Whoa there, big fella," Mark said to the tow-headed boy. "It seems you ran into the army."

The small boy, with a makeshift bow in one dirty hand, peered up at the tall officer. His big blue eyes widened. "Are... are you an Injun?"

"Yes, I'm an Indian, or at least I'm half. Are you?"

The boy stared, saying, "No, I'm play-acting. It's my turn to be an Injun. I don't like real Injuns." He ran back around the corner.

Mark stood still a minute, his jaw set, thinking of how honest children were.

He continued to his parents' quarters, as he had scarcely seen his mother since he left for Prescott. Yvonne had always made him feel better by offering encouragement, but he didn't choose to tell her of his probable meeting with Victorio. After giving her a hug, he gathered up his books and personal belongings. Returning to his room, away from the rising heat of the day, he unbuttoned his shirt and loosened his boots. He would arrange his things later.

The combination of school and the keen insights of his father and mother, as well as his relationship with his Choctaw grandfather, had given him an early understanding of the Indian people. Mark knew them as he knew himself, but there was always more to learn about the Chiricahuas.

He mulled over the recent escapades by the Apache leader and his tribe, and then wrote his report on Waddell and Simmons.

Afterward, he went for that long-needed bath. Bone-weary, he welcomed the chance to rest his tired muscles. The only way he could erase the dreaded thoughts of meeting with the colonel the next day was to replace them with Jerry Whitfield's words—*long golden hair, creamy skin, and blue eyes.*

~~~

Mark's mind raced as he entered Colonel Blair's office. "Sir, I have my report as you directed."

"Yes, I'll take that. Sit down, Lieutenant. Three days ago, an Apache rider brought a message with Victorio's refusing the ultimatum to remain at San Carlos. They want to return to Ojo Caliente. If forced back, Victorio plans war. He's ready to talk, but only to you."

"Sir, I haven't seen Victorio in some time, and then, I was pretty young. But I'll do what I can. For some reason we formed a kind of bond."

"That's why you're the only one who can deal with this. I considered not going through with such a talk—just push them bloody well back. But I have my orders. You meet in two days. Damn their insolence!"

As the colonel fumed, a fiery gleam came into his eyes. "Washington says send them back to San Carlos, but if the opportunity arises, I'll wipe out the lot of them." His narrow face hardened. "By God, I'll show them, as well as those fools in the capital."

Mark thought Blair accepted the Apache refusal as a personal affront, rather than impertinence from a hostile tribe toward the United States. Nor did "fools in the capital" escape Mark. "Sir, do I understand correctly? If the Apaches do not return, we will destroy them?"

"You heard correctly, Lieutenant."

"But sir, that isn't our duty to—"

"To annihilate an enemy of the United States? They have had every concession. The government took care of them on the reservation, and now what do they do? Kill, plunder, and defy the army. Nomadic dogs! The country will be better off without them. I can tell you, McCrae, I will crush this myth of Apache invincibility."

"Sir, may I remind you of what you will be up against if you persist in this plan?"

"Lieutenant, are you challenging my authority?"

"Not at all, sir, but I've studied the Apaches. The Spanish invaders couldn't conquer them. They're unsurpassed in their cunning. They know every drop of water and sprout of vegetation in Arizona and New Mexico Territories. I've not heard of Victorio's band engaging in torture like other tribes, but they excel in ambush and surprise attack."

The colonel's face offered no expression.

What is he thinking? He isn't listening. "You can't mean to kill all the women and children, sir."

Blair rose, leaned over the desk and spoke with sarcasm. "If you are quite finished, Lieutenant McCrae, I'll tell you why I can do just that. Women and children... spawns of evil, I'd say. Get the whole bunch of them, and we'll have no more trouble. Logical, isn't it? Let me tell you, McCrae. I know something about the Apaches. They murdered my sister and her entire family. I know what we must do!"

Arguing with Blair was out of the question, but he wanted to end the colonel's tirade. He couldn't help wonder if this ambitious man planned to make him a dupe for an already arranged plan at slaughter. "Yes, sir," Mark said. "I believe Victorio will cooperate... as long as our government does."

"Tuesday, Lieutenant."

Mark saluted and left. Stopping at his father's desk in the outer office, Mark related his orders to him.

"Son, get the color of the situation as soon as ye can, and try to pinpoint some kind of solution. And remember, ye may think ye understand the Indians' problems, but they won't know that. They'll see ye as a half-blood bluecoat."

With that bit of wisdom given him, Mark felt need for a shot of whiskey, although he didn't particularly like the taste.

While walking, his thoughts went to what his father had told him about Blair's background. A West Pointer who rose to full colonelcy at the Battle of Bull Run, his reputation for arrogance and his refusal to adhere to strict orders reduced him to the rank of major at the conclusion of the war. With the opportunity of being elevated once more to the rank of colonel, he accepted the position at Hellsgate. He was determined to rebut the attitude of the powers-that-be in Washington that John Blair wasn't worthy of his post advancement.

Mark thought that must have been the origin of Blair's bitterness, not that it made him like the colonel any better.

He turned the corner and passed a group of men bunched around a tub and a large pile of potatoes. Condemning those who put them into such a position of abuse and ill-gotten work, one man following another tossed peeled potatoes into the tub. Grumbling men also worked in the stables, their protesting expletives adding to the foul air.

Almost to his barracks, and planning to have that drink after all, Mark overheard two army wives conversing on a porch.

"I declare when I used a fan back home, who'd ever think I'd be using one of the lovely things out here in this Godforsaken land."

Mark tipped his cap.

"How do, Lieutenant. Mighty nice day, wouldn't you say?" one of the ladies asked in a high-pitched voice.

"Yes, ma'am, it is that."

Continuing toward his quarters, he heard one of them say, "Such a nice young man. His mama's a fine woman. I had my doubts at first, her being Indian and all. But she's taught me everything I know about tatting. Took me some time to admit it to myself."

"Or to anyone else for that matter," her friend replied crisply.

Chapter 16

Overhanging rocks of crumbling limestone partially sheltered the closed basin, where stern-faced elders sat in a circle around a brightening flame. The women prepared the evening meal in the traditional routine of over a hundred years.

High in the mountains on lost trails and in deep gorges, the collected Apaches banded for a council. All present watched the dominant figure pacing in their midst, his thundering voice like a mountain storm.

Draco, giant firebrand of Victorio's band, called upon the tribe to strike while the White Eyes were unprepared for attack. "Are we women sulking in the brush, hiding from a drunken warrior that we do not take what is ours? We are Chiricahuas! They take goods from us and send them to Las Cruces. Who does this to us? Agents and traders seek to make the Apaches pick up bones they throw. Do we fear this band of bluecoats?"

A murmur of hostility arose from the seated men, and the fanatical young warrior spoke on.

"Now we have a taste of leaving the reservation. Other tribes will follow. Mimbreños, Coyoteros, Mogollones—all the rest." Draco expounded in a release of pent-up fury. "No matter what the White Eye colonel says, we must strike soon. Now!"

His brutal face wore a mask of hate. A scar along his temple flared as a souvenir of a past encounter. At the conclusion of his speech, he folded his bronzed arms across his broad chest and surveyed the circle of men.

Victorio approached the group, stopped and listened. He stepped into the circle. The Apache leader stood silent, fingering an amulet hanging from the rawhide thong about his neck. Close to five-feet-ten-inches, he appeared taller. A red headband kept back the graying hair resting on his shoulders.

Gazing past the other men, he stood immobile then spoke. "Draco talks as I once did in the days of my youth. He is a great warrior, but a warrior does not win battles with only the strength of his arm. The Apache must use cunning and wisdom. I will try to guide the path of my people. But if we must, we will die fighting before we go back to San Carlos. Is land of death!"

Reacting to those words, the others again broke in and raised their voices in approval. The upraised hand of their leader stilled them.

"We will meet with bluecoat McCrae and hear him speak."

~~~

Meanwhile, inside his room, Mark opened a drawer and removed a full bottle of whiskey. He poured two fingers into a tin cup and downed it in one gulp. His eyes watered from the sudden shock of the fiery liquid. *I still don't like the taste.*

Not unlike other billets of rough frontier posts, his room held a neat single bed, washstand with metal basin and pewter pitcher, and a large wooden trunk bound with iron, all common furnishings for an unmarried lieutenant's quarters.

Before Mark went to West Point, he owned a small collection of cherished books. Those he couldn't acquire for himself, Colonel Hardin had loaned him or sometimes gave to him. Mark planned to place them on a rough plank bracketed to the wall over the bed. *The Iliad* and *The Odyssey*, works of Voltaire, Thomas Paine, plus books on grammar and mathematics. The required books on cavalry tactics would complete the four feet of shelf. The Bible his father had given him lay on his desk.

Mark ambled toward the low bed and flopped onto the blanket-covered mattress. Hands behind his head, he stared at the beamed ceiling.

At that moment, he heard a rap on the door.

"Lieutenant McCrae? Mind if I come in, sir?"

"Door's unlocked."

Jerry Whitfield entered and tossed his cap on a table. He grinned at Mark's prone figure and glanced at the open bureau drawer. "Here you are, resting your carcass and partaking of liquid refreshment. You do this while I meander around the stronghold of the U.S. Army, trying to appear regimented. I'd sure like a drink, sir."

"Help yourself. Cut the sir and call me Mark."

Jerry poured one and sat down, tipping his chair against the wall. "Well?"

Mark looked falsely surprised. "Well, what?"

"You know what I mean, sir," Jerry exploded. "We saw that Indian ride in the other day. Rumor has it he carried a message from the big leader himself. What's it all about?"

Mark had the impression his visitor wanted the answer to be that Victorio planned to fight. "I'm to meet with Victorio this Tuesday morning. You may see action soon."

"You mean they refused to go back on the reservation in spite of knowing we would come after them?"

"Can you blame them?" Mark sprang from the bed and walked over to the window. "But he wants to talk to me all the same."

A tight smile lit up Jerry's tan face. "How soon do you think we'll take the field?"

Mark's jaws tightened as he kept his back to the junior officer.

"What's wrong, sir?" Jerry asked.

"I said cut the sir! I'll tell you what's wrong. That maniac of a colonel wants to destroy all the Apaches he can lay his hands on. Granted, Victorio may deserve punishment, but really, what has he done? They're fighting for their land as you would fight for yours." Mark smashed one fist at the wall, giving vent to sudden anger that swept over him. "What's wrong with the Indian Agency is the question."

"I didn't mean to get you riled, but isn't that why we're here? To keep them in line?"

"Yes, but to keep them in line fairly. Sometimes I can't help myself getting riled—I don't know which self that is. I am white and Indian. I am also a soldier."

Jerry said nothing.

"Usually I'm not violent in my opinions and certainly not toward a commanding officer. I know how you feel. You want to put your book tactics to a real test. Everyone is like that in the beginning."

"What do you mean, 'the beginning'?"

"I've heard of the wars from my father and grandfather, and from instructors at the Point. Heard the whine of too-close bullets and the death screech of a mount. The only soldiers the politicians see are those marching down the street in Washington on the Fourth of July, never the battered men dragging in from a fight in the field, or a horse with an empty saddle."

"But it's our duty to carry out orders," Jerry said. "I don't understand you. Would you have me make nothing of myself because it meant killing a few Indians?"

Taken aback at Jerry's statement, Mark rationalized that the lieutenant was oblivious at what he'd just said. Mark ignored it. "We've broken more promises than we've kept. If we go along breaking our word to anyone just because they're not white, what does that say about us?"

"Lieutenant, I've made it clear to my family, whom I respect a great deal, mind you, that I do not choose to follow in my father's footsteps as a Boston banker. In order to prove myself to him, I plan to become a colonel with my own command. If I seem impatient to you, so be it."

"Give it some time."

Jerry picked up his hat and stomped out, not without saluting.

For several minutes Mark stared out the window. Finally he lay back on his bed and thought himself to sleep.

~~~

In the orderly room of headquarters, a corporal on duty sat scribbling the click-clack message from the telegraph. "Sergeant McCrae, this here's for the colonel."

Allie rose from his desk and stepped to the far side of the room. He peered over the operator's shoulder and swore. "All we get is trouble."

He entered the colonel's office. "Pardon, sir, but this wire just came in for ye."

Colonel Blair read it and, frowning, tossed it on the desk. "You read this, Sergeant?"

"I did, sir."

"Nothing we can do about it now but send an escort to Clear Springs and fetch my niece. My wire for her to remain at Fort Davis apparently arrived too late to stop the stagecoach. I'll send Lieutenant McCrae. Tell him I wish to see him. That's all, Sergeant."

~~~

Mark awoke with a clear head. He prepared the iron basin for his shave and scraped stubble from his angular chin. A steel comb made his thick hair presentable. He stepped outside and gazed about the awakening post. Remembering he didn't have supper the night before, he started toward the mess room.

The sutler, John Higgins, maintained an eating area in his small store at the fort. Mark decided to eat there instead. An aged Mexican woman turned out some fine meals, and Mark had the feeling he wouldn't be disappointed in one of her breakfasts.

Higgins wrestled with a barrel of vinegar as Mark approached. "Whew! Well, bless my soul, Lieutenant McCrae." He set down the barrel with a sigh. "I heard about you and the sergeant landing Waddell and Simmons. A job well done, sir."

"Thanks. The effort succeeded, I'm glad to say."

Higgins was a friend of Allie's and had been in America so long, he'd lost all but a touch of his Irish brogue. Allie and Lafferty made a pair of his best customers. The three of them formed a sort of drinking club. Mark never found who won out, nor where his father placed in the contest. He felt sure being first wasn't his objective, especially since he had told him he rarely drank before coming to the Territory.

"Too early or too late for breakfast?" Mark asked.

"Lieutenant, that woman would fix you anything you wanted, even at midnight. Ever since she heard you were back from West Point, she's just been waitin' for you to wander in. Wish I could get along with her like you do."

The shapeless old woman finished placing knives and forks on a table as Mark entered.

"Ah, Elena, the prettiest sight I've seen since returning to the Territory. *¿Cómo estás?*"

"*Muy bien.*" A grin appeared on her lined face. "Señor Mark, let me see you. You look so fine." Elena pulled out a chair. "Sit." She hurried to the kitchen. In a short time, she returned with steaming plates of aromatic dishes: huevos rancheros, a small steak on the side, and *bisquetas.*

"Is it as tasty as it smells, Elena?"

"I hope so! *Uno momento.* I bring you café." She returned and continued the conversation. "The lieutenant takes his food like a young colt returning from the empty desert."

Almost finished eating, Mark heard Higgins say, "Yes, the lieutenant's having breakfast."

The corporal, his manner stiff and militaristic, walked over to Mark. "Lieutenant, the colonel wants to see you, sir."

"Breakfast was great, Elena." Mark gulped down the last of his coffee and left with the corporal for headquarters. "See you later, Higgins."

The colonel stood in his familiar pose with one hand behind his back and peered out the window. "How long would it take you to ride to Clear Springs, McCrae?"

What has he got in mind now, Mark wondered. "Alone or on patrol, sir?"

"A squad and a light carriage."

Mark paused, then said. "About two hours or so, sir."

The tip of Colonel Blair's long cigar glowed brightly. "I want you to escort my niece from Clear Springs. She arrives from Washington sometime Thursday afternoon. Amanda is like my daughter, and I expect you to give her safe escort."

"Yes, sir. I will be glad to." *At least I think I will.*

"But get this business settled tomorrow with the Chiricahuas," the colonel added. "I don't trust them."

Chapter 17

Mark brought out the big bay on Tuesday. Checking over his sidearm, he headed toward his patrol. He and the men were on their way to Mark's first meeting with Victorio. Just thinking of it made him anxious.

By noon they neared the meeting place. Mark left it to Allie to set up camp in a spot with an unobstructed view but with protection, should they need it.

Mark continued riding, and Chiricahua scouts soon surrounded him. The warriors led him to a large brush hut, facing west, as always. Victorio stepped out. Recognition passed between them.

"Mark McCrae, I have known you since you were a cub. You have grown into young manhood."

"Victorio, it is good to see you. Are you well?"

"I am well in body, yet my spirit is troubled. Come. We talk."

Mark hesitated. "My Apache is only fair, Victorio."

"Do not worry. I will do my best to translate."

Once inside the hut they sat in a circle. Victorio spoke. "Naiche, Dark Cloud, Draco, this is my friend, Mark McCrae. He will listen to you speak and hear your message from Geronimo." Only the slender Chiricahua, Naiche, who was the son of Cochise, and chief of the Cochonen Apaches, stood.

Naiche, with straight nose and chiseled features, stood with arms folded. He stared at Mark. "I ask our brothers to drive out all White Eyes from our lands. We will continue raids wherever need takes us. I have come to hear your answer. Then I decide."

Mark was aware Victorio and Naiche's bands were not close, but after all, they had the same goal. "I can tell you what I know at this time."

"Say your message, Mark McCrae."

Mark turned toward the group, with Victorio translating as best he could. Drawing on his nerve, he said, "This may not all be a good thing you ask." He hoped he had not already insulted them. "The bluecoats will fight any attempt by you to drive the settlers from this land. This is something our people must resolve, or many young men on both sides will die."

Victorio paused. "Can bluecoat give reason for this not to be? Agency tell us we can live in Ojo Caliente... then they sell land. Promises no help when broken many times. They force us higher to Tularosa River but send no blankets in winter."

Draco asked in a voice swathed in contempt. "Lieutenant McCrae of bluecoat army, what say you to that?"

Mark started to reply, then stopped. He thought fast to come up with an answer. "First, I know San Carlos is not livable. I have a plan. If the government will send you back to Ojo Caliente, limits will again be set on how far the settlers and New Mexicans may go toward your land. I ask you to give this much thought before it is too late."

"How can you, one man, say this will be?" Victorio asked.

"I can't promise. Before the agreement is final we must get our president in Washington to agree. It is up to more than one person in Washington. Then Colonel Blair from the fort will tell it to you himself. Find patience until all questions can be answered."

An elder spoke up, "Victorio, you say this soldier McCrae will make things once more favor us. But he is like the rest, a traitor to his people. He wears the uniform of the Long Knives."

Victorio arose from his blanket, eyes flashing. He stood straight and deadly as an arrow. His thin lips turned down in an expression of ruthlessness—or sadness. "McCrae speaks straight. We must give his words more thought before we pick up the lance. His words offer us safety." He turned to Mark. "You wait. We will council. Then we have food."

Mark stepped outside the hut toward the fire pit. He smelled the meat cooking and thought the tantalizing aroma could awaken a dead warrior.

After what seemed hours, Victorio came forth. "It is true, the bluecoats are many. We agree to hear your colonel speak his words—before the sun sets in three days.

Mark breathed a sigh of relief but noticed dissatisfaction on Draco's face.

After a full meal, the women passed around old tin cups of black coffee. Those wanting it sweetened dipped their knives into leather containers of golden wild honey that the women had brought from the cliff overhangs. Some of the men let go loud belches announcing their full pleasure.

"Stay until morning, my friend," Victorio offered.

"Thank you for your hospitality, but I must leave. My men expect me at camp." Mark said goodbye, and as he walked toward his horse, he heard footsteps from behind him. It was the warrior, Draco. "Your words may fool older ones," he called, "but they do not fool me, half-blood."

Offering no response, Mark mounted the bay and reined her to the near-invisible trace leading to his patrol's camp. He wouldn't forget Draco's menacing voice.

Mark concentrated on his possible fate, fully aware he had presented his own plan, and not the colonel's, to the Apache. He wondered what Blair would say.

Less than a quarter mile down the trace toward camp, Mark guided Belle in order to miss a fallen tree branch. He didn't see the hole made by some desert varmint. Belle stumbled and with front legs flailing, went down, taking Mark with her. He put an arm out to break the fall, but he hit a boulder.

~~~

Victorio returned to the fire. As he stared at the smoke spiraling upward from the low-burning embers, he grew transfixed. After several seconds, he arose from his place. He left the fire and followed the same path Mark had taken. His own sentries seemed startled by his departure, but he walked past them, saying nothing.

The chief soon glimpsed the bluecoat's horse standing by Mark, who lay on the trace, unmoving. Victorio examined the young soldier. Then, finding the horse intact, he managed to get Mark across the saddle. He continued leading the bay down the narrow trace to the soldiers' encampment.

Steel-shod hooves on solid rock resounded in the darkness.

~~~

Mark regained consciousness at the sound of Jeb's voice.

"Halt!" the corporal said, drawing his Colt as the sounds came closer. "Allie, quick! It's the lieutenant!" They helped Mark from his horse and got him onto a blanket by the fire.

"I know I saw an Apache bring him in," Jeb said, breathless. "And I didn't dream it!"

Still dazed, Mark said, "I remember falling. Sure got the wind knocked out of me. Is Belle all right?"

"Fine. She's just fine," Allie assured him.

"But how did I get here?"

"Why, Lieutenant, that Indian right over there brought you in on yore horse."

Mark glanced in the direction Jeb pointed. "I don't see anyone."

The Indian had vanished like smoke in the wind.

By morning, Mark awoke with a headache. Pushing himself up, he walked over to the small fire and poured a tin of coffee from the blackened pot. As he leaned over, an object fell from his pocket. Reaching down, he picked up a leather pouch of jerky. He knew he hadn't put it there. Now the identity of his rescuer became clear. When he was a boy riding in the mountains, lost and hungry, he had accepted beef jerky from Victorio.

Allie hunkered down on the opposite side of the fire and reached for a cup while the rest of the men rumbled about. "I'm glad to see ye on your feet, Son." He grimaced after tasting the bitter coffee. "Sure an' begorrah, 'tis worse than the pinther juice served up by the bloomin' sutler. I should've made it meself. But it does take the nip from the air."

He took another swallow and tossed the rest out. "So what do ye think? I'm guessing a fight is nearing. Am I right?"

"May be, and we might not be able to do a blessed thing to prevent it. Victorio agreed to talk with Blair, and we only hope Washington's response goes along. Otherwise, more terrorizing of the settlers and raids will continue." He stopped long enough to notice the men had readied themselves for leaving, even without his orders. "I guess everybody got ahead of me this morning. All right, men. Time to move out."

Mark felt the relief of the troops as they headed away from the immediate vicinity of the Apaches. The slow column wound its way through the rough terrain, thick with saguaro, and projections of jagged knolls crossed the deeply gashed washouts. Loose tumbleweeds rolled along, as though accompanying the soldiers.

To Mark, this seemed like home. The tranquility of the land would fool only the newcomer. It was a place he had come back to, but he would never forget the years spent in Red Oak with his grandfather during the war. In those times, the Choctaws were his family and friends. He wondered if the Apaches would ever again exist in the beauty of the land they had always known? The encroachment of advancing whites was inevitable. As a soldier, he followed orders, regardless of the outcome. At least, he planned to.

Halting the men on the slope near the fort, Mark ordered them to shake the alkali dust from their clothing and to appear sharp upon their return.

~~~

From the forward guard rampart, the sentry called, "Patrol's coming. Open the gates."

"Hold it!" Lieutenant Jerry Whitfield climbed the ladder two rungs at a time. He could tell by the alarmed look in the sentry's clear hazel eyes that he had startled him. "Who told you to open the gates, soldier?"

"Why, no one, Lieutenant. It looks like our men in blue, so I thought—"

"How do you know it's not a trick—the enemy in stolen uniforms. It's happened before. From here on out, call the OD when more than one man wants entry. Understand?"

The trooper stood at rigid attention. He swallowed hard. "Yes, sir!"

Whitfield turned away from the trooper beside him and gazed at the approaching men. No one sat a mount quite like Mark did, he thought, a man born to the saddle. "All right, Private, give the signal to open them now." Whitfield climbed back down.

~~~

The big gates opened, and the patrol clattered into the Fort.

"Good showing, men," Mark said. "Dismiss the troops, Sergeant."

They broke formation. Some made straight for the sutler's store and the waiting liquor, soldiers' liniment for weary bones.

Mark knew they spent much of their wages on whiskey. "I don't know, Top, they must save all month to buy it."

"Aye, a quarter of 'em will end in the guardhouse on charges from drunkenness to who knows what, but in this wilderness, it's vent for stored energy. I tell ye, when they're sober, each one is as fine a fighting man as ye can find in the country. Not much less even when drunk."

Mark walked Belle to headquarters, rubbed her neck and gave the reins to the orderly who stood waiting.

"The colonel wants to see you immediately, sir."

"I guess this is soon enough." He proceeded inside and stopped at the colonel's open door. "Sir, Lieutenant McCrae reporting from special assignment."

Colonial Blair put aside a territorial map. "Come in, Lieutenant, come in. Sit down. Now, from the beginning. Tell me the outcome of your mission."

"Sir, I think it was successful, although I may have overstepped my authority."

Blair looked up sharply. "What do you mean by that, McCrae?"

"Well, sir, as we know, foremost on the Apaches' minds is they want to be at Ojo Caliente. It is their land as it has always been. Our meeting resulted in a kind of compromise, and they want you to tell them yourself, as I did. If we replace agents and guarantee no more settlers will intrude, they will stop their plan for war."

"Suppose you tell me how we can accomplish that?"

"Those are their conditions for further talk, sir. Victorio forced the results. Not all of them agree, especially a hotheaded warrior called Draco. He thirsts for blood, no matter what we decide. Victorio wants you to look into their eyes and tell them of the plan. I told them you will have to get orders from Washington."

Mark had no idea what the colonel's reply would be, nor when he would offer it.

Colonel Blair sat a moment, leaned toward his desk and sighed. "Very well. I will chance it, but there is no guarantee. In the meantime, we will have this scheduled meeting, but we won't have our answer from Washington by then."

"Sir, Victorio knows, but he wants to hear from you that we'll try. And thank you for understanding. I knew I took authority, but had you been there, you would—"

"Lieutenant. I said we're going to try it your way."

Mark's nerves tightened at the colonel's strident tone.

"I will inform the sergeant to choose a patrol. He'll have to make sure no one is the nervous type and gets us all killed. That's all, Lieutenant."

Chapter 18

Amanda Blair's pert hat flew off, and her parasol fell to the ground as she landed most unladylike on her backside. Gathering her ruffled petticoats and green taffeta skirt around her, she drew herself up from the dusty street.

Placing the hat on her flaxen curls, she snatched her parasol, and with eyes blazing, stomped up the steps to the saloon "Knock me down, will you, you drunken beasts!"

The two men ignored her tirade and continued their brawl.

"If you have no manners, I'll teach you some," she screamed, pummeling one of them on the head and shoulder with her parasol.

"What the hell?" The man waved his arms to block the rain of blows. His distraction created the opening his first opponent needed to send him sprawling.

The man delivering the last blow straightened. "What's the trouble here?" he demanded.

"You know very well what's the trouble. I was on the boardwalk when you drunken men pushed me down the steps. Why, I could have been seriously injured."

"Whoa, only one of us is drunk—that one lolling over the rail there. I caught him cheating at cards and thought to give him a lesson."

"I don't believe you." Amanda started for him again. "You smell like a stinking barroom!"

"Now, missy. I'm sorry you landed in the dirt, but... hey, hold on there." With one arm he succeeded in stopping her from thrashing him, and with the other, caught the flailing parasol.

"Let me go!"

"Well, lookee here, a regular wildcat. Guess I'll have to see to it you don't hurt any more of us fellers." He released her and grabbed the parasol, breaking it in half.

"Oh, you'll pay for this. My uncle will see you punished."

The man blinked at the fiery young woman before him. "Punished? Who's going to do what to me?"

"My uncle is the colonel! He will have you jailed for this insult."

"So you're army, huh? You listen to me, woman. The army busted me out, so I got no liking for it *or* your uncle. But mebbe now I can still get a little pleasure back." He wiped his mouth on his sleeve. "Come 'ere, missy, let's give us a kiss."

~~~

Mark and the detail arrived in time to witness the last of the scene, which had already brought out the town's bystanders. He wheeled Belle to a halt in front of the hotel. Leaning a little forward from the saddle, he shouted, "I suggest you let the lady go!"

"Well now, is the big important lieutenant plannin' to rescue the girl and run Lafe Logan out of town?"

"That just might be true, mister. I said release her!" Mark drew out his .45. "Then clear out!" The half-blood's voice resonated with killing realism.

"Okay. Okay." Logan put up a hand and backed away. "She may not be worth a fight at that. I'm goin', but that woman had no cause."

"No cause?" Amanda cried. "This blundering fool knocked me down in the dirt and broke my parasol."

"Apologize to the lady, or I'll beat you myself and it won't be with a parasol."

"You think just because you—"

"Logan!"

"All right, all right," he grumbled. "Sorry, ma'am. I'll go." He disappeared into the crowd.

Dismounting, Mark couldn't help laughing at the pretty girl, perky hat askew. "Miss, are you hurt? Do you need a doctor?"

"Stop laughing. It isn't one bit funny, whatever your name is," she blurted, as she shook the dust from her skirts.

"Lieutenant McCrae at your service." He suppressed further laughter into a broad smile. He watched her push the hair from her face and readjust her dainty hat, its flower slightly crushed.

Her expression tempered, she almost cooed. "Lieutenant McCrae, my name is Amanda Blair, and I want to sincerely thank you for your intervention with that horrid man."

Mark hesitated in disbelief. *I know her, but I never expected... It's clear she doesn't recognize me.* "Miss Blair, I can't believe these townspeople would have allowed Logan to carry out his intent."

"Lieutenant, am I to assume you are my escort?"

"Yes, ma'am. And I suggest we get started."

"Oh, please, Lieutenant. I'm exhausted. Of course, I'm anxious to see my uncle, but can't we please wait until morning? I couldn't ride another mile today."

Mark hesitated since they hadn't prepared to stay overnight. There wasn't much he could do about it. "I understand. I'm sure your uncle will, too. Since this is the hottest part of the day, waiting would probably be a good idea."

"Then would someone be so kind as to fetch my travel cases at the stage office? We can pick up my trunks in the morning."

"I will see to it." Mark turned to the soldiers, who had watched the entire episode. "Private, escort Miss Blair to the hotel then bring her luggage from the station."

"Yes, sir."

Mark had counted on Allie to survey the crowd and rooftops for any of Lafe Logan's friends who might have a mind to draw a weapon. "Top, looks like we'll be staying a while."

"If that's the case, I'll gather the men and we'll have a bite to eat at the restaurant. No cook on this mission. Just me coffeepot." He grinned.

"You go ahead. I'll catch up with you. I have something very important to attend to."

~~~

Amanda headed for the hotel, escorted by the private. "I'll bring your luggage right away, ma'am."

"Thank you. I'd appreciate that."

Amanda noticed a well-dressed individual on the walkway but did not acknowledge him. He appeared intent on joining her—somewhere. He removed his hat and brushed off the brim.

Amanda stepped toward the door then looked back. She felt anxious but couldn't help watching him, ready to scream if necessary.

Still following, the man had only four steps left to the hotel entrance.

An older drover of sorts, with skin like leather, leaned against the outside wall. He casually stuck out his booted foot just as the dapper man passed by. The latter fell flat on his face.

"If I were you, I wouldn't do what you're thinkin'," the crusty drover warned.

The man pulled himself to his feet and made a fast departure.

A voice called from the dispersing crowd, "C'mon, Zeke. We're leavin'."

The drover took a deep drag from his cigarette and, exhaling a soft curl of smoke, ambled down the steps to join his three friends.

With the episode over, Amanda quickly entered the hotel.

The desk clerk, a robust man with a string tie, obviously a little tight for his neck, began running his finger down the worn ledger as Amanda approached the desk. "Good day, Miss. Will you be wanting a room for the night, or longer?"

"One night only." In her most charming way she added, "May I sign now? It's been a long day, and I'm very tired."

"Of course, Miss. Are you traveling alone?"

"Yes, my chaperone wasn't feeling well, and she stopped off in Gallup to visit relatives. I didn't want to wait. My room, please?"

The clerk glanced again at the register. "Ah, Room 2. This is the nicest and airiest we have." He turned the book around, and Amanda entered her name, writing Washington, D.C., as her address. "Actually, my local address is Fort Hellsgate where my uncle is commandant. Are you acquainted with Colonel Blair?"

He nodded, as if to understand why the young woman before him would be in a town like Clear Springs. "Only by reputation," he replied. "I'll show you to your—"

"Don't bother. I can find it." She reached out for the key. "When the soldier brings my luggage, would you have him bring it up, please? And also, would you be so kind as to let me know when my escort calls for me in the morning?"

"Yes, ma'am. If you need—"

"And one more thing. Might I have your best supper sent up? And a bath drawn?"

"Certainly, Miss Blair. We aim to please."

"Thank you. You're very kind." She wearily climbed the stairs.

~~~

Mark noted his father had chosen the most defensible spot in a wooded area outside town.

He found a pile of leaves for a bed and used his saddle for a pillow. *She doesn't remember me... and still as haughty as before.* He tried to force himself from thinking about her. *What would she see in me anyway? Besides, Whitfield's made it clear he has his sights on her.* He listened to the night for a while, the soft gurgle of a nearby stream aiding his progress for sleep.

Only when Mark became aware of the coffee smell did he waken. *Top will bring that coffeepot whenever he can,* he thought, smiling. The morning sun's rays slanted across his eyes, fully arousing him. He stood and stretched. After a second cup, he said, "Well, I guess Miss Blair has had enough beauty sleep for one night."

"I'll get Jeb to bring up the carriage," Allie said. "By the way, what do you think of the colonel's niece?"

"What do I think? She's about what I expected, being the colonel's niece. But right now, I'd best ride on in and fetch her." Minutes later, he looped Belle's reins over the tie bar. He walked up the steps, strode to the front desk and looked around. "Now where's that clerk?"

The man from the day before suddenly materialized from a back room. "How do, Lieutenant?"

"Good morning. I've come to escort Miss Blair."

"She asked me to inform her when you arrived, Lieutenant. I'll help with her luggage."

Carrying a package under his arm, Mark followed him up the stairs and rapped on the door.

The petite young woman appeared, flashing a smile.

In as normal a voice as he could muster, Mark said, "Miss Blair, your uncle's compliments, and my own. Have I arrived too early?" He leaned the package against the wall.

"Oh, no. I've had my breakfast, so I'm ready." She stepped over to the dressing table, closed her vanity case and handed it to Mark. "My other luggage is right here by the door."

"Something else," Mark said. "Our roads are sandy, and I wouldn't want you to soil your dress." *What a fool thing to say.*

"Let me just fetch my duster from the wardrobe."

Mark helped slip the full-length wrap on her shoulders. Being so close to her, he didn't escape the scent of her perfume. He could find her in a room full of women, with the lights off. Thank you. Lieutenant…?"

"McCrae. Mark McCrae."

"Yes, of course. Lieutenant McCrae."

The clerk cleared his throat and picked up the luggage. "I'll just take these bags downstairs."

"Oh," Mark said. "Miss Blair, I have something for you." He retrieved the package he brought from Morton's store.

"For me?" Amanda accepted the long parcel and quickly opened it, to find an ivory-colored parasol. "Why, Lieutenant, thank you. What a delightful thing for you to do, but it wasn't necessary."

"It may not be as special as yours, but Mr. Morton at the General Store said it's the best in Clear Springs."

"How charming. I do believe it's trimmed with Battenberg lace. Thank you, Lieutenant."

"That was the least I could do. Shall we go now?"

When they reached the front porch, Jeb Speck had just pulled the carriage up to the steps. A slight cloud of street dust swirled around the large dark wheels.

"Your carriage awaits, m'lady," Mark said.

"Thank you. Oh, no white mice?"

"White mice?"

"To pull the carri... oh, never mind."

Mark extended his hand to assist her. When he took a step back, a glimpse of ankle and an inch or two of calf rewarded him for his courtesy. He hoped his face would hide the flush he felt creeping up from his neck.

Chapter 19

After two hours of riding, Mark espied the fort's flagpole over a stand of oak trees. He had learned that when Amanda's parents died, her uncle had raised her. The colonel saw to it she had the best education a New York private school offered—the best of everything. The best of Hellsgate might be disappointing.

Once they entered the post, Mark directed Jeb to drive to headquarters. He dismounted and assisted his charge from the carriage.

He turned to one of the men. "Private, will you see if Colonel Blair is in his office?"

"Yes, sir."

As if with a snap decision, Amanda turned straight toward Mark and threaded her arms around his neck. She stood on her toes and planted a kiss on his cheek.

Caught off guard, he gently released himself from her grasp. "What was that all about?"

"For the ride to the fort and the lovely parasol. It was something I wanted to do ever since you saved me from that horrible man. Was it so bad of me?"

"Not at all. I'm sure most of the men staring out the barracks enjoyed it almost as much as I did."

Amanda laughed. "I hope you don't mind being seen with someone so shameless. I must rest before dinner, and since there will surely be many young men there, I must look my best—hussy that I am."

Mark wasn't quite sure how to reply, so he didn't.

The colonel burst out the door, a wide smile across his face. He gave his niece a bear hug and lifted her into the air.

"It's wonderful to see you," he said. "Did the lieutenant take proper care of you?"

"Yes, of course," she said, blinking up at Mark. "He was an excellent escort, although he couldn't do anything about the morning sun. Uncle John, I'm so glad to be here."

"Not as glad as I am to have you, but I'm sure you're tired. Your room is all ready and waiting."

Mark reached down for Belle's reins, figuring his part in safely conducting Amanda to Hellsgate was successful.

"Uncle John, will the lieutenant be joining us for supper?"

Mark felt a little embarrassed.

"Uh, well... Yes, of course... Lieutenant?"

"Certainly, Colonel. Thank you, sir."

"Come along, my dear. I'll take you to your room now."

Mark walked to his quarters, thinking, *I've known a few girls in my lifetime, but this one seems pretty damned pampered to me. Sure hasn't forgotten how to flirt.*

~~~

After her uncle left, Amanda unpacked her luggage. In deciding what to wear for supper, she tried on two different dresses. Choosing one, she said aloud, "He's so good-looking. But he's an Indian. He seems familiar... but how can that be?"

She took her time bathing and getting ready, making sure every curl on her head was in place. When the colonel rapped on her door, she realized just how much time she had taken to get dressed. It seemed as if he had just left.

When they arrived at the officer's mess, Mark waited inside the entrance.

"Oh, Lieutenant McCrae," the colonel said. "I'm glad you're here. I didn't quite finish filling out some forms that must be attended to. Would you please take care of my niece until I get back. I hope to return shortly."

Without waiting for a reply, he leaned over and kissed Amanda on the cheek. "I'm sorry, my dear. I promise I'll be back before dessert."

"It's all right, Uncle John. Please don't worry about it."

As he walked down the steps, Mark said, "I think your uncle tipped off the cooks you were here. It never smelled this appetizing before."

"He did mention earlier about having something special. But before we eat, may we sit for a moment? I'm curious about a few things."

"Fire away, but I'm a hungry soldier." He led Amanda to the table and pulled out a chair for her. "You have a twinkle in your eye, so I'll try to be prepared."

"I wonder, well, I know nothing about you except you are a lieutenant in the United States Army. From your appearance you have Indian blood, but how did the two come together—that is, if you don't mind my asking."

"Well, I can answer that, and no, I don't mind. My parents are here at the fort. My father's a soldier, and back in Indian Territory, he married a young Choctaw woman. So, you are dining with the great grandson of a Choctaw leader and the son of an Irishman and an Indian mother. It's that simple. Have I answered your question?"

"Why yes, I guess you did, but I thought I'd hear a story taking me at least through supper."

"Speaking of food, maybe we'd better have ours. Excuse me. I'll see what I can find."

Mark moved over to the serving table and filled a plate.

As he chose what he guessed Amanda would like, Jerry Whitfield stepped up beside him. "If you'll pardon my saying so, sir, it didn't take you long to set your sights on the colonel's niece."

Mark blinked in surprise at his Jerry's bluntness. "My sights? I'd like to clarify that. Her uncle asked me to escort her from town, and then to eat. The colonel had business to attend to. Following orders, Jerry, following orders." He grinned, hoping the explanation satisfied his friend. "Besides, why not join us?"

"No, thanks, I've finished. I will say hello to her, though."

They walked back to the table. "Amanda, remember me? Jerry Whitfield?"

She glanced up at him and with a slight hesitation, said, "Jerry, of course! It's been a long time. How have you been?"

"Very well, thank you. I must say you look lovely."

"Thank you for the compliment. Mark, here, fetched me in town, and we're waiting for Uncle John."

"Amanda, I wonder, might I see you tomorrow, to talk over old times?"

Mark sensed the obvious implication but stood there, still holding their plates.

"Why, yes, Jerry, that would be fine, just as long as Uncle John doesn't keep me unavailable."

"Then I look forward to tomorrow." He turned to Mark. "Lieutenant, enjoy a pleasant evening."

Mark made no response and promptly placed their supper on the table. "I chose a little of everything, since I didn't know what you'd like."

"Thank you, Mark. I'm famished."

Amanda began eating and continued until she finished almost all her meal. She looked up to see amusement on Mark's face. "Oh my, where are my manners. Well, as I said, I was—"

"I know, you were famished. Now, is there anything else you want to know?"

"As a matter of fact, there is. I can't believe you received all your schooling at the post. Did you become a first lieutenant through the ranks? Now that should take us until Uncle John gets back."

"Only if I give you boring details." Mark told her of his grandfather in Indian Territory, and then of how he gained an appointment to West Point. "And now Colonel Blair thinks my heritage will help in peaceful negotiations with the Indians."

"Very well. I'll accept that. You do have a way of over-simplifying your explanations."

Amanda paused a moment. "But wait. If you were at West Point. Mark McCrae... McCrae. The Christmas Hop! Yes. Yes! Now I remember."

Chapter 20

Allie stopped in the mess room where he hoped to find Lafferty.

"And a fine mornin' to ye," Allie said. "Lafferty, I have here an invite from the colonel to go on a twenty-five-mile ride to talk peace with a bunch of Indians. And ye even get t' act like a soldier. But don't fire your rifle without a direct order from the colonel. Is that understood?"

"I've been in this army longer'n ye have and never did anything without an order. I suppose ye want breakfast after hiking all the way over here?"

"Ye are a true Irishman knowing the mind of another. But I have me breakfast eaten. 'Course, I might have a couple those biscuits. Now, is the coffee worth drinking?"

"I made it myself and if you keep raggin' me, I'll pour it on your biscuits." Lafferty turned around to reach for a mug. He filled it from one of two large pots of steaming coffee.

Allie accepted the coffee and immediately blew on it. "I hope you're available to put out this fire. Thing is, I must move on to explain the importance of this mission to the chosen few who'll be going with us."

"I'm sure they'll be looking forward to it. Are you certain you want to tell them about the Indians?"

~~~

"Lieutenant McCrae? Can you wait up a minute, sir?" A private chased Mark as he left headquarters. Breathless, he skidded to a halt and saluted.

"Yes, what is it, Dolan? It must be important."

"It is, sir. Well, not real important, but Corporal Speck and me, we wanted to go into town today. An' we wondered if you and Sergeant McCrae might want to go with us? I mean, the corporal said it was all right to ask you. He said you wouldn't mind." Dolan felt self-conscious to be asking his superior to go to town with them, or anywhere for that matter.

"Can't think of a reason not to," Mark replied. "The day's already showed signs of being a scorcher, but town may be cooler than here. The sergeant's on duty, though."

"Then I'll find Corporal Speck, sir," Dolan said. "We'll meet you at the stables."

Dolan took off to the barracks. He opened the door and called for the corporal. Lanky Jeb Speck still lounged on his bunk, one of many bunks that lined the walls of the barracks.

"What'd they say, kid?" Jeb asked as he swung his legs to the floor.

"By golly, the lieutenant said he'd go with us. Can ya imagine?"

"That don't take much imagination. He's not one to flaunt his rank." Jeb reached for his cap, then his gun. "C'mon, let's go." They hurried out of the barracks and headed for the stables.

~~~

Mark already had Belle saddled and started in on Jeb's sorrel.

"Here, Lieutenant, I'll get that," Jeb said. "A lieutenant oughtn't to be saddlin' up a corporal's horse."

Mark grinned. "Doesn't matter. I was the first one here." He relinquished the task to Jeb and mounted the bay. "You know, this ought to be a real pleasant day."

The route into town was saguaro-lined. A few shanties stood close to the fort, most of them occupied by Mexicans. Being outside the fort's walls, but still near, offered relative safety. Mark remained silent for a while as they rode. "Speck, you know that Indian scout you waved at back there in front of his cabin? Rockin' Horse, wasn't it?"

"Yes, sir, Lieutenant, Ol' Rockin' Horse. Why?"

"We weren't so far away I couldn't see him cleaning his rifle. Like a new Winchester."

"A what, sir?" exclaimed the red-haired Private Dolan. "Dang. Where'd he get a Winchester, much less a new one?"

"I could have been wrong," Mark said, "but I don't think so."

"Who is that scout, anyhow, Lieutenant?" Dolan asked. "I've seen him around ever since I got here."

"Corporal Speck can give you a better answer than I can. All I know is he's an Indian and he speaks English. He was here when I came back from the Point."

"I know a little about him. Mostly Navajo. We call him 'Rockin' Horse,' because he sits on his porch in that rockin' chair. Speaks Navajo and some Apache, Spanish, and English. Mebbe more of each than he wants us to know. Colonel Hardin found him somewhere. He's been a big help to us more'n once."

"Let's have our time in town. I'll talk with Colonel Blair about it later."

Silence filled the second hour's ride, which Mark enjoyed, since Jeb had spent most of the first hour telling stories about his home in Kentucky.

Laid out like many frontier towns, Clear Spring's businesses lined up together. Included were Miss Elsa's "hotel" for women behind the buggy repair shop, and that building stood offside of the Silver Nugget Saloon. The saloon had its girls and rooms upstairs, but Miss Elsa's joy ladies were strong competition. The Morton brothers ran the General Store, the relay station, and the livery stable. There was a dining establishment, sheriff's office, and the one respectable hotel.

"We better tend our horses," Mark said. "There's a trough in front of the Silver Nugget."

"I tell you what, sir," Jeb said. "I could eat about anything, but there's not one thing in the saloon worth gnawin' on. What say we eat at that rest'rant then get a drink or three before we leave this town?"

"If it suits you, let's do it," Mark said.

The restaurant offered a couple choices for a noon meal— stew and goulash. Mark perused the two. "Look both the same to me." But after they finished eating, Mark leaned back in his chair. "Now that's what I call tasty. Was this your idea, Dolan?"

"Yes, sir, I guess so. We're glad you came with us."

"Well, I hadn't been here at midday before. Things seem to be picking up in little ol' Clear Springs."

"If you don't mind waitin', sir," Jeb said, "I'd like some a that apple pie I seen on the counter." He walked over to get a slice, gave it a savoring sniff and glanced out across the street. He moved closer to the window. "Now that's plumb curious. A wagon full of... coffins?"

Mark peered outside and watched the driver enter the General Store. "Why would somebody be peddling pine boxes in pine country?"

"That don't make any sense."

"Maybe some poor fool thinks he really can sell them here," Dolan commented. "But Sam Morton keeps them made up in advance, any size a body'd need."

"I dang sure ain't gonna reserve one for my body," Jeb replied, finishing off his pie.

Mark scrutinized the corporal from head to toe. "Narrow and long, I'd say."

"That's what my mama always said, sir. 'Son, you're gonna be a pole when you grow up.'" Jeb laughed. "She sure knew what she was talkin' about."

They paid their bill and ambled across the dusty street to the Silver Nugget. Mark stopped by the wagonload of pine boxes and reached to open one of the lids. "Nailed shut. Guess so they won't fall off." He slapped his hand on one of the coffins and leveled a thoughtful gaze across the rest of them. He turned and joined his companions.

They entered the Silver Nugget and sat at a table in the front. "Far's I know," Jeb said, "nobody ever found a silver load in these parts, but it does make a catchy name for a saloon."

A painted lady with almost orange-colored hair and a tight satin dress to match walked over with three glasses and a whiskey bottle. She gave her attention to Mark. "Hello there, good-looking. What can I do for you, besides bring you this drink?"

"Just a beer, thank you. That's all." Mark thought she seemed disappointed at his response.

"Uh, a beer for me, too, ma'am," Dolan said.

The woman gave Dolan a motherly smile and turned her attention to Jeb. "What about you, Slim?"

"Leave a glass. I'll have whiskey." After one gulp, his eyes widened. "Dang, that sure burnt off the pie I just ate." He wiped his mouth with the back of his hand. "Funny, no matter if the weather's cold or hot, whiskey'll warm your insides."

The painted lady dipped an almost curtsey and sashayed off to give the order to the bartender.

"Lieutenant, " Dolan said. "That feller in the wagon's leavin'."

Mark shifted in his chair to see the man in dark gray riding off. "Did you see his face?"

"No sir, not his face. Had sort of sandy hair... young. Near tall as you."

"A friend of yours, is he, Lieutenant?" Jeb asked.

"Something about the way he carried himself going into the store. But no. I don't know him."

After the two finished their beers, and Jeb his second whiskey, they proceeded down the steps to their horses.

"Hold up, Corporal. Would you go ask Morton if this guy tried selling him coffins? I want to check on something."

"Yes, sir." Jeb nodded and struck out for the general store.

Mark and Dolan strode a few feet, stopping at the spot where they first noticed the wagon. "What do you think about these tracks, Private? Set pretty low, wouldn't you say?"

While Dolan considered the question, Jeb returned. "Lieutenant, the man went in there all right. Morton sells his coffins for two dollars apiece. This fella wanted twice that. Sounds like he checked with Mr. Morton just for the town's benefit, knowin' he wouldn't sell any."

"Curious," Mark said. "From the tracks in this dirt, those boxes weren't full of feathers. But right now, I've got Victorio on my mind. We best get back to the fort."

Chapter 21

Morning came a little at a time until the sun's first rays, with bright slashes of pink and red, slanted through the tall sparse trees.

"I have fought the Long Knives," Victorio said, "the same as Geronimo and Cochise.

"Cochise is dead now. We burned out the settlers, destroyed crops, stole their horses and fought bluecoats on the plains. They still beat us. We must not make such mistake again. As a man, if this Mark McCrae has same thoughts he had as boy, he is friend."

At the mention of Mark's name, the giant Draco raised his head, showing the fierce hatred that seemed to attune his ears to the words of his leader.

Victorio did not cast his eyes about the upturned faces. His followers did not question his word. Saying nothing more, he stepped out of the circle and walked away, his ragged red shirt hanging well past his waist. A breechclout exposed his legs to his knee-length deerskin leggings.

After the meeting, Draco stopped Victorio near his hut. "My chief, your words are wise, but the young men thirst for blood of Long Knives."

"You have much hatred for McCrae." It was a statement, not a question.

"Phah! The seed of a traitorous woman and a dog of a White Eye," spat Draco. "I hate all half-bloods. No matter the tribe."

"Yes, but McCrae is friend."

As Victorio entered the hut, Draco muttered, "He is still a bluecoat."

~~~

"Scouts out!" The colonel assumed his position at the head of the patrol.

By noon, the troopers arrived at the designated meeting area. Colonel Blair pointed to the base of a wall of boulders about thirty yards from the Treaty Rocks.

"Lieutenant, if trouble starts, this is all we have for protection, providing there's time to take advantage of it. Station a sharpshooter at the highest point. Tell him to down any Apache that makes an unfriendly move." After a long pause, he added, "We'll take five men with us. Five stay here. Alert them that at the first sign of trouble they are to move for cover behind these rocks and not wait for an order."

"Yes, sir. Let's hope there's no cause to worry." When Mark gave the order to the last man, he noticed a dust line straight on. "Sir, up ahead. They're Indians all right, but I can't see who's leading them."

"I judge them to be about one-and-a-half miles distant. They'll be at the rocks soon."

Mark noticed a twitch on the side of the colonel's face, which he took to be a sign of nervousness. *He's got to handle this properly, or I don't know if I can rescue him.*

"Lieutenant, I want to make sure I address these people so as not to offend them."

Mark grasped the opportunity to give the colonel assurance. "Sir, I suggest you get right to the point. They respect that. The Indian depends a great deal on the tone of your voice, so speak as if you believe what you say. And don't forget to look them in the eye. That's about all I can tell you, sir."

"Very well. We will proceed." He signaled for the five soldiers to follow.

The Indians drew near—no more than ten or twelve—with Victorio and two others riding almost stirrup-to-stirrup in front.

We're about even in number, Mark determined. He extended his right palm in greeting.

The chief did the same.

"Victorio, my friend." He introduced Colonel Blair, who seemed to have composed himself.

After introductions of the other Apache leaders, Juan D'Oro and Dark Cloud, Victorio said, "Colonel Blair, it is good we meet together here... for peace."

"And it is good to talk with such powerful leaders," Blair answered with a strong voice.

Juan D'Oro spoke. "Victorio say you need to hear from your great white leader about more settlers taking our land. I tell him we give you time, but we do not know how much time."

"Soon we will hear from Washington," the colonel replied. "We have asked for the home you want. But if boundaries of San

Carlos are pushed farther north, you will no longer suffer the heat of summer. To keep peace, the law must not be broken."

Victorio spoke in deliberate tones. "Victorio does not break law. My people will be satisfied. Our land is Ojo Caliente. We go to San Carlos only if boundaries please us."

Dark Cloud seemed to accept this. "We care for our young men same as you."

Juan D'Oro consented with a nod.

"Then it is settled," the colonel responded. "None of us wants to lose our people. We will meet again here in six suns, after we get word from Washington."

Saying their farewells, the Apaches turned their horses and rode out.

"Well, that was a brief enough meeting, Lieutenant. I'm not sure I believed what I said. I still don't trust them, but if it works..."

"It sounded acceptable to me, sir. I'll say one thing more to Victorio and catch up with you." Mark turned and rode a short distance with the chief.

"What you said before was true, Mark McCrae."

The lieutenant felt a sense of relief at Victorio's words. "I am glad to hear you speak this way."

"You see, young soldier, not all Chiricahuas as bloodthirsty as White Eyes think."

Victorio paused. "But Draco... his son wanted to be warrior. Bluecoats kill him. Draco's anger boils within."

"We have all known sadness, my friend. We hope word from Washington will be what we ask for."

They gestured goodbye to each other and departed.

Mark, heading back toward the patrol, viewed Colonel Blair and the men turning in the direction of the fort. They had just passed a second large boulder stand when, out of the corner of his eye, Mark caught a small reflection of light.

He turned to his left to see an Apache up on a ledge grasp his bow and let fly a metal-tipped arrow at the colonel's exposed back. Colonel Blair slumped forward.

Mark, having drawn his rifle, wheeled his horse in time to see the Indian aim again. Steadying his sight, Mark dropped the Apache into a rolling dust heap. He raced ahead to join the patrol.

"The colonel's hit!" Jeb yelled.

Allie, riding next to Blair, scrambled off his horse. "Here, Jeb, help me get him on the ground next to that rock. Easy now, we want to lean him on his right side, so I can see better. Some of you men scan the area."

Mark climbed from his mount. "What can I do to help?"

"Not sure yet." Allie drew a small knife from his pocket and ripped through the colonel's clothes. "It went through, back to front—just barely. At least it is low and on the side."

"Dr. Wilcox ought to be doing this, but the ride back is too jolting to leave it in. Get bandages from the wagon. Wet some of 'em down. And if any among ye has whiskey, bring it over."

"I got some, Sergeant." One of the men fetched an almost full bottle from his saddlebag.

"Is he gonna be okay, Sergeant?"

"How bad is it?" another questioned.

Without answering, Allie grabbed the fiery liquid. "This'll help." He slanted Blair enough to get whiskey down him.

Pallor sheathed the colonel's skin. With a grimace, and his body shaking, he swallowed the whiskey.

"Take a little more, sir. Then I'll pour it on your wound. It'll burn like fire but nothing compared to having a piece of wood pushed through your innards without it... Mark, I could use your Bowie."

Mark handed it over. "There must be something I can do."

"Jeb, ye keep him still. He can't turn while I trim off this shaft in back."

"Mark, I want ye to put your fingers flat on each side of the arrow right at his body, so the wood won't twist while I'm cutting it. He's lucky it went through, or that tip might already be off and floating around inside."

He angled the knife above Mark's fingers at the arrow's entry, then drew the sharp blade toward the end of the shaft. He sliced off most of the hard reed. "Get me a thong from me saddlebag. Somebody! I need a good grip. Let's turn him. Gently now."

He took the thong and wrapped it around and under the arrowhead.

"There's just enough to catch hold of, and the tip's still on firm. Some of his insides'll cling like a vise t' this wood."

"Hang on, Colonel. This is going to hurt like hell."

"Well, if that's as bad as it gets," the colonel wheezed, "get on with it."

Allie grinned at Blair's response. "Here we go, sir." He inched out the arrow with one hand. Pressed down on the exit wound with the other.

Blair clinched his jaws. When the arrow slid free, he passed out.

"There. That does it. If the point was poisoned, we'd know by now." Allie doused both entry and exit wounds with whiskey and cleaned them as best he could. He wadded wet bandages, pressing them against the ragged wounds to lessen the bleeding.

He and Mark carried the colonel to the wagon, and with Jeb's help, propped him sideways against a rolled saddle blanket.

Allie wiped his brow with his bandana. "He seems comfortable enough, but he probably doesn't know it. Mark, did you see who did this?"

"A hotheaded cohort of Draco's, no doubt. Not only did I see him, I shot him before he could get off another arrow. First Indian I ever killed."

"Bound to happen, sooner or later. May not be the last. But don't ye think Victorio and his followers were already gone and never knew anything about what happened here?"

"Yes, I saw them leave. But our first priority's laid out right there in the wagon. Our second is taking that Indian back to Victorio. He needs to know why I shot him, or we'll lose any of his trust we may have gained."

"Good idea. Maybe take one of the men with ye, though."

"I'd rather you had all of them with the colonel, to make sure you get to the fort safely. Besides, nobody would expect me to be coming back."

"If ye say. I only hope we get the colonel to the fort with no further damage to him."

Allie reined Blossom to the wagon and settled down by the colonel for the tedious ride.

"I'm thinking he feels no pain, thanks to the whiskey. Maybe tomorrow his major hurt will come from a helluva hangover."

"Let's hope so. I'll catch up with Victorio and will be back at the fort by the time you are." He mounted his horse and called over to Jeb. "Corporal, you'll be driving this wagon. Try to avoid rough ground."

"That's my intent, sir. But you know, even when you try, you can't."

"One more thing, Top. Maybe I should have my Bowie, not that I expect problems."

Allie reached over for the knife and gave it to him. "Like I said, Son, be cautious. Go ahead and expect trouble, then be grateful if it never comes."

~~~

When the gates opened for the patrol, Allie headed straight to the post hospital. As soon as they got there, the fort's doctor, Dr. Wilcox, directed Blair's removal from the wagon.

"Sir, I hope I did it right," Allie said. "I did all I knew how."

"We'll soon know, Sergeant."

"I gave him whiskey the two times he came to."

After instructing the men to transfer the colonel to a bed, the doctor removed the bandages. "I'll give him laudanum to take care of his pain."

"Major, what's your opinion?"

"Doesn't seem to have lost a lot of blood. Couldn't have said that about a bullet wound. Seems you did a decent job, Sergeant. I can't tell for sure until I check him over. Now, all of you, wait outside while I tend my patient."

Some sat on the steps, while others leaned against the porch. By that time other men from the post had gathered. All seemed nervous.

"It's close to getting dark. Mark should've been back by now," Allie said. "I sure hope he didn't meet up with that Draco. Still think he should've had someone go with him."

The soldier designated as sharpshooter spoke up. "If I hadn't left my post so soon, maybe this would never have happened."

Startled at the man's words, Allie stared at him. "The colonel ordered ye to. Now put it out of your mind."

"Why do you suppose those Apaches done that?" Jeb asked, "We were getting all lined up for peace."

"I wish I knew. I bet a silver eagle Draco knew it was going to happen, but not Victorio. I guess we couldn't expect all of 'em to get civilized at once." Allie continued to pace.

"Quit fidgeting," Jeb said. "The doc will be out in a minute. See, here he comes."

Dr. Wilcox stepped to the door. He paused before giving a statement. "I can safely say the arrow missed all the important parts."

"So ye think he'll be all right, sir?"

"What I'm saying is, I think he'll make it, barring an infection, which is always a concern. But I believe the iodine will take care of it. That and alcohol."

Allie leaned inside. "Doctor, I just heard him say something."

Wilcox turned back to the mumbling colonel.

"Sounded something like 'damned Apaches,'" Allie said.

"Well now, Sergeant, I'd like to think that's good news."

~~~

"Gates open!" the sentry yelled.

Mark rode through but not at a swift pace. He dismounted and walked Belle the rest of the way. He noticed the men milling in front of the hospital didn't seem dejected.

"Here comes the lieutenant," Jeb announced.

Allie grinned when he saw Mark. "I was getting worried, Son. What took ye so long?"

"That's a story, all right. But what about the colonel?"

"He's sleeping right now. The major says he'll need a day or so to know for sure. A prayer or two sure wouldn't hurt. But what happened with Victorio?"

"Water first. My canteen's empty." He turned to one of the men. "Private, would you take care of my horse? She's pretty tuckered."

"Yes, sir. I sure will."

"I'll be along directly."

Allie handed his canteen to Mark.

He drained it, then sat on the steps. "I went right to where the Indian fell." With a sigh, he took off his cap and ran his hand through his hair. "He was gone. A dark circle had dried in the sand, so I never doubted I hit him."

"What do ye think happened?"

"From the size of that circle, I don't see how he could've survived."

"But where was he, Lieutenant?" Jeb asked.

"That's the odd part. I saw tracks, like his horse took off, but then I noticed tracks of a second horse. Somebody came for him."

Allie said, "It would sure spoil things if the chief thought we'd killed one of his warriors."

"As much as I wanted to go to Victorio right then and explain, I figured I'd be ambush meat before I ever got there."

"We'll find out the answer soon enough when we go for our next meeting."

"About the colonel, does Amanda know?"

"She doesn't. You can tell her now if ye want, or wait till tomorrow."

"It's already late. I'll do it in the morning, but I want to see him before I leave." Mark stood and stepped inside the hospital. He glanced over at the colonel, and thinking he slept peacefully, let out a sigh of relief.

"Lieutenant," Dr. Wilcox said, "you never can tell about an arrow wound. Sometimes, for the seriousness of them, they turn out to be relatively minor. Other times, infections occur that we can do nothing about."

"Thanks, Major." Mark left to tend to Belle's needs before heading for bed, all the while hoping the colonel would come out of it, and soon.

~~~

"Oh, why didn't you tell me last night, Mark?" Amanda, already ahead of him, quickened her steps.

"Aside from the late hour, your uncle was asleep. The only thing you could have done was worry about him all night."

When they reached the hospital, Amanda rushed through the door Mark held open for her. She passed two other patients, one asleep and the other with a splint on his leg. The major stood by her uncle's cot, checking his temperature.

"Dr. Wilcox, is he—"

"He's going to be all right. You can visit him if you like, but don't stay long."

"Oh, thank you, Doctor." She rushed to his side, with Mark following. "Uncle John, how are you feeling? I'm so worried."

"About as sore as a man can get, I guess. If it weren't for the sergeant and the lieutenant, I might not be feeling at all. Wilcox told me what you two did for me."

"Not me, Colonel. The sergeant did it."

"I never trusted the Apaches, McCrae. There for a while I thought I was wrong..."

Mark didn't comment.

"Uncle John, I'll hear the whole story later, but right now I'm glad you're alive. I had to see for myself. We'll let you rest, but I'll be back real soon. Thank you for your help, Dr. Wilcox." She leaned over and kissed her uncle on the forehead.

As they left, Amanda glanced around the small hospital. It had its shortcomings, even though the doctor did what he could. The place was drab, but any fort hospital in the desert would be.

"Mark, the doctor doesn't have enough help. I know he has a steward, but he needs more. Perhaps it's time I helped someone besides myself. Beginning tomorrow, I'm Nurse Blair."

Mark grinned when she made the determined statement.

~~~

The following evening when Mark dropped by to see the colonel, he wasn't surprised to see Amanda had kept her vow. She had immediately busied herself in the hospital. She'd fashioned a nurse's cap from white material Mark's mother gave her. Concerned for her uncle, she stayed by his side until he showed definite improvement.

Amanda asked him to walk her home. When they reached her quarters, she said, "Mark, sit with me for a while."

He had no idea why she seemed nervous.

"Uncle John ordered a porch swing some time ago, but until it gets here, two sturdy barracks chairs will have to do."

Mark fitted his lean frame into one of them thinking how glad he would be when the swing arrived. *That will be much friendlier. Yes, it will.*

"You know, hearing my uncle pay his thanks to you made something quite clear to me. I know I'm right."

"You usually are." Mark smiled. "But what—"

"Please listen until I finish. In trying to make up for the loss of my family, Uncle John gave me all the advantages. Having him almost killed opened my eyes." Amanda paused, blinking back a tear. "I guess I've become spoiled with everything I ever wished for... even some things I never thought of having. It was natural to dream of continuing the same life."

Mark wondered where this explanation would lead and squirmed uneasily.

"Now, I realize other things are important—no matter whether a man's rich or poor, as long as he's a virtuous man... and Mark McCrae..." Her voice trembled. "I care for you. And I will even more tomorrow." She rose from her chair, straightened her skirt and patted her hair. "There! I've said it."

No admission could have surprised Mark more. He knew how he felt but hadn't known Amanda's feelings. Standing, he reached for her.

She resisted, but only a little.

He kissed her for the first time. "Amanda, I don't ever want to kiss anyone else. How are chances of my placing five ponies in front of headquarters?"

"Do they still do that in Arizona? Just five?"

"A twinkle in your eye makes me think I need to be on guard."

"Have no fear, my warrior. Just be prepared—twinkle, twinkle."

He continued holding her close. "But what about Whitfield?"

"We did meet when I was here last, and we spent some time together, but there's nothing between us, really. Jerry should know that by now."

"Then, what if—"

"What if what?"

"Never mind. It's not important." His thoughts churned. "I should go." He walked down the steps of the veranda. *Is she leading me on, or does she really see past my heritage?*

~~~

Before the echo of the last bugle call, Mark was on his way to headquarters. He took a seat in the war room and waited for the colonel to make his appearance. It was obvious to him Blair was impatient to return to work. He also thought the doctor might not have approved. When the commandant walked in, still pale, he quickly made a head count.

"I see we're missing two men. Sergeant, have the bugle sound assembly again."

In one minute the bugle sounded loud and clear. The tardy drifted in.

"Gentlemen, when you hear that call, you come running. If you don't understand this order, tell me now and I'll see that you do."

Allie whispered to Mark, "I think he's feeling near his whole self again."

The colonel took another sharp sweep of the room. "These orders are perhaps the most important from Washington since you came to Hellsgate. I will have them posted, and you damn well better become familiar with them.

"Word has come that Geronimo and the Nedni leader, Juh, have been persuaded to go to Camp Apache in San Carlos. It's my guess Victorio knows of this, but our main concern lies with him. At any rate, the officials have said Victorio and his people can live at Ojo Caliente."

"Sir, do you believe they will be allowed to stay on the reservation this time?" Mark asked. "They've been promised this before, for as long as the mountains and rivers exist."

"It came as a surprise to me too, Lieutenant. Frankly, I don't know what they have in mind. Our business now is to inform Victorio of the orders. We leave at dawn Saturday. Just remember, we don't know what to expect in view of our last experience." With that, he dismissed the men.

Mark remained after the others vacated the room. "Excuse me, Colonel, but this ride is twenty-five miles each way. Are you sure you feel up to it?"

"The doctor put so much padding on me, I scarcely know I'm wounded. For the time being, we'll try the road of peace, although I must say the arrow didn't help. Accordingly, I should shake Victorio's hand. Except they tell me Apaches think that's a strange custom."

"Sir, are there any other details I need to know?"

"None. We know what we're going for." Taking a deep breath, he added. "I admit, when first coming to Hellsgate, as you could probably tell, I was in no way a friend of the Chiricahuas, nor did I want to be. I still feel the same, but talking to Victorio cast a different light. That doesn't mean I forgive the Indians for what they did to my family—"

"Colonel Blair, I want you to know about Draco. Victorio has told me soldiers killed his son."

Blair remained silent, his expression sobered. "Then we have similar feelings, he and I. Don't we, Lieutenant?"

"Except Draco is unrelenting with hatred and revenge."

"I'll say no more, except this treaty must be successful. Tell Sergeant McCrae to proceed with the roster detail."

Mark left and stopped at his father's desk. He said in his best Irish accent, "Da, the colonel asks ye to select the detail for our special mission. Do ye think ye can handle that, Sergeant?"

"I have everything under control. Now begone, ye young snapper, or I'll ignore the bars on your coat. I was a 'Da' before ye were a lieutenant, and don't forget it." Feigning a throw of his inkwell, Allie added, "That does it. Now off with ye... Sir!"

~~~

Mark counted the thin mica windows and rapped on the third one. Amanda peered out and pointed toward the end of the building. Not wanting to alert anyone else to his presence, Mark slipped through the back door.

Amanda stood there to greet him.

Looking both ways down the hall, Mark stopped at the threshold. "Do you have an escort for evening mess? I mean supper."

"Are you volunteering yourself, Lieutenant?"

"Why yes, ma'am. I always go tapping on windows until I find a lovely lady who will dine with me. Tonight, you're the lucky one."

"You big tease! I'd better not find you tapping on any windows but mine."

"I'll know I'm safe as long as your eyes twinkle, but we'd better leave before the colonel finds me at his niece's bedroom door."

Chapter 22

Blair chewed the end of his unlit cigar and assumed his usual stance at his office window. "McCrae, I want you to go into town and send this message off to Washington."

"But sir, we leave for our meeting with Victorio tomorrow." Mark saw no reason for his being the messenger.

"Lieutenant, the wires are down somewhere between here and Clear Springs. Washington answered only two of my three questions." The colonel seemed to need only slight cause for anger, and this was as good a cause as any.

Mark knew what to expect, but asked anyway. "Sir, what have you in mind?"

Blair faced him. "It isn't every day the lines go down, McCrae. Considering the importance of this message, I don't want any doubt in its delivery. If you leave now you can be back by late afternoon. I have also written a personal letter, which will serve as a backup."

"Yes, sir. I'll return as soon as possible." He accepted the letter and message from Colonel Blair and was out the door.

~~~

Mark was tempted to doze and let the bay take him on into town. That idea stopped short about two miles out when Belle's ears perked. He glimpsed the sun's rays shifting through the mesquites before settling on the barrel of a Spencer rifle, leveled off straight at him. He drew his .45.

At the same time, a rough voice called out from the brush. "Okay, soldier boy, Injun, or whatever you are, drop your gun."

A bullet whizzed by Mark's left shoulder.

"I'm takin' that horse!"

Reining Belle to a sliding halt, Mark fired into the sound then dodged. He made a prime target. With no exchange of fire, he figured there were only himself and the bushwhacker, unless it was a trap he didn't want to ride into.

He backtracked to the far side of the heavy growth. Mesquite stands could loom up in the desert, usually with nothing inside but small vermin and slithering reptiles. He removed his Springfield from its boot and laid it across his saddle.

Some of the boulders between the fort and Clear Springs rose so high the sun shaded the stunted prickly pear flanking the trail. In order to reach the spot from which his assailant fired, Mark rode between the stand of boulders and the mesquite brush.

"Soldier, I'm hurt."

Mark dismounted and ground-hitched Belle. Ever heedful of a ruse, with his rifle in the crook of his arm, he used his Colt to separate the branches and crept to where he had a good view. A man sat against a tree, a stream of blood trailing down his sleeve. He was well-leathered from the sun, probably not as old as he looked. His skin had the color of old bronze, with the patina of a hundred years.

The man looked up. "Now you don't hafta kill me, soldier."

"I'd have killed you the first time if I could've seen you. Now you hold right still," Mark ordered, pointing his revolver at the wounded man. He reached for the Spencer. "That your last shot? You should have aimed better."

"I'm bleedin', soldier. You gonna help me or not?"

"Well, I can't very well leave you here to die." Mark laid down his weapons and turned the man to examine his wound.

"I wasn't aiming to kill you. Wanted to scare you enough to steal your horse."

"You came pretty close to me by not aiming." Mark ripped the man's drenched shirtsleeve. This doesn't seem so bad. But you still bloodied the sand."

"You're a fine one to talk. You ruined my shirt. It's the only one I have."

"A shirt's the least of your worries, friend." He ripped off another strip. When a small sack of tobacco fell from the shirt pocket, Mark wrapped and bound it onto the wound.

"What're you doin' with my tobacco? You loony?"

"Pressure." Mark went for his canteen and handed it to him. "No more questions. Just answers." He rocked back on his heels, still suspicious. "Why do you need a horse so bad you'd shoot me for it?"

The man groaned when he moved sideways against the tree. "My no-good partners stole mine and ran out on me."

Mark rose to his feet. "Where are they now?"

"Could be anywhere. We had an argument and they took sides against me. Cyrus, he's plumb crazy. Big and dumb and crazy."

Mark rubbed his hand across his jaw. "Well, I've business in town and I'm not keen on riding double. But guess we will. Otherwise, you'd have to take your chances with the gilas."

"Gilas? Huh! Wish you hadn't ruined my tobacco," he complained. "I could sure use a smoke."

"And what you'd likely do is make an inferno out of these mesquites."

Another groan. "Thanks anyway. Never thought I'd be grateful to an Injun."

Mark gave him a searing stare.

"Sorry, soldier. Honest. I shouldn't a said that last."

There was something likeable about the stranger, but Mark couldn't put a handle on it.

With his last step from the thicket to bring Belle closer, he barely saw what hit him. No time to draw.

A figure dove from a horse, swept into Mark, crashing him to the ground. At first glance, it reminded him of the grizzly back in Prescott, except this grizzly rode a sorrel. Mark decided he was being attacked by strongman Cyrus.

At first he thought it might be an even match, but it turned into a grappling fight. Mark couldn't get enough leverage to land a fist anywhere that counted. It was pure luck the second time they rolled over. The man's hand rammed into a prickly pear. The attacker yelped and loosened his grasp.

Mark scrambled for his Colt.

The stranger roared forward, knocking the revolver into the air. Mark ducked under the man's arm and then smashed his fist into Goliath's neck.

It merely staggered his assailant.

Cyrus glared and brought up his bludgeon of a hand. With a short uppercut, he lifted Mark off the ground.

The blow launched Mark backward. He caught his breath and rose to his feet, swayed, then felt another punch gash his brow. Mark had to work his way back into this fight. He blinked several times to clear his head.

In a flash, he spied two men on horseback, less than fifteen yards away. One sat upright in the saddle. Couldn't make out his face. The other, a wiry individual, one leg crossed over his saddle horn. He smoked a cigarette, grinning, as if at a peep show. Mark figured they were the other partners.

Cyrus lowered his head and came at the lieutenant like a runaway stage. Mark caught him charging and hammered a right cross with the man's jaw as the target. He thought he heard a bone crack and hoped it wasn't his.

Mark's opponent's cheek split open, blood spattering. He dragged himself up and lunged again, slamming his fist into Mark's stomach.

Mark folded over an instant but came up this time with all the power in his right hand to smash Cyrus's nose. He didn't know how many more blows he could take, or how many he had left to give.

The wiry figure on horseback flicked away his cigarette. "I've seen enough of this," he yelled. He raised his rifle and fired.

As Cyrus sprang at Mark, a shot rang out. The bullet, obviously meant for the lieutenant, struck the big man between the shoulder blades. He grabbed Mark's upper arms in an attempt to stand. Eyes staring in disbelief, he slid to the ground.

Mark wrenched away and reached for his gun, halfway covered by the man's body. He thumbed back the hammer. Two shots fired simultaneously—one from the wiry partner and the other from Mark. A shooter fell—the one on the horse. The other man rode out.

Cyrus was dead. The other partner appeared to be, but Mark took a close look at him to make sure.

The stranger Mark shot earlier staggered out from the mesquites. "Soldier, you sure were somethin' to watch, an' I didn't help ya none. That's not my style."

"Thanks for the thought anyway." Mark removed his cap and emptied his canteen over his head. His nerve endings were tied in knots as he sat down to catch his breath. His tension eased. "Is that extra horse over there yours?"

"Yeah, the roan." The man clicked his tongue. "Come 'ere, Barney." The roan trotted over and nuzzled his shoulder.

"Well, we better get on with it." Mark got to his feet and searched the partners' saddlebags. "I know you can't do much, but maybe you could help a little with this dead weight. Just stand close so I won't drop them." They finally managed to drape the dead men over the horses.

"Sam Morton might buy the horses and gear. And unless you can think of something better to do with the money that's in here, it's yours."

"I could sure use the money all right. Besides, I've got a bad yearnin' for some worthwhile tobacco."

"Enough about the tobacco. You need a doctor. Riding may start that wound to bleeding again."

"You said yourself it wasn't that bad. Besides, do I have a choice?" He reluctantly accepted Mark's help in mounting his horse.

"I'd say you got the short end of the stick from your so-called ex-partners, Mr...."

"The name's Aloysius Ezekial Berne. Mother was Irish. Pa, German. You can call me Zeke." He paused, tilting his head. "You thinking on turnin' me in?"

Mark grinned. "No, guess not. I don't think I could turn anybody in with a name like Aloysius." He tossed the man his rifle and more cartridges from Cyrus's saddlebag.

"Soldier, I don't mean to be nosey, but you're a half-blood, ain't cha?"

"I don't need reminding."

"Now, hold on Lieutenant. You seem to be edgy about the subject."

"It's not that simple. I'm proud of my heritage, but it splits my loyalties."

"Well, the way I think of it, you're one person, not two. You'll figure it out some day."

Mark turned his horse. "We best be going." Before they arrived in Clear Springs, Mark spotted a crew of telegraph linesmen putting their tools away. He rode closer and called, "What was it? Apaches?"

"Most likely," one of the workers replied. "Wanted the copper for jewelry. But the line's ready for use now—at least until next time."

Once in town, Mark directed Zeke to the doc's office. "I'll meet you at the sheriff's as soon as I send this wire." If all went well, the answer to the colonel's message would be at the fort any time, and he hoped, soon.

Mark explained the situation to the sheriff, and he agreed to take care of the dead men. In a few minutes, Zeke walked into the sheriff's office, having had his arm patched up. It was obvious he had stopped at the general store, since he sported a new shirt.

"Maybe we'll run into each other again, Aloysius. That's a fine name, by the way."

"Like I said, make it Zeke, if you don't mind," the cowboy replied, patting Mark on the shoulder before leaving.

On the way back to Hellsgate, Mark chuckled, shaking his head at the thought of Aloysius E. Berne. He noticed clouds wrapping around the early moon, and as he expected, a light rain fell. It did little more than settle the dust, giving the evening a fresh desert smell. He stretched and realized his bones ached. His lip stung from the souvenir Cyrus gave him.

"At least I don't have to worry about any renegades," he muttered. He remembered the time Victorio told him why Apaches didn't attack at night. Some people thought it was because of snakes. But Apaches believed if they killed at night, at their own deaths, they would walk the spirit trail forever, never resting in peace.

Chapter 23

The message from Washington arrived the next day, as Mark hoped. That night he slept sporadically until dawn. He splashed water on his face and ran a comb through his hair. *Best thing about being Indian, I don't have to shave so often.* After dressing, he strapped on his service revolver. He then pronounced himself ready for a delicate mission.

As Mark and the soldiers exited the gates, a private rushed after them. "Lieutenant McCrae, beggin' your pardon, sir, but this letter came for you yesterday. I plumb forgot to sort it out, and you weren't around—"

"Don't worry about it, Private." Mark noticed the return and figured it was only one of many the school mailed out to graduates. He stuffed it in his pocket. Victorio was uppermost on his mind now.

Colonel Blair led the patrol and headed north, away from Clear Springs. The sun scorched from the sky, making its presence known.

"Heat's up," Allie remarked. "Ye could roast an egg in the sand."

Jeb rode alongside. "Dang, you could roast the whole chicken."

"I hope we're at the Treaty Rocks first," Mark said. "I prefer facing forward when the Apaches arrive."

Jeb brightened. "You mean like a card shark in a barroom corner?"

"I see what ye... Wait a minute," Allie said. "Over yonder, by the Mortons. Sure is a whirly. Looks t' me like horses riding off."

Mark turned to look. "In a hurry, too."

Allie rode up a horse's length to the colonel. "Sir, just north of town, by the Morton place. What's that seem like to ye, sir?" He pointed to the dusty plume rising in the stillness.

The colonel shifted in the saddle to get a better view. "It doesn't look like smoke."

"Sir, do ye think we ought to check this out? Especially since we saw a bunch of horses."

"All right, go ahead. Take a couple of men. Lieutenant McCrae, you stay with me."

"Sir, if anything's wrong at the Mortons', I'd like permission to go."

"McCrae, I need you to see this through with Victorio, and I don't want you delayed."

Mark watched the dust spiraling upward. "Sir, we'd be angling off less than a mile. We can catch up and be there at about the same time."

Colonel Blair relented. "Very well, you and the sergeant go. Take Speck and Private Dolan in case you run into trouble. And McCrae, we can't afford you much time. Be quick about it."

"Yes, sir." Mark wheeled Belle around to meet the others. "Get a move on. That unknown whirlwind needs seeing to."

~~~

In that instant, Blair thought he had made the wrong decision.

"Sir," Jerry Whitfield said, "maybe I should've gone, too."

"We have problems of our own, Lieutenant. Let's get on with it."

"All the same, sir, I'd rather not be in the middle of those Apaches without Lieutenant McCrae."

"Are you insinuating I can't handle this myself, Whitfield?"

"No, Colonel. I only meant the lieutenant knows this Victorio, and he can—"

The colonel spurred his horse up the incline.

"Damn," Jerry muttered.

Not certain of what he thought the lieutenant said, the colonel ignored him.

The troopers continued without incident toward the Treaty Rocks. They stopped only to rest and water the horses. Green grass would soon become sparse, giving way to Apache country.

They arrived early, as the colonel planned. His command was sharp. "Men, remember, this is a peace mission, so don't get trigger-happy. I'll personally shoot any soldier who fires without an order. When the Apaches arrive, form a half-circle with the open side toward the boulder field."

Jerry rode up to the colonel. "Sir, I'm sorry about what I said earlier. I didn't mean—"

"It's all right, Lieutenant. McCrae should have been here by now," he added, wiping sweat from his brow. "Place yourself where you have a view of the trail, and let me know the minute you see him."

"Yes, sir."

Blair realized he was on his own when Victorio and his followers came over the horizon. Outriders of the other bands followed to their right.

The whooping of the Chiricahuas, with bows and arrows, some with lances, created a nervous stir among the troopers' mounts, and the troopers as well.

Blair knew arranging this meeting was difficult enough. Now, even with the successful bartering with the government, it might still fail. He wouldn't mention the arrow incident, for fear it would complicate matters.

As Victorio moved closer, the colonel felt his tense muscles tighten even more. He had the feeling the leader would blame them for shooting one of his men.

The chief said nothing, but searched the faces of the half-circle of soldiers. "Where is bluecoat McCrae?"

"The lieutenant will be along." Colonel Blair strained to see if he could spot Mark in the distance. "We can still go on with our business. Washington has agreed to terms."

"That may be, but I agree to meet with you and Lieutenant. Where is he?" Victorio demanded.

Blair's thought mirrored the Apache leader's. *Where the hell is McCrae?*

Chapter 24

"Dust's settled at the house, but it's trailing to the north," Mark said, as they headed toward the Morton place. It was no more different than any other settlers', except Mrs. Morton managed to grow a flower or two close to the porch. She had potted flowering desert cacti sitting on the porch.

"At least we know it's no fire," Dolan said.

"Something's happened here. That's for sure." Allie pointed to a horse, struggling to rise up on all fours.

Jeb skidded up to the animal. "Look it. That rope around his neck musta caught on the fence. He's got hisself a broke leg."

"That's Sam's horse," Allie said.

Jeb already had his gun drawn. "Lieutenant, you want I should shoot him?"

"Do it."

One shot put the animal out of his misery. "Dang, I hate to see that happen to a good horse."

"Couldn't be helped. But about those horses we saw ride out... Hold on! If this one's Sam's, the Mortons should be home. Top, you and Dolan check on the barn. Speck, come with me."

Mark and Jeb took the porch in one leap. In the parlor, they saw a woman lying on the floor, her blue-flowered dress spattered with red.

"It's Mary Morton." Mark stooped to examine her more closely. "Not dead long. Stabbed three or four times."

They peered into the other two rooms but found nothing. "That's it for in here. Let's go, Jeb."

A pale Archie Dolan came out the barn door, vomiting, barely missing Allie's boot.

Allie looked up at Mark. "It's Sam. He's dead."

"I seen dead men before, Lieutenant, but not somebody I knew so much."

"Private, sit down in the shade and take it easy. I don't like this. We need to find answers."

"You think Indians?" Jeb glanced around the barn as if an answer were there.

Allie wiped his brow. "Maybe."

"But they weren't massacred, just kilt."

"That might be to throw us off," Mark said. "Morton's General Store was the only one around, so he had to have savings. Top, I think you said he didn't like banks and kept money buried out here?"

"That's the rumor I heard."

"The house was so tore up, couldn't tell if they took anything." Jeb said. "Maybe we ought to see if it's been dug up somewhere."

"No time for that," Mark replied. "If the money's gone it's gone, and if it's here, it is. Besides, Indians wouldn't have known about any money."

Finding a place as close to shade as they could, the men buried Mary and Sam Morton in shallow graves.

"This'll have to do," Mark said.

Allie crossed himself. "Thank the Lord they didn't have any little ones. Sam's brother will take care of it and put markers on. But Tobias usually rides by here, and he and Sam go in to the store together."

"In that case, I'll write a note for Tobias. We can't wait for him." Mark hurried back into the house.

Jeb turned to Private Dolan. "You doin' okay?"

"Uh, yes...Sure, I'm okay. I got caught by surprise, that's all."

Mark returned in a couple minutes.

"Now that we're done here, Son, ye need to go," Allie said.

"I know. The way I see it, we've taken about an hour. It would've taken two for the patrol to get to the Treaty Rocks. The trail may be cold already. If we see it's taking too long, I'll double-time back to the Treaty Rocks and let you three finish the job."

Jeb peered at the tracks. "Some shod and some not."

"And ye know, Sam had four or five horses in that corral. That's why it's most likely renegades."

"We'll ride a ways and see what we find," Mark said.

About a quarter mile out, toward the direction they had seen the last of the dust trail, they found clear tracks. "As far as I can tell, there are only four Indian ponies, plus the Mortons'."

"They moved fast. Let's get going."

Hoof prints led them across low brush around great stands of saguaro. The men lost the marks through a stretch of tall grass.

"The way I see it, we have two choices," Allie said. "They wouldn't go back where they've been and certainly not south toward Tonto Basin. I say we take a chance and ride on north."

The morning grew hotter. Any breeze had died out.

Mark noticed Dolan guzzling from his canteen. "Private, I know your canteen's full now, but we don't know for how long."

"Yes, sir. I wasn't thinkin'."

Jeb said, "Allie, I think we've picked up tracks again."

"Aye, that we have. Son, I doubt the colonel can settle that peace thing without ye."

"These tracks look to be going parallel toward the Treaty Rocks. If they are, I can at least ride that way, and then branch off and meet with the patrol."

They continued through uneven terrain, with tracks leading into a narrow gorge.

Allie squinted into the morning sun. "That gorge has plenty of hidey holes."

"I rode into it once before going to the Point," Mark said, "then later on, I met up with Victorio."

The trace led to a mass of rocks on one side, at which spot the gorge expanded to a width of about thirty-five yards. Scrub oaks seemed to be rooted in solid stone all the way to the rim.

Jeb gazed skyward. "We can see what's behind and before us. I'm not sure about the top, not with that glare."

Mark took the forward position.

"You think they're in here, Lieutenant?" Dolan asked.

"This is where the tracks led us." After riding a short distance, Mark stopped. "Over to the left... makings of a fire, but not started."

"Aye, and the smell of tobacco's still lingerin'. They saw us most likely. We best keep eyes and ears open."

Mark thought that was exactly what they should do. Nervous at every unexpected sound, even at the flutter of a bird's wings, he led the foursome farther into the gorge. The side walls merged into large, broken boulders where a single path worked its way toward the plateau.

"Lieutenant," Jeb called, "If we start up there and them Indians see us from the top, we won't have any more of a chance than a frog in a dry well."

"That's the chance we take, Corporal. They sure didn't leave the same way they came in." Mark guided Belle up the slant, scanning the high rim and crumbled rocks. "They may be gone by now."

He turned to see Archie Dolan following a few yards behind. "Careful. We don't want a landslide." Mark thought if anything other than anxiety raced through the private's mind, it was probable he'd be better off with the colonel and his men.

From the rim above, an Apache came into view and aimed his rifle. Dolan, holding his weapon, pulled his horse to a quick halt, causing him to slip. The mount faltered down the incline. When the young soldier jumped from his horse, the momentum compelled him to run several steps before he could steady himself enough to level his weapon.

Mark fired a split second before Dolan. One or both shots felled the Apache. "Take cover. Gotta be more than one up there."

Fifteen feet in front of Mark, an Indian charged, panther-like from the shelter of the limestone rocks. Before Mark could prepare to meet the Indian's flashing knife, Allie fired. The bullet whizzed through the air, contacting nothing.

The Apache executed a leap, carrying him to the next ledge where he seemed to vanish. "If they can dodge like that," Allie said, "a dozen of 'em can hold off our whole army till we die of old age. Flush him out, Jeb. I'll cover ye."

Jeb moved over to the other side to do just that when out of nowhere, the Apache leapt down onto him.

Allie shot once, straight at the Indian's headband, sending both men tumbling from the horse.

Jeb scrambled to his feet.

"Good goin', my friend. That's two of 'em. We got part of what we came for."

"Well, dang it. You said you were going to cover me. Just how much of me did you plan to cover?"

A taunting screech sounded from the plateau, as a large rock came crashing down. "Watch it." Mark yelled. "On the ledge!"

Before the sergeant could shift in his saddle, the still unsteady Jeb Speck fell to the ground.

"Jeb. Jeb!" Dolan yelled.

Mark took dead aim at the tall figure framed in the bright Arizona sun. With the glare in his eyes, he hesitated.

Allie called out, "C'mon, shoot, Son! It's him or us."

Mark squeezed the trigger. "I missed! I had him in my sights, and I missed!"

Allie jumped from his horse and dragged Jeb to safety.

"Dolan!" Mark shouted. "Take aim across the upper edge. If another one peers over, at least one of us ought to drop him. Don't throw away any shots."

"Yes, sir."

After a short silence, hooves pounded over solid ground. Mark lowered his rifle into the boot. "Sounds like they're moving out." Dismounting, he rushed over to Jeb.

"How is he, Top?"

"He's barked up pretty bad."

"I can't see, Lieutenant. Guess there's too much blood in my eyes."

Mark saw no blood, just a large knot on Jeb's head.

"Private! Bring that whiskey from me saddlebag." Allie reached for Jeb's bandana. Pouring water from his canteen, he washed Jeb's face, then padded the wet cloth on his forehead to slow the swelling.

Dolan sprinted over with the whiskey. "Is he gonna be all right, Sergeant? Is he?"

"We'll have to wait. His head's too hard to hurt for long." He held the bottle to his friend's lips. "Here. Now, drink this."

With grim humor, Jeb muttered, "That can't be yours. You never carried such high-grade stuff."

Dolan hovered over Allie's shoulder. "You're gonna be all right, Jeb. The sergeant'll take care of you. Sergeant, did you see the size of that Indian the lieutenant shot at?"

"Aye. I have a hunch it was Draco. Mark might a nicked him, or they'd still be after us."

He removed the damp cloth from Jeb's forehead and freshened it with water.

"Dang it, Allie, why do ya hafta put that bandana over my eyes? I sure don't feel very good. Got some churnin' in my stomach."

Not a comment Mark wanted to hear, not with a head injury. "Just hang on, Corporal."

He looked up and perused the sun's angle at the top of the gorge. "My time's running out. Top, can you and Dolan take care of him?"

"I'd say so. We'll wait a few minutes, then head out for the fort."

Mark put his hand on the private's shoulder. "Try not to worry. He'll be all right." He knew Dolan was anxious. He had joined the army after his parents died, and Jeb had taken him under his wing like he was his own son.

Mark had a last swig from his canteen. "Here, Top, in case you're slowed down too much, you may need the rest of this."

"Thanks, Son, and luck be with ye."

Mark turned Belle to exit the way they had entered. He headed toward the meeting place, all the while watching for any surprises.

Chapter 25

Mark rode the lathered bay into the area of the Treaty Rocks. The next minutes shifted to near quiet as Mark watched heads turn toward him.

"Colonel!" Whitfield said. "The lieutenant! He's here!"

It took only one glance for Mark to sense the colonel's relief. He turned immediately to the Apache chief and thought quickly of what to say to him. "Victorio, good fortune can meet us all on this day."

"You have come, McCrae. You kept your promise."

Mark tried to stay calm. "Will you sign the papers, Victorio?"

"First, before we talk," Victorio said, looking Blair in the eyes, "It pleases me the colonel has recovered from his wound a Chiricahua foolishly delivered. One of my warriors saw his cowardly act and brought his body to me. Such a thing will not happen again."

"Your pledge is accepted, Victorio," Colonel Blair replied. "Now, I want to show you what we have from Washington."

The Apache chief motioned for the other leaders to ride nearer. After exchanging a few words, Victorio said, "We listen. This does not mean we will agree."

Unfolding the paper from his uniform pocket, the colonel began, "Our president in Washington sends this message. You have two choices. The first is that settlers will not cross the Little Colorado River to the south, or encroach on any part of Indian land within ten miles. They live on land only outside that boundary."

Mark studied Victorio's face to see any trace of acceptance.

Colonel Blair continued. "The Army will investigate the actions of Indian agents whom you say are still treating you unfairly. I expect you know Geronimo and Juh have taken their people to Camp Apache in San Carlos."

Victorio ignored the statement. "First is no choice. What is other choice?"

"The other is the land in Ojo Caliente will be open to you. Our president signing this agreement makes it official. He asks our Apache friends to likewise put their marks on the paper."

Victorio looked at Mark. It was obvious the chief wanted him present—the one bluecoat he trusted. It was not so much the Indians found fault with the agreement. "Why is choice? We want as before, to live where grass is green and streams are clear. Game is plentiful."

The three leaders turned to one another. Their expressions showed doubt at the Colonel's words.

Mark wondered if they didn't decide now, would there be another battle stemming from the Treaty Rocks? Wasn't this what they wanted?

"McCrae, we trust your words more than actions of Indian Agency. Your colonel says something will be done. Can you also say?"

"We will do our best. This is what the new agreement will take care of. Washington formed the Agency. Some agents take your blankets, sell your good beef and leave you the spoiled. I don't have to tell you that. We will keep our eyes on them from now on."

Victorio addressed the other leaders.

Mark saw decision cross their faces. For him, it was enough.

"We will go to Ojo Caliente. We think this mean not forever, but we will try."

Mark understood the Apaches' mistrust. White-Eyes had stolen their land right from under them. *Why wouldn't they have doubts?*

One of the men brought out the field table from the transport wagon and placed it on level ground. All dismounted. Victorio signed first. Juan D'Oro, Dark Cloud, and Naiche followed by signing their marks. The small group then sat in a circle and smoked the pipe of peace.

After a time, the participants rose and said their farewells. Mark and the colonel prepared to leave the Treaty Rocks for what they hoped would be their last visit.

"Sir, you know the Indians usually respond to decent treatment," Mark said. "If we hold up our part of the bargain, they will not break theirs."

"It isn't up to us. All we can do is intercede." Blair barked out the command to take formation. "Men, by twos, right turn." He took his place in front and bellowed, "Forward!" The procession headed for Hellsgate.

After a few minutes passed, the colonel asked, "Now Lieutenant, would you tell me what took you so long? We came close to having this whole deal turn into a bloody disaster."

"Sir, it's not simple to tell. I can give you details later, but we found Mr. and Mrs. Morton murdered. Speck's injured. The sergeant and Private Dolan will see he gets to the fort."

"The Mortons murdered? But who would kill them, and why?"

"Indians, sir. We downed two, but the others got away."

"Well, I'll be. Here we were making peace with the bunch of 'em, and they sneaked off to kill the settlers. I told you we couldn't trust them."

"Sir, I feel sure they were renegades, with Draco in the lead."

"Corporal Speck, how bad is he?"

"I can't say for sure, sir. Major Wilcox can check him over as soon as they get him to the fort, and I pray they do."

"I'm glad you made it, Lieutenant. There for a while, I thought we had trouble."

"Thank you, sir. I had concerns myself."

As they rode along, Mark tried to relax. One thought nagged him. Where was Draco?

Chapter 26

The troopers were less than an hour from the fort. "Colonel, seems we have a welcoming committee of one."

"He's in a big enough hurry. Ride out and see what's up."

Mark touched Belle on the flank, and she loped toward the soldier.

The oncoming rider halted his winded horse beside Mark. "Lieutenant, quick," he gasped. "The colonel's niece—"

"What about the colonel's niece?" Mark reached over, almost dragging the soldier from the saddle. "What about her!"

"She had a new recruit drive her into Clear Springs, sir, to go shopping or something. About an hour ago the carriage came back to the fort, empty. No sign of Miss Blair or the recruit, Lieutenant."

Mark's pulse pounded. "Why'd she go off like that? She should've waited!"

"Well, you know, sir, if you pardon me for saying, Miss Blair has a mind of her own. She insisted. But Sergeant McCrae, he'd just come back with Corporal Speck and left out soon's the carriage came in."

"Wait for me, Private." Mark raced to give the message to the colonel.

Blair's face drained of color. "Lieutenant, we'll take a detail of men into town. I've got—"

"Sir, they've already done that. I'll go to Clear Springs. I promise, I'll bring her back... safely."

The muscles in the colonel's jaws tensed. "Whitfield, take another couple men and ride with him. And McCrae, find my niece!"

For the first time since he'd known him, Mark believed the colonel was scared—not uneasy, like with the Indians, but really scared. Mark felt beads of perspiration on his brow as he and the soldiers headed toward Clear Springs.

Belle lit out as if spirit-possessed. About five miles outside of town, Mark slowed down and pointed to the left of the narrow road. "By that stand of cottonwoods. Do you see it? We better have a look."

Riding the short distance, Mark realized what he feared was true. A soldier lay dead from a bullet wound. "God help him."

"It musta been the recruit what took Miss Blair to town, sir," one of the men said. "He never had a chance."

"I'm going on in. You take this soldier to the fort, then come back as soon as you can."

The grim discovery fanned Mark's building rage. He clutched his reins so tight, his knuckles whitened as he rode Belle on the straight stretch to Clear Springs.

Allie stepped out of Morton's Relay Station when the soldiers approached.

"What did you find out, Top?" Mark asked, before he had even pulled Belle to a halt.

"Tobias said the morning stage picked up three passengers. A young woman answering Amanda's description boarded the stage with an unlikely sorta fella."

"What fella? I can see why a man would abduct Amanda. It's the 'who' that worries me."

"Three sorry individuals had reined up across the way. They didn't go anywhere until almost time for the stage to leave. The whole thing didn't sit right to him. Miss Blair being so pretty and all, and nervous. The man just didn't seem like somebody she'd be traveling with."

Jerry added, "Besides, Tobias never saw her before, so he wouldn't have known who she was. But there's no sign of the soldier who drove her."

"We found his body. Two men are taking him to the fort."

Allie shook his head. "I don't see how we missed him."

"He was off to the side by a copse of cottonwoods," Mark said. "Now, figuring the time, we have to make up some miles. The stage has to change horses at Warner's Station. We'll head there."

With no delay, the detail covered the distance to the station by four o'clock. Mark briefed Warner on the situation.

"Lieutenant, I have fresh mounts for your men. They can change them on their way back."

"I appreciate it. But what can you tell me about the stage and its passengers?"

"Well, there was two men and a woman, plus the driver and shotgun. One of the men, Weatherby, was on his way back home to Virginia. The other'n didn't seem like much 'count to me.

Don't know his name. The wagon tongue needed replacing, but since I didn't have a spare, I only repaired the broken one."

"What about the woman. Was she all right?"

"I dunno. Funny thing, though, the little lady didn't eat a bite. Say, Lieutenant, you'd best eat something yourself. There's no place else to stop for quite a spell." He pointed to a water pump at the corner of the station. "You can fill your canteens over yonder. Then go right on inside. The wife'll fix you something to eat."

Mrs. Warner, a cheerful woman who wore her long hair in braids around the top of her head, appeared to enjoy preparing meals for unexpected soldiers. "Now you eat all this stew you want. It's made early, and I have plenty of time to prepare for the next stopover."

"Thank ye for the food, ma'am," Allie said. "We'd best eat standing up—can't stay long enough to sit."

Mark reached for a couple biscuits, took a bite of one and stuffed the other in his pocket. "We really don't have time—"

"Nonsense," Mrs. Warner huffed. "Here, take this slice of cake. You can eat it on the way."

"Thank you, ma'am. I'm obliged, but I'm fine." He adjusted his cap and turned to leave.

"Men, time to move out."

"One thing more, Lieutenant," Warner said, "The driver's Eli Powers. He's a good man. Never lost a gold shipment for Wells Fargo yet."

Mark stopped. "Gold shipment? You mean the stage carried gold? They didn't tell us that in town."

"They don't usually spread it around, but under the circumstances they shoulda let you know. I tell you one thing, Lieutenant. Loyd Fore's riding shotgun, the best safeguard against a holdup in the Territory. There's no better shot."

"Thanks again for your help. We've got to be going. Top, you sure you don't want to leave Blossom and pick her up later?"

Allie shot his son a piercing glance. "Not on your life. If somebody took Blossom, I'd never get over it. Besides, she can run a week without stopping if she's a mind to. Eli Powers won't know we're following, so he won't be driving that fast."

"I figure we have two, three hours to make up, so we best leave out."

As the day grew longer, Allie commented, "That stage is behind now on account of wasted time with the axle. We'll ride all night, with just rest stops. With some luck, we'll catch up."

"Seems obvious those three men Tobias saw in town were in on it," Mark said. "They knew about the gold. Kidnapping Amanda was just a bonus."

~~~

Loyd Fore sat on top of the stagecoach. The first shots came with no warning from out of a stand of chaparral. Fore turned in that direction as horsemen came roaring through. He fired his rifle, spilling two hijackers right off.

After his next shot, lead blasted his shoulder. All he could do was flatten himself and hold on with his good arm.

"Loyd, you all right?" the driver called.

"It came too quick, Eli. I'm no help to ya. Keep movin,' and fast.

The stagecoach churned down the trail with Loyd knowing he could do no more.

~~~

Weatherby reached for his Colt and leaned out the stagecoach window. He leveled off at the hijacker riding up behind the stage. The hole he put in him went in like a dime and came out like a twenty-dollar gold piece.

The other passenger jabbed his revolver into the shooter's ribs. "Drop it, friend," he ordered. But it didn't work that easy.

"I should have known," Weatherby said, "you're one of them!" He tried to change positions to shoot again, but a bullet blew through him.

Amanda huddled in the corner.

Weatherby reached for the door strap to hold on, but no use.

"That wasn't smart, mister," the passenger said, shoving the dying Weatherby out the door.

~~~

Mark didn't realize how close he and the men were to the stage until shots rang out just over the crest. He demanded more speed from the borrowed sorrel.

The holdup man began climbing out the stage window while Mark reined in from the other side. The lieutenant slanted off his horse and caught hold of the window's edge. Bringing himself through, he lunged for the man, grabbed his legs and dragged him back inside. He realized who he was—the drunk who'd accosted Amanda when she first came to Clear Springs. "Lafe Logan, you bastard!"

Logan kicked Mark in the face, throwing him off balance. He leaned back to fire, but in the chaos, his bullet veered through the top of the stage. He started for the window again and climbed to the roof.

Intent on freeing Amanda, Mark managed to double wrap the coach blanket around her and over her head—enough so she could see and still hold the blanket together. Opening the door, he yelled, "All right, Amanda. Jump and roll with the fall—you can do it." *I hope to God I'm right.* "Now!"

Mark saw the fear on Amanda's face as she grasped the blanket and tumbled out, rolling over and over.

Gunfire had terrified the shying horses. They raced blindly out of control toward the horizon, a thin misty line against the sky.

Mark scrambled to the top of the stage. He saw the wounded man, shirt drenched in red, still holding his rifle. *Has to be Loyd Fore.*

Lafe Logan was the only live member of the holdup gang left. He was obsessed with trying to unbuckle straps on the brassbound chest of gold.

"Logan, you crazy fool!"

"It's all mine now, Mr. West Point. I told you I'd get even," he screamed. "It was easy taking your girl."

Mark caught sight of the other man, slumped on the wagon tongue, a bullet in his back—reins clutched in dead hands. Nothing left to do but tug him over so he would drop to the ground. With stopping the coach Mark's priority, he frantically tried to reach the reins, then realized that misty line at the bottom of the sky took on a different picture now—the rim of a box canyon. He clambered up to the seat.

The horses kept up their frenzy as they neared the canyon's edge. Mark pulled Loyd's foot from around the luggage rack, the only thing that kept him on the coach. "Loyd, you have to jump. It's your last chance."

Near unconscious with loss of blood, the wounded man gave a weak grin, and more fell than jumped.

At that instant, the wagon tongue snapped with a loud crack, breaking the traces as if they were threads. The released animals lit out, and by sheer luck, made it to the safety of the road. As Mark leapt to the ground, he shouted, "Logan!"

The stage teetered on the ledge of the box canyon.

Logan clutched the chest of gold as if frozen. He yelled, "I still have your girl! Now who's the fool?" His features went rigid when he realized his fate. His screams hung in the air.

Mark watched the stagecoach falling over the cliff as if in slow motion. "Wells Fargo can pick up the gold. The devil can pick up Lafe Logan."

Chapter 27

Mark had no further interest in the stage, Logan, or the gold shipment. At the sound of hoof beats, he turned to see a soldier riding toward him, leading a horse. In a flash, he mounted the sorrel and headed for Amanda.

"She'll be all right," the private called after him, his voice fading into the wind.

Three soldiers had stationed themselves along the road, with Allie huddled over the colonel's niece. "She's shaken and bruised up but no broken bones that I can tell."

Mark brought his horse to a halt. Dismounting, he gathered Amanda in his arms. *She's so limp.* "Amanda! I was afraid I'd killed you."

Her long hair disheveled, she lay covered with dirt. "You have a gentle touch, Lieutenant."

Reaching down, Mark slipped his arm beneath Amanda's back and helped her stand.

Her legs buckled. "I guess it's worse than I thought."

Mark lifted her to his horse then turned to the men. "See about those dead back there. Bring 'em in. And find the stage horses!"

When Mark arrived at the way station, Mr. Warner stood waiting.

"Guess luck found you, and I see you found your young lady."

Mark climbed from his horse then assisted Amanda. "I found her all right. Fore got a bullet, and we lost Powers. Miss Blair has injuries as well. Suppose you could let us fix them up so we could get back to town? Fore's in a bad way."

"I reckon we can do our best. It must've been some ruckus for Loyd to get shot and Eli killed. Let's get him inside. We lost a good man."

"Don't worry, Fore," Mark said. "The sergeant knows what he's doing. At least, that's what he tells me."

"Don't guess I have much choice, Lieutenant." Fore grimaced. "I sure hate that about Eli. And my wife's going to be peeved. She just got these store-bought pants for my birthday."

They placed the patient on the cleared table so Allie could get to work removing the bullet.

Mrs. Warner moved the lamp closer to Allie and handed him laudanum from her medicine box. She reopened it when she took one look at Amanda rubbing her knee.

Mark helped her over to a chair. "Here, I'll get you some water."

"Lieutenant,' Mrs. Warner said, "there's a pitcher of cool water on that table over there."

"Now then, young lady, let me see that knee of yours. Ah, it's bad swollen." She removed cloth strips from the box. "I'm wrappin' this tight until the doctor can examine it."

Amanda let out a squeal.

Mrs. Warner stopped immediately. "Oh, I'm sorry, Honey."

"No, no, that's all right. Please go ahead."

Mark brought over a cup of water.

"Thank you, Mark." She drained the cup. "I must have swallowed part of the road."

Mrs. Warner continued with her nursing, bringing out a bottle of green liniment. "I'll just touch up these scrapes on your face and hands. It's goin' to hurt a mite. I'm sorry, but I can't help it."

Amanda winced when the tingling liniment touched her cheek. "I appreciate everything you're doing, Mrs. Warner."

"You are so welcome, dear. Just be sure to have a doctor in town tend to it."

Jerry had been watching the entire procedure. "Amanda, are you going to be all right? You had quite a spill back there."

"Yes, I will, Jerry. Thanks. I hurt all over, but I'll be fine, thanks to Mark."

"Oh, yes. Thanks to Mark." With brisk steps, Jerry left to go outside.

Mark noted his crisp response, and then looked at Amanda. "I'm just thankful you're in one piece and not broken ones."

Allie began tending Loyd's wound. "I've taken out a share of bullets, but ye'll be better off with a real doctor. I don't take after diggin' so deep in your shoulder." He helped stem the bleeding with a cloth dipped in cold water and removed as much dirt as he could.

"Thanks, Sergeant. I'm just glad to be here."

"Here you are, Sergeant McCrae," Mrs. Warner said. "This bed sheet's old but clean. I keep it on hand for injuries that seem to crop up."

"Thank ye, ma'am." Allie padded the wound and placed strips of sheet around Loyd's shoulder, crisscrossing it chest to back. "There, this ought to work till the doc can do it right."

Mr. Warner withdrew tobacco and cigarette papers and offered some to Mark.

Mark rarely smoked but now thoughtfully rolled a cigarette and twisted the end. He inhaled deeply, exhaled and watched the gray swirl before him. Turning from the doorway, he asked, "Mr. Warner, you had any trouble with Indians recently?"

"Could be," he replied, rubbing the stubble on his chin. "About two weeks ago, we heard some unusual noise out by the barn, but I figured it was just a varmint. Then it got quiet. Next mornin' a couple of mares was missing. I saw shod tracks. That wouldn't be Apaches."

"Renegades could have been riding stolen horses. I suggest you stay cautious. I've heard of Indian raids not far from here."

"Will do, Lieutenant. Say, come around here to the back. I've got a sturdy buckboard, if that'll help. I can spare it a while, but I'll need the horses returned pretty quick."

"Thanks. We sure could use that kind of help. I'll make arrangements to return everything as soon as we get to town."

As they brought the buckboard to the front door, Mark looked up to see the troopers bringing in the dead men, as well as the stage horses.

"Lieutenant. We got 'em," one of them said, "and the horses had stopped by a stand of trees not far from where the stage went over."

"Good work. Two of you stay here and bury the hijackers. We'll take Weatherby with us."

They made Loyd Fore and Amanda comfortable up near the driver and placed the covered bodies of Eli and Weatherby at the other end.

"Amanda, if you'll keep an eye on Fore, you can let us know if we need to stop."

With a slight frown, Allie scanned the gray-marbled sky. "'Tis a soft day, it is. But it can't rain. It'd rot the cactus and drown the sagebrush."

His forecast proved wrong.

~~~

Mark called for the buckboard driver to halt. "Whitfield, better get out your blanket."

They removed the blankets rolled behind their saddles and covered Amanda and Fore. "These won't hold back the rain, but maybe they'll help a little," Mark said.

Allie dismounted and brought his blanket around. He placed it over Amanda.

"No, no, cover Mr. Fore. He needs it more than I do."

Since the soldiers hadn't carried their issued raincoats, they were all drenched before they finally rode into town.

In one stride, Mark vaulted the steps to the doctor's office, only to find him gone. He ran across to the General Store. "Tobias, have you seen the doc? Loyd Fore needs him.

"Why, he ought to be returnin' in just..." Tobias glanced out the door at the buckboard. "Oh, Lord, not Eli." He looked up the dusty street and pointed. "There, Lieutenant. Doc's coming yonder."

Allie and Jerry carried Fore into the doctor's office.

"Can you take care of him, Doc?" Mark called. "Got a bullet in his shoulder."

"I'll sure do that." The doctor hurried into his office. "Now, let's see here, Loyd. What have you gone and done to yourself?"

Loyd groaned out, "I personally didn't do a damn thing to myself."

Mark returned to Amanda and helped her from the wagon. "You need to have your knee looked at."

"It isn't that bad, really. I ache mostly." She held her arms against her chest. "I'd like to have dry clothes first. Besides, I was coming into town to shop before all this happened."

With his arm around Amanda's waist, Mark helped her walk, or almost hobble, next door to the General Store where Tobias's wife had all the answers.

"Now go in that room over there," she directed, "and get shed of those wet clothes." She reached for a quilt. "Here, wrap up in this. I may not have your exact dress size, but you can't ride to the fort in soaked clothes. You'll catch your death, and as wet as you are, you may already have a head start." Mrs. Morton returned to the front of the store, chose a simple calico dress and carried it to the back room.

Mark heard Amanda say, "Thank you. This will be perfect." *She'd probably say that even if it wasn't perfect.*

He told Tobias about the gold and gave directions as to where the coach ran off the cliff. "The stage horses worked enough for one day. They're out at Warner's."

"Wells Fargo will thank you, Lieutenant. They'll see the gold is picked up right away. I'll take care of Warner's buckboard and animals. But Eli. Things sure won't be the same."

Mark walked to the back room. Hesitating to go in, he called, "Is everybody decent?"

"Almost," Amanda answered. "You can come in." She gathered the blanket closely around her. "Now don't you use this as an excuse to throw me off another stagecoach, Mark McCrae."

Mark couldn't help visualizing the Indian custom of having a bride share a blanket with her warrior. He snapped back to reality. "But it was the only way I knew to save you."

"Ha! The least you could have done was jump with me. Now, out of this room."

With Amanda properly fitted in a new dress, she reluctantly agreed to have the doctor look at her injuries. She accompanied Mark back to the doctor's.

He examined her cuts and scrapes. "I'm giving you this liniment to use once a day on your scrapes. Let it dry and don't touch, even if they itch. As for your knee, it's almost popped through the bandage." He reached for a roll of tape. "I'm going to re-tape it—not too tight, but just enough to give you support. Lieutenant, can you see she stays off her leg for a while?"

"I think she might take those orders from you better."

"All right then, Miss Blair. Those are my orders."

With that, Mark swooped her off her feet and carried her outside.

Chapter 28

After more than two hours devoted to traveling the muddy road back to the fort, Mark knocked on the door of Colonel Blair's office. The colonel was overwhelmed at seeing his niece safely home. "Lieutenant, I can't thank you enough. I'll see she is well-taken care of."

Mark reported the events of the last two days. "Amanda can tell you anything I left out, sir." He smiled at her then hurried to his quarters. He tossed his grimy uniform on a chair and prepared for a bath. For only a moment, he thought he had dropped something, but he was too tired to look. Even the bath could wait.

Mark had no trouble sleeping, but once morning came, he had his bath and wondered why he waited. Half dressed, he peered into the hazy mirror on his shelf. He splashed a little Bay Rum on his freshly razored face and ran over in his mind what he would say to Amanda.

Instead of rapping on her window, he entered by way of the duty office, walked down the hall and stood at Amanda's door. Mark wondered if he was prepared for this. His knuckles in midair, he hesitated then knocked.

"Come in. It's unlocked."

Mark entered to see her in a rocking chair, her leg resting on a stool.

She looked up with a bright smile. "Back doors aren't good enough for you? A handsome lieutenant frequently calls on me, but he taps on the window first."

"I hope the colonel won't know I'm here."

"Don't be silly. You're merely visiting an invalid." She pointed to a chair. "Here, sit."

"I can't. I keep thinking of how close I came to losing you. Amanda, do you have any idea what I want to say?"

She paused before answering. "I might, but I've wondered when you would say it."

"I'm not sure there's an answer to my question." Mark paced while trying to gain courage. "It isn't so bad when a white man marries an Indian girl. It isn't the same the other way around. What would your friends back home think?"

"Mark, listen to me—"

"And the colonel. I know your uncle respects me as a soldier. That doesn't mean he wants his niece to marry me."

"Let me worry about my uncle."

He turned to look at her. "I can't imagine my life without you, but it would never work." He squared his shoulders and started for the door.

"Well, don't I have anything to say about this?" Amanda rose from her chair and hopped on one foot toward him. She lost her balance and fell.

Mark turned just in time to catch her.

She wrapped her arms around his neck. "Oh, Mark..." Her voice trailed off as she kissed him.

He pulled back, his hands on her shoulders. "Now that's something I could linger over for a very long time."

"You're such a fool. Do I have to propose?"

"You mean you will marry me? And the only hurdle is your uncle's permission?"

She kissed him again.

~~~

Mark strode into headquarters and found Colonel Blair perusing his report log.

Blair laid his pen aside. "Come in, Lieutenant. Come in."

Moisture spread on the palms of Mark's hands, but he couldn't stop now. "Sir, may I have permission to speak, man to man?"

"Of course, McCrae."

"Colonel, for some time now, you have, I mean, well, sir, I think you recognize I'm a capable officer and have performed my duties satisfactorily under your command. Those are my qualifications from at least one standpoint."

"Qualifications for what, Lieutenant?"

The muscles in Mark's throat tightened. He swallowed hard. *Say it, McCrae!* "Sir, I'm asking you for the hand of your niece in marriage."

Silence.

Why doesn't he say something? "Sir, I know how you feel about Indians—"

"Lieutenant, I do respect you as an officer and as a man. And I know Amanda has a mind of her own—always has. But she's too young to know what's best for her. I'm sorry, McCrae. I can't give my consent."

Mark felt warmth flooding his face. His gaze locked with the colonel's. "Why don't you go ahead and say it, sir? I'm a half-blood, and you don't want that for your niece."

Blair stood, his hands flat on the desk. "Think, man! What can any soldier in the Territory give her? This is no life for a young woman, and certainly not my niece.

"But, sir, I'm not just any soldier. Graduating at the top of my class at West Point must count for something. I can take care of Amanda, and she loves me! She wouldn't stay here if she didn't want to."

"McCrae, if you love her, you'd think about her needs and not of yourself. And she *needs* to return to the East. Museums, parties, culture—and safety. It's all there for her. As soon as she recovers from her injury, I'm sending her back to Washington. You're dismissed, Lieutenant."

Mark had nothing left to say. Anything else would be a flimsy rebuttal to the colonel's reasoning. Reluctant, he returned to Amanda's quarters. He tried to trade his emotions for logic.

~~~

"The least I can do is report back to you, Amanda. That is, if your uncle doesn't object."

"Are you saying he didn't give his permission?" Her eyes expressed the emotion she obviously felt.

"Why should he? Yes, I'm a soldier, and I'm white. But no matter the reason he gives, what really matters is I'm still an Indian."

"It isn't because of you. He never wanted me to come out here in the first place. I can talk to him."

Mark wished he could share her optimism.

"It will work out. It has to." Placing her book on the side table, she continued. "I'm on my way to roll bandages. I can do that sitting down."

"Roll bandages?"

"You remember. When Uncle John was recovering, I promised Dr. Wilcox I'd help when he needed me. I studied a little nursing in school. I can surely offer assistance."

"Amanda, listen to me. Your uncle will send you back east to keep us apart."

"Not once he realizes how much I'm needed. He won't send me away!"

"Perhaps we should drop it for now. I can't see him changing his mind." Mark departed before she could respond.

Back in his quarters, still discouraged from Colonel Blair's adamant refusal, he noticed a corner of something under the bed. He reached for it—the folded letter the private had given him earlier. *Must've been what I dropped this morning.* He scanned the lines, trying to absorb the contents.

~~~

Amanda opened the door and exclaimed, "You're back. What happened?"

Mark drew a deep breath. "How would you like to live in the East after all?" Noting her surprise, he reached out and drew her close to him. He repeated the question.

"Do you want to live in New York, at least for a while?"

Amanda looked baffled. "Is this a prank, Lieutenant?"

Still in disbelief, Mark shook his head. "Can you believe it? After all the trouble I stirred up as a cadet, they want me to return."

"Return to West Point? I don't understand." She spied the letter in his hand. "Here, may I see?"

He held out the letter. "The superintendent is offering me a position as a sword master. What do you think, Mrs. McCrae?"

"You know I would go anywhere with you. Uncle John can't help but say yes now," she squealed. "You'll see it wasn't you he objected to."

"If the colonel approves, will you agree to an early wedding? "They want me there in four weeks. We wouldn't have much time."

"That sounds beautiful."

~~~

As Mark took the second step onto the porch to his quarters, a voice startled him.

"So, McCrae, I've been thinking. Now you've rescued the colonel's niece, I guess you'll be captain before I see a new stripe."

Mark questioned what he'd heard and turned toward the voice.

Jerry Whitfield, arms crossed, leaned on the corner post.

"Whitfield? What kind of remark is that?"

"Well, I guess you can take it any way you want."

Mark stepped down. "Frankly, I don't want to take it at all."

Jerry tilted his head and glared. "You wouldn't have paid attention to Amanda unless I told you about her. When she first got here, you finagled your way into meeting her stage in town."

"What?"

"Next thing we know, you're the big hero."

"That's a real nice speech, Whitfield, but in no way could I have not paid attention to her. Just don't talk so loud everybody in the fort can hear you make a drunken fool of yourself."

"Why you... I'm not drunk!" Jerry took a stance and threw a punch at Mark's jaw.

Mark staggered, then drew himself to full height. He shoved Jerry back into the post.

Bouncing off it, Jerry came at Mark with a swinging blow, splitting his lip.

Fed up with bruises and split lips, Mark let go a left jab.

Jerry pressed his hand to his mouth. "You could have busted my teeth, you half—"

"Go ahead. Say it!" Mark, ready for a real fight now, rushed head-on, ramming his shoulder into Jerry's chest.

Jerry pushed against him but skidded backward in the dirt. Each throwing punches, they grappled their way to the front of the building. Mark maneuvered Jerry over to the horse trough and propelled him into the water. He'd planned to loosen his grip, but before he knew it, Jerry grabbed his sleeve and pulled Mark in with him.

Both men splashed and spluttered before Mark scrambled out. "What did you call me?"

"A half... baked gladiator," he said, lifting one foot over the edge of the trough.

"Oh, of course. I must have misunderstood. I don't believe that for a minute." Mark pushed Jerry right back in. He shook his still wet head and ran his hands through his hair.

Jerry succeeded in climbing out this time. "Mark, you know I wouldn't call you a... a—"

"You damn-well would." Mark stepped out of the way of the dripping soldier. "I want to drip in my own standing space."

Squeezing water from his soaked clothes, Jerry said, "I don't like the idea of you taking my girl away from me."

"I didn't know she was your girl."

"I told you once how I felt about her. She never gave me a second thought after she saw your admirable self. But I wasn't giving up easy."

They stared at each other. Glowered.

Mark began to think they were getting nowhere. He tried a new approach, knowing he couldn't stay angry with Jerry for long. "See here, Whitfield. I sure hope I didn't loosen those pearly whites of yours. What say we dry off and go for a beer at the sutler's? Take it or leave it."

Mark sloshed off in his boots.

"Hey! Wait for me."

After settling down for a beer at the sutler's, the two decided they'd best mend fences.

Such a decision didn't require much conversation. Mark shook Jerry's hand, and they left to get out of their still-wet clothes.

Mark returned to his quarters to change, all the while wondering what he would say to the colonel. *Third time today I'll be in his office. What do I have to lose? Except Amanda.*

Chapter 29

Dr. Wilcox reached for the scissors.

"Go to 'er, Doc."

The gauze dropped from Jeb's face.

"Open your eyes slowly. Corporal, I said slowly. The light will be bright." Dr. Wilcox turned to close the shutters.

"Doc, I can't see nothin'. Everthin's a cloudless sky. You told me—"

"What I told you was, you might regain your sight. And if you did, it would be some time coming." Wilcox placed the scissors on the table and peered into Jeb's eyes. "You'll have to be patient, maybe pray a little. You do know how to pray, Corporal Speck?"

"Sir, of course I can pray!" He rose from the chair and pawed the air with his hands. "But I can't see nothin'." He grew somber and sat back down. "Gawdamighty, sir. What good's a blind soldier? Soldiern's all I know."

"Jeb, you said 'cloudless'. Is it light or dark?"

"Well, it's... wait a minute. Allie McCrae, did you just come in here?"

"Can you see me, Jeb?" Allie's voice was jubilant.

"Dang it, I lost my sight, not my nose. I can smell that pipe of yours a mile away."

Allie patted his friend's arm. "Don't worry, the major knows what he's doing."

"Well, I owe you thanks, but if I can't see, you may's well left me back at the gorge."

Dr. Wilcox gathered up the bandages. "Corporal, I want you to lie down and rest. Keep your eyes closed until I come back to check on you. Sergeant, you can sit with him, but make certain he obeys my orders."

"I assure ye I will, sir."

~~~

As soon as Mark opened the door, Amanda pounced on him. "What did he say? Tell me."

"Your uncle said Victorio and his people should be content now. They have permission to return to Ojo Caliente."

"I already know that. I mean about us."

Mark knew what she meant. "I'm getting there. First, the colonel agreed to West Point. Then, out of the blue... no, not quite that fast. He thought about it and said he would write to the commandant at West Point and request the best cottage available."

"Then we can set the date," Amanda exclaimed, limping in circles while she counted off the various points in planning a wedding. "Let's see... How about the twentieth of July? I'll talk to the priest today, and then order my dress. It will have to come from San Francisco, but your mother could help me plan, and—"

"Whoa, just a minute," Mark said. He grasped her in his arms and planted a kiss first on her forehead, eyes, then lips. "There I go, lingering again. I'm going to ask Whitfield if he'll stand up for me. He saw you first, and he may say 'no.' We've patched our differences, so we'll see." One last kiss on the tip of her nose and he was gone.

~~~

The next morning Amanda awoke to the whistling of a mockingbird. She peered out the window, thinking she and Mark would be gone when the leaves of the few trees within the fort's confines would have turned to gold.

The news of their engagement traveled about the fort as if carried by personal messenger.

Amanda, with great help from Yvonne, began taking care of all the details of a wedding.

After much persuasion, Lafferty agreed to ice a wedding cake. "Yes, Miss Blair, I'll be glad to ice it for ye, but don't expect me to be puttin' any sugary posies on top."

"Never mind, my dear," Yvonne said. "We will have plenty of food, and small desert flowers in the center of the cake. It will be grand."

Amanda called upon the few ladies at the fort to give their opinions and suggestions.

Each one of them had something different to offer. As each day passed, she felt satisfied everything would be perfect but became worried when her wedding dress hadn't arrived. Two days before the wedding, she cried, "Mark, what shall I do? They promised it would be here in time."

Putting his arms around her, he said, "It doesn't matter what you wear. You'll still outshine any girl in the Territory."

Tears brimmed in her eyes. "I'm about to be married, and I don't even have a wedding dress!"

~~~

Mark left his fiancée in anguish. He hastened to headquarters to telegraph Clear Springs.

After receiving an answer, he walked to the stable and saddled Belle. Settling his tall frame in the saddle, he exited the big gates. He steadied the pace of his mount and headed for the small town. He considered his mission—the package waiting at the General Store. The proprietor had wired he wouldn't close until Mark came for it.

With time to himself, his thoughts drifted to the colonel. As other frontier post commanders often did, Blair used excuses to hold dress ceremony inspections. It raised the men's morale. Mark decided the colonel enjoyed standing on the porch of the brick headquarters, smoking his imported cigar and gazing out on the well-tended parade ground with its whitewashed stones. The colonel never relented in his desire to further his command.

Still, he's changed.

A mixture of landscapes decorated the area around Fort Hellsgate, in an otherwise sandy desert choking out almost everything but saguaro, creosote bushes, and cholla. The plains allowed an open terrain as far as a man could see. Vegetation would spring up among boulders. This particular morning in the desert brought an uncommon stillness with only Belle's hooves scuffing the loose gravelly earth.

Mark rode an hour or so, thinking how lucky he was to marry Amanda. An unusual sound interrupted his thoughts. For once, he heard something almost before his horse's ears perked up. "Did you hear that, Belle?"

He listened closely and heard it again. *Not a desert bird's call. The distant howl of a wolf?* He couldn't be certain. Mark had an urge to investigate but wondered if he had time. The cry seemed almost human. He veered off to his right toward the faraway sound. A dog's bark intervened over the original cry.

Distinguishing a form in the distance, Mark picked up speed. Not until he rode closer did the little Indian girl come into view, a dog standing beside her. He scanned the plains before him. His

Choctaw grandfather had taught him to see more by not staring directly at an object, but by looking from side to side. He saw nothing suspicious so continued to ride toward the child, whom he thought to be about six. His heart skipped a beat.

The child dragged a cornhusk doll. Blood had spattered her fringed buckskin dress. At Mark's approach, she drew back, her dog snarling.

He again gazed in all directions. Something had to be very wrong for a little girl to be alone in the desert. He dismounted, taking a piece of beef jerky from his saddlebag to quiet the spotted dog, which refused to leave the girl's side. It snapped the jerky from Mark's hand. After taking a second piece, the small dog allowed him to come nearer.

Mark knelt with his canteen of water. Although obviously frightened, the little girl drank between rapid breaths. "*Enjuh*," she said.

He knew enough Apache to know the word meant "good." He patted her shoulder and noticed the deep scratch on her arm, caked with dirt and dried blood. Pouring water on his bandana, he rinsed the wound with a gentle touch.

She seemed calmer and no longer as scared.

Pointing to himself, Mark called his name, then he pointed to her. He repeated the process, "Mark."

The child at last said, "Siki" and pointed to herself.

Well, that's the first step. "All right now, Siki, I'm hoping to take you to your family." Apache children did not usually run away from home. Mark wondered where home was. It would be northeast, not as far as Hopi country. If a small group of Indians had made camp, perhaps Siki followed her dog and became lost.

Lifting the girl to the saddle, Mark climbed up behind her. The little dog yelped alongside the horse, then quieted and trotted after them. If the Apaches did make camp, chances were they chose a spot near the small lake at the base of Verde Mountain.

Mark and the child passed a boulder field where tiny artesian rivulets seeped, disappearing into the thirsty sand. He rounded a curve, and as they approached a grove of cottonwoods, a rustling sound greeted them. A great white owl flapped its wings, flying from one branch into the seclusion of another.

The child seemed terrified of the white owl, a foreboding omen to an Indian. She turned and hid her head in Mark's chest.

Even the omen did not prepare him for the sight on the other side of the trees. "Mother of God," he uttered. He tensed at the sight of the bloody scene. The silent bodies of four Apache women and three children lay strewn near the clear lake. One baby still lay in the willow *tsach* carried on its mother's back. Their clothing indicated a fierce struggle. Three of the women had been shot in the head, and the youngest, her throat slashed, was tied to a tree.

Mark drew in a deep breath, barely controlling his fury. He felt more sickened than angry. Dismounting, he lifted Siki to the ground and indicated for her to stay behind. He needed to assure himself none of the victims survived, or if so, he wanted to help. He soon knew they were past any help he might give.

Siki dashed by him toward one of the bodies. Wailing, she threw herself by the woman's side. Apaches taught their offspring to be brave and not cry. Mark thought this little one had been brave long enough.

He tried to console her. "Siki, your mother's spirit rests. Here, come with me." Leading her away, he wondered how she had escaped death.

He knew the Apaches would return, and even though he was of mixed-blood, they would think he was more soldier than Indian. It didn't matter—he was Choctaw, not Apache, which was no better for him. Right now, he had concern for Siki's wound, which had begun to bleed. Spying nopal plants nearby, he split some of the leaves. After cleansing her arm with water from his canteen, he bound the fleshy side of the leaf to the wound. He hoped the old remedy would work.

Showing no fear, Siki allowed him to help.

Then he saw what he had expected. Five Apache braves rode down from their timbered cover. *How long have they been watching?* Mark hoped long enough. He knew not to show his revolver. Perhaps one of them could speak at least a little English or Spanish—maybe not.

Mark's Apache was only fair. Still, he had to convince them he did not commit these cold-blooded murders.

The Indians needed only to look at the women and children before they charged toward Mark. He had never felt real fear before, but if it meant every muscle in your body tied in knots, then this was fear.

Two Apaches leaped from their mounts, one grabbing him from behind, his arm about the lieutenant's neck. Mark twisted around, but the Apache's hold grew tighter. The other drew his knife, obviously ready to drive it into Mark's chest.

Siki, babbling in rapid Apache phrases, clung with both hands to Mark's arm.

Mark believed Siki could be his only hope.

A third brave ran to the child, hoisted her up, even as she cried out again. "Unh, enjuh, enjuh!" and pointed to the soldier.

The man Mark thought might be Siki's father questioned her. She repeated, "Enjuh." She pointed to her arm, then again to Mark. The father said something to the others, and the braves loosened their hold.

One Apache, still mounted and holding a rifle, spoke. "Bluecoat, if you saved this child from harm, say what happened here."

Mark breathed a sigh of relief at hearing English and hoped they would understand his Apache. He described how he found Siki and then came upon the scene. He held his breath that they understood.

The Indian again spoke to the others and said no more to Mark.

He hoped that meant they believed him.

Siki's father asked her if she knew where the evil ones went. She indicated west, telling them what Mark took to mean "four white eyes," not soldiers. Her explanation seemed to satisfy them. They believed his story.

The Apache knelt by Siki's mother and placed his hand on her shoulder for a brief moment. He rose and mounted his horse. Four braves checked their old muzzle-loading Springfields before departing.

Mark understood that one brave would remain with the child and watch over the women's bodies until the others returned. He had no intention of talking them out of it. It would be impossible to stop them even if he wanted to. He knew the Indians had only one thing on their minds—to avenge the deaths of their women.

As a white man, he could easily kill the murderers for their atrocity. As an Indian, he suffered with the braves, and as a soldier, he proceeded with caution.

Seeing wisps of smoke-curls in the distance, Mark envisioned the white men sitting around a fire at that moment, never suspecting what was in store for them. He rode along with the Apaches, thinking of what he might say to them before he headed for town.

Their leader drew rein and looked at him. "Bluecoat, you do not come."

"But you—"

"Not your concern. You leave now."

Mark knew they were right. And, he needed to be on his way. He remained still as he watched the four horsemen heel their mounts and ride across the plains toward the smoke. He did not understand their innate ability, but Apaches would be able to sense whether they came upon four murderers or just drifters warming themselves by a fire.

With reluctance, the lieutenant turned back. He needed to accomplish his mission soon, or be in deep trouble when he returned to the fort.

~~~

Rail-hitching his horse in front of the General Store, Mark took the three steps in one.

Tobias said, "Lieutenant, I'm sure glad you telegraphed. I plumb forgot to let you know this package was here."

"Don't worry, Tobias. Thanks for waiting for me, and I guess I neglected one important item. I need a ring. A gold one. It would be small."

"I have exactly what you need, Lieutenant. Let me just go to the safe." He returned with three rings.

"They all look about alike, but I think I'll take this one. Seems it shines the most."

"Oh, they're all the real thing, Lieutenant." He brought out a cloth and gave the ring a quick once over. "There, how's that?"

"Perfect," Mark said. He paid for his purchase, pushed the ring down in his pocket and hurried out with his wrapped treasure under his arm. He mounted the bay and rode down the dusty street. At the edge of town, he suddenly stopped. The echo of faint rifle shots carried in the still distance.

One... Two... Three... Four.

The Apaches had carried out their vengeance.

~~~

The sky showed very little moon, but Belle knew the way to the fort. Only a mile short of Hellsgate, clouds darkened, sending down one of Northern Arizona's occasional torrents. Mark let forth a chorus of swearwords—some he didn't know he remembered. *I'll never understand women. They're just as married in calico as lace.*

With sharp raindrops stinging his face, he reached for his slicker to cover himself, as well as the valuable package. Riding against the fierce downpour would soon be impossible. Mark needed refuge before dark. As he neared a thicket, he decided to take shelter. *Sometimes there are small vermin and slithering reptiles in mesquite stands.*

Mark led Belle under the limited protection of the trees. With his saddle for a pillow, he tried to rest. Rain trickled through the branches, and he pulled his blanket close over him. As he lay there, he thought of Siki, hoping she was safe from further harm.

He began to doze when Belle nickered. Rain had slackened into a sprinkle, promising a better day. Mark's unplanned detour to Verde Mountain had delayed him getting home. He knew Amanda would be worried. He saddled his horse, and just in case of more rain, again covered the package.

The earth wouldn't crust over without a couple days of sunshine, so he still couldn't make good time. Eventually, Fort Hellsgate loomed in the distance. As he came close to the fort, he could see the silhouette of the corporal on duty. He signaled him to open the gates.

The rain had totally stopped by the time he rapped on Amanda's door.

"Just a minute." Amanda pulled open the door. "Mark! What on earth are you doing here so late?"

He handed her the package. "I believe this is yours, young lady."

"Mine? But what? Wait and I'll open it." She hurriedly untied the string. "Oh, Mark," she squealed, rising on her toes to hug him. "How did you manage this?"

"One question at a time. It came in on the stage two days ago, but Tobias was waiting for somebody to pick it up."

"Oh, thank you. Thank you. I love you, Mark McCrae. I hope it wasn't too much trouble!"

"No. No, no trouble at all." He grinned.

"I do thank you, but you'll need to leave now. I have to try it on and you mustn't see it until our wedding day."

"I think that sounds like an order, so I'll go." Confused over such a superstition, Mark left, ready to turn in for the rest of the night.

~~~

Holding the dress, a teary-eyed Amanda ran to the McCraes' quarters.

Allie called out, "I'm coming. I'm coming."

As the door opened, Amanda exclaimed, "I'm sorry, Sergeant. I know it's late, but may I please see Mrs. McCrae?"

"Of course, ye—"

"Yvonne interrupted, "Whatever is wrong?"

"Mrs. McCrae, I'm so sorry, but my dress is here. I mean I'm not sorry it's here, but it doesn't fit. Mark rode all the way to town for it. Please forgive me for disturbing you, but can you help?"

"Come in, my dear. Let me see." Yvonne reached for the dress. "Allie, would you leave us for a few minutes?"

Allie left the room so Amanda could try it on.

Slipping into the dress and having Mark's mother fasten the many delicate buttons, her joy faded. "See, it's too large in the waist. And I even sent the store my measurements."

"Not to worry, dear. I can take it up. They probably didn't believe anyone would have a waistline as small as yours."

"It's gorgeous, as I knew it would be, but the length..." She broke into a smile. "I'll have to wear ten petticoats to make it short enough, or I'll fall on my face."

"This dress will be perfect," Yvonne said. "I've never seen such lovely lace. And imagine, all the tiny pearls and satin rosebuds."

"It's much prettier than in the magazine."

"Amanda, would you consider wearing the wedding necklace of my family? Mark's ancestors have worn it, as I did at my marriage. Here, let me show it to you."

She reached for a small, decorated box from a drawer. "It is of no great value, only something special carried from Mississippi by Mark's grandmother."

Amanda cradled the delicate necklace. "Of course, I'll wear it. Thank you, Mrs. McCrae. It will be a beautiful wedding. Nothing can change that now."

~~~

One of the soldiers who could play the hand-pumped organ told Amanda he had limited knowledge of wedding music. But when she asked if he could play "Ave Maria," his face brightened. He even knew a few measures of the "Wedding March."

"Then please just repeat those measures until we're standing in front of the priest."

The next morning, guests filled the small chapel. Wives at the fort had on their best Sunday clothes. Yvonne wore a lovely beaded Choctaw dress, which Mark knew she wore only on special occasions. And this occasion was very special.

He now understood why his bride was so concerned about her wedding dress. Seeing her walk into the chapel and down the short aisle made him forget to breathe. He smiled at the memory of the pretty and indignant girl sitting in the dusty street of Clear Springs. Mark knew then he could never let her go.

The priest took his place in front of the blissful couple. Clearing his throat, an obvious ploy to draw Mark's attention from Amanda, he began the ceremony.

When will he come to the "I do" part? Mark worried.

Commotion from outside shattered the jubilant occasion. The door burst open. A man stumbled into the chapel, a wide spread of red soaking through his shirt. "Colonel Blair... Where is he?"

A soldier rushed after him. "Colonel, he galloped over here soon's I told him where you were."

Colonel Blair started for the intruder. "Tell me, man! What is it?"

"Indians," he gasped. "Attacked the ranch. Dunno who all's dead."

"Whose ranch?" the colonel demanded.

"Shults Double Bar S. I'm foreman—name's Broder. Stole all the stock, horses, cows."

"Get this man some help," the colonel ordered.

Allie reached for him before he fell to his knees.

Amanda clung to Mark's arm. "No, wait, Mark, let them take care of it. Please."

All his hopes and dreams stood before him in a white wedding dress. The thought of ending Draco's assaults crisscrossed with his love for Amanda.

"Give me a minute. It will be all right." Loosening her hand, Mark moved closer to the wounded man.

Amanda, tears streaming, waited.

"How many in the party?" Colonel Blair asked.

"Ten maybe. Big Apache leadin' 'em. They snuck up on us... maybe renegades."

"Sergeant McCrae, employ a patrol and be ready to move out. By God, won't that Victorio learn?"

"Sir, Victorio had nothing to do with it, " Mark said. "According to the foreman, it was a 'big Apache.' That could only be Draco. I'm going after him."

"McCrae, Whitfield can take charge."

"If they're attacking the ranchers, Colonel, they'll take a swath through the whole Territory. We've got to stop them. Besides, I have a personal interest in Draco."

"Mark! You can't leave now."

He turned to see Amanda, her expression pleading. "Mark, this is my wedding day. Our wedding day! If you go, I might not be waiting when you come back."

"That's up to you, of course, but I hope you'll be here." He took her in his arms. "You would never be able to respect me if I didn't go." He cupped her face in his hands and kissed her tear-stained cheeks. "Save some cake for me, my love. And when I return, all the rest of the days will be ours."

Chapter 30

Father and son leaned over to study the territory map on Colonel Blair's desk. Mark traced a path southwest, the closest side of Verde River. "Sir, whatever we learn at the Shults spread will determine where we go next."

"And ye know, sir, the Apaches will continue to slaughter ranchers unless we stop them."

"Sir, if we take a patrol," Mark said, "we might all wind up dead. Colonel, I'd like to go with a couple of men. If there's only a dozen as the foreman said, I think we can handle them."

"Three of you?" The colonel furrowed his brow. "I don't know, Lieutenant. That firebrand renegade they call Draco is vicious. It's risky."

"It is, sir. But I think we can outsmart them. Twenty soldiers can't sneak up on a band of renegades. They'd know we were following them before we knew we were even close. After nightfall, three of us could snake into their camp and surprise the lot of them."

"All right, then." Blair sighed. "I'm glad you're so sure. Besides you two, who do you want?"

"Speck says he can see," Allie said, "but he's not steady enough."

"Nobody's a better shot than young Private Dolan. Let's go with him," Mark added.

The colonel rolled up the map. "Then it's agreed, but I can't afford to lose any of you. And Lieutenant, you're leaving my niece behind. You better be damn careful."

Mark hurried to his quarters and threw off his dress blues. He was aware his father was the toughest sergeant in Arizona Territory, and he also knew the area. Mark changed into buckskins before Allie and the private arrived at the front gates.

Once the men had gathered, Allie turned to the sound of his name.

Jeb Speck came rushing away from the remainder of the wedding guests. "Allie McCrae!" He shook an angry finger. "You stubborn Mick! You ain't goin' without me."

"Next time, me friend. I'm sorry, but ye gotta heal up better."

Mark took the lead, and the three soldiers rode out, leaving a cursing Jeb Speck standing by the gates as they closed in front of him.

~~~

Mark knew the Double Bar S covered well over 2000 acres southeast of Clear Springs. Some desolation, and not many mountains—a fairly level trail.

"Lieutenant," Dolan said, "How come these folks settle way out here anyway? Seems t' me there'd be safer places."

"They depend on the army to some extent. Those uneasy about the Indians reroute themselves to California or move on up to Oregon. The ones staying generally have more fear of cattle rustlers than Indians. Guess they hadn't counted on Draco."

Dolan shook his head. "If I wasn't a soldier, I sure wouldn't live here."

Morning sun gave way to the drizzle of the day before, and the men pulled out their slickers. Tracking Indians on the desert required the best of hearing, but rain shifted importance to other senses.

"There's been more spring rains in three weeks than I've seen in a whole summer," Allie said. Almost as he spoke, the drizzle stopped, and everything became still. "We've made good time, under the circumstances."

Late afternoon brought them within sight of the Shults ranch. Mark reined his horse at the top of the hill. The ranch house, corrals, and outbuildings stood in a broad basin.

"That's really something, Lieutenant."

Mark scanned the area. "Hold on. See those buzzards circling? I don't think they're searching for a dead cow, not that close to the house."

"It's quiet down there. So quiet, ye can almost hear it."

"I bet big trouble's ahead. That rail fence is broken all up," Dolan whispered, ready to spur his horse.

Allie motioned the private to wait. "Easy, it could be a trap."

"Cover me." Mark said. "Likely I won't need it, but I'm going in."

"Aye. We'll ride as far as those trees." Allie drew his rifle.

Cautious, Mark rode down to the ranch house. Two bodies lay at the corner and another on the far side. Hearing no sound except the clucking of a few chickens, he dismounted.

One victim by the house had drawn his weapon, but it did him no good. He had taken a bullet in the face. Glancing toward the empty corral and feeling secure nobody was around, Mark turned to signal the men.

Rifles in hand, Allie and Dolan approached the yard. They ground-hitched their mounts and followed Mark to the barn. Another man lay dead.

"Oh, Lordy." Allie let out a low whistle. "They sure must have been taken by surprise."

Dolan glanced back at the house. "Never had a chance, did they, Lieutenant?"

"I'd say that. What I don't understand is, they were all shot. Someone's been supplying the Apaches with rifles."

"Ye got that square on target. Best we see what's in the house before we tend to digging."

Mark led the way up the front steps. A flowerpot of red geraniums had spilled out on the porch. Inside, embers still smoldered in the stone fireplace.

"We better give the other rooms a once-over," Mark said.

"Not as messed up as I'd supposed, Son. If they wanted anything in the house, they must have found it right off. What do ye make of it?"

Mark shook his head. Back outside, he paced across the front porch, gaping toward the clearing sky. "What I make of it is, somebody wanted it to look like whites did the killing. They didn't burn it out, and they took no scalps."

Dolan stood at the doorway. "That's like the Mortons, except Mrs. Morton was stabbed, an' we know they was Indians did it."

Mark stepped off the porch. "Enough talking." He spied two shovels leaning against the house and gave one to Allie. "Private, get that fork over there. We need to get to work."

At first, the damp earth made five graves easy to dig. Yet, beneath the soft surface, the job took longer than expected. The task finally completed, Allie dropped his shovel and wiped his sleeve over his sweaty brow. "I guess if ye two don't mind, I'll say a word."

Nodding in agreement, Mark and Dolan stood in silence.

"Lord, I'm askin' ye to bless these men and rest their souls in eternal peace in the Celestial City of Heaven. We thank ye for our daily blessings, Lord. Amen."

Mark put down his shovel. "Maybe we can brew up some coffee before we leave."

Dolan looked as if he had something to say and finally did. "Lieutenant, do you think maybe we could eat some of those biscuits settin' on the stove? I know it doesn't seem right, they being meant for somebody else and all, but I'm pretty hungry."

"It's all right, Dolan. We can do that."

They went inside, and after having biscuits and their fill from a steaming pot of coffee, Allie said, "We don't even know which one of those men was Shults, or even if he had a wife. But seeing the remains of a cobbler over there makes me wonder."

"They didn't all the way ransack the house," Dolan said. "According to that Broder fella, they was mainly interested in the stock."

Mark concentrated on something out the window. "Those clothes hanging on the line. I never knew a hired hand that wore inexpressibles before."

"That accounts for that pot of geraniums. Well, if there is a Mrs. Shults, where do ye think she might be?"

"That sort of begs a major answer, Top. We'll water the horses and get moving." Out by the barn, Mark studied the tracks that led from the corral. Even with a humid day, they had crusted over. "There's some not shod. The others must be stolen."

"Appears to be around twenty horses kind of bunched up at the front," Allie said, "then more strung out one by one. We'll have to ask Broder how many cows are missing."

"A white man had to be involved in all this."

"What makes you say that, Lieutenant?"

"First, the rifles came from whites. Apaches are more interested in horses than cows. The more they have, the better their image. Must've had a deal concerning all the stock. Wouldn't surprise me if cattle brands are being changed right now."

"I bet a painted pony you're right," Allie said.

"We best go now. Let's move." Mark sat taller in the saddle to take in the expanse of the Shults' land.

"But rustlin', that's for the law to take care of, isn't it, Lieutenant?" Dolan asked.

"Normally, it is, but the army's concerned with Indians, and we're army."

Allie made note of the dew-sparkled grass swaying in the breeze. "Ye know, it's blowing in from the north. If we get close to them, the horses won't pick up our scent."

A few uneventful miles passed while they rode through the cactus swells of the desert. Allie suddenly stopped. "Mark, wait. I think I have something here." He leaned over to a young sapling and picked off a piece of cloth, ragged on one edge. "If I know what I'm seeing, this is a piece off a woman's dress."

"Guess that answers our question. We've got to be careful or Mrs. Shults' life won't be worth a dime."

"It's not worth a shield nickel as it is."

As they slowed to a walk, the afternoon dissolved into near dusk. "They're gonna have to stop sometime, aren't they, Lieutenant?" Dolan asked.

"They'll stop and tend the horses. Probably make camp for the night. At least, there's no chance of losing them—not with all these tracks."

"Lieutenant, you think we can sneak up on them t' night?"

"It all depends on where they have the woman. If she's in the center of camp and they see us first, we'd manage to get her killed. And they'd most likely make us watch. One thing's sure, they'll make camp by water."

"Aye, that they might. It'll be dark any time, so let's just hope she's on the outskirts."

Mark noticed the tracks led into a stream ahead, banked by aspens. "Dark or not, we need to rest ourselves and the horses."

"This oasis came along at just the right time."

Mark led the way by the tree-lined bank. "We'll ride alongside the creek and watch for tracks when they come out. They can't be far."

The breeze picked up, floating the scent of smoke toward the three riders.

Mark briefly studied the other side of the wide stream. "I don't see tracks, but we'll cross here and stay put by that ledge backdrop." The water's gurgling concealed any noise the horses' hooves might make.

When they dismounted, Allie moved farther along in the moonlight, returning quickly. "Their remuda is just up ahead. Not nearly as many as I expected. Can't see anything else."

Dolan kept his voice low. "They're probably settled down for the night."

Mark handed his reins to his father. "I'm going to caution up there and find out."

"Ye want me to come along?"

"Better only one snake at a time." He removed his boots and pulled his moccasins from his saddlebag. "Main thing, I want to check on the woman and see where Draco is." He loosened the strap on his Bowie. "I won't be long."

"Sir, we're ready if you need us," Dolan whispered.

Mark moved several yards upstream, listening for any sounds from the camp. He heard only Apache, not a hoped-for white voice. He dropped to his stomach, hand-pulling himself a few inches at a time—creep and freeze—as his Choctaw grandfather taught him.

Long grass twisted like rope under his body, making it difficult to hold his rifle in the crook of his arm. He lay still, listening. Finally, a voice said, "Draco be there with horses by morning. With more warriors, we be at—"

"I know, I know," interrupted a gruff voice. "We'll be at the Walter's ranch in five days. That's five suns from now, you stupid dolt."

Damn, Draco's not here. He probably took the rest of the horses. It was clear now a white man was involved. He parted the grass with one hand and spied the encampment in a low area. Eight Apaches slept in a semi-circle by the fire. *Broder said a dozen. Some must've gone with Draco.*

The Indian who had been talking walked away and bedded down, leaving the white man's back toward Mark.

He managed only the partial sight of a woman tied against a tree.

The man moved over to her. "And you, girlie, a pretty honey-haired thing like yourself, you'd be surprised how much you'll bring south of the border." He leaned over, attempting to kiss her.

She shrank from his grizzly beard.

"Now, girlie, there's no need to pull away. You'd best be nice to me, or I'll turn my friends here loose." He grabbed her by the shoulders and roughly kissed her.

"Stay away from me, you—greasy animal."

Throwing his head back, the man laughed and returned to his place by the fire.

Intent on observing the scene before him, Mark scarcely heard the whisper moving in the darkness. But when he did, he grew as still as the earth beneath him, and with a slight turn to his side, he slipped the Bowie from its sheath. He shifted over on his back and held the knife, blade up with both hands, close to his body. The faint sound grew nearer, then waned.

He relaxed, exhaling the breath he'd seemed to hold forever.

Suddenly the Apache turned and lunged.

Mark froze for an instant. Then, with a grip on the Bowie, he thrust upward.

The Indian couldn't have seen the knife that plunged into his throat. Blood funneled out as he fell against Mark.

He lay still, praying the flowing creek covered any noise, including the pounding of his heart. Feeling safe, he rolled the Indian away and dragged him downstream. He hoped he was the only one on watch. If any of the others came looking, they'd find three armed soldiers first.

He dipped his knife in the water and wiped it clean on the grass. He crept back toward Allie and Dolan, one soft step at a time. "When they've fallen asleep, we'll do what we came for."

"What happened up there, Son?"

"There's one less Apache to worry about. He was silent. Probably meant to pick us off one at a time."

"What about the camp?"

"It's Mrs. Shults all right and a white man. We have to take him alive, or we won't know who's responsible for the cattle rustling. Getting the woman across the border may be a one-man operation—his, but he may be in charge of the rustling, too."

Mark waited for what he thought was enough time. "They should be asleep by now. We'll walk our horses upstream as far as we dare and rein them to those aspens. Any nickering, and the Indians will think they're theirs. If we have to take off in a hurry, I'd rather ride than run."

"Dolan and I'll take places opposite each other," Allie said. "Maybe we'll fool them into thinking there's more of us."

"I'll try to wake Mrs. Shults without scaring her to death. If it doesn't work, send in lead. I won't be taking my rifle."

He crawled into the camp, making his way toward the woman. He knew Apaches could hear noises no white man could, and a white man could imagine enemies where none existed.

But Mark knew his enemies existed right in front of him.

Before the captive realized Mark was there, he covered her mouth with his hand. She was younger than he expected. He put his finger to his lips, signaling her to stay quiet. She remained silent, fear in her eyes. As soon as he removed his hand, she gasped.

An Apache stirred.

Shapes and shadows constantly changed with the campfire's glow.

Mark slid behind the tree, pulse racing. Reaching for his .45, he pushed himself to one knee. Then the soft whistle of a night bird sounded.

The Apache stopped, turning in that direction. After what seemed an eternity, he settled down.

Waiting a couple minutes, Mark cut through the girl's ropes, then helped her stand to get her bearings before starting up the incline. At the top, he pointed to the horses and whispered, "Wait there. If anything goes wrong, mount the big bay and ride like the wind to the fort."

Dolan and Allie had laid out their Colts and ammunition in front of them and aimed their Springfields at the right targets.

Mark slithered back down the incline and hoped to be as successful in his second attempt.

The difference was the man wouldn't want to come and was a lot bigger. He slept on his back, with his hat drawn over his eyes. His snoring kept Mark undetected. Crouching, he jammed a hand over the man's mouth and pressed his .45 into his side. The fat man gargled something but quieted when the muzzle went deeper.

The plan was working. But just when they were up the slope, the fat man's foot slipped, dislodging gravel. Gun in his back or not, he let out a howl. Mark pulled him down. The Apaches scrambled to their feet. Mark slammed the barrel of his .45 against his prisoner's head. If he got out of this, he wanted to make sure the fat man went along with him. The knock on his head would immobilize him, at least for a while.

Mark spun around and fired. Two Indians fell. At the same time, shots came from the soldiers above the campsite.

Another volley. Mark felt a horrific pain, like a hot branding iron on his leg.

Dolan dropped the one who shot Mark, plus one trying to put out the fire—leaving four.

Another bullet opened the air alongside Mark's ear. *That was too close.*

Allie put a hole in the head of another one racing toward him, but not before a bullet creased his own sleeve, coming out at the shoulder of his coat. "Lordy, that singed the hair right off me arm."

Luck was on the soldiers' side since they were in the dark and had a clear view of the Indians in the campfire's glow. Dolan reloaded while Allie took aim, hitting his target.

At the break of a twig, Mark realized an Apache had sneaked out from camp during the firing. He turned to see a sharp weapon aimed at his skull.

Two volleys cracked from behind him, both tearing through the Apache. He flung his arms above his head, tomahawk sagging from his hand. He rolled down the incline toward the fire.

"Dang, Lieutenant! You oughta have your hearin' checked," a voice blared out. "Uh, sorry, sir."

When Mark pulled himself back, he squelched a groan. "Speck, what in God's name are you doing here?"

"Well, Lieutenant, if your daddy can't take care of you, I guess I'm gonna have to."

The last Apache lost his battle with Private Dolan.

Mark raised up, pain tearing through him. He grabbed at his leg.

Allie and Private Dolan came flying across the grassy ledge. "Mark, what's happened to ye?"

"My leg just got in the way of a bullet."

Allie pulled off Mark's moccasin and ripped his pants leg. "Dolan, get that whiskey from me saddle bag."

The young private took one look at Mark and raced off.

Allie glanced up and saw Jeb moving toward them. "Jeb, what in Hades? You're going to be court-martialed for sure."

"No, I ain't, dang it. Colonel Blair let me come. Thought I'd never find you. Good thing I followed the smoke. If it'd been your pipe, I'd a found you sooner."

"I'll thank ye to leave me pipe out of it, but I'm grateful to ye for being here."

Mark glanced up and saw the girl. "Are you all right? I hope I didn't hurt you, dragging you up those rocks."

She held her arms against her chest, visibly shaken. "I, I'm fine, just some scratches. I'm really grateful."

There was just enough moon to see. Allie ripped Mark's pants leg and washed the blood away with water from his canteen. He took the whiskey from Dolan and dashed a quarter of it on his wound.

"Just so you'll know, Top. That hurts."

"And just so ye know, I'm sorry."

The girl tore off a strip of her dress for a tourniquet.

Allie glanced around at her. "Are ye hurt in any way? I didn't mean to pass ye by."

"I'm all right. I'm more scared than hurt. Don't worry any."

Allie continued working on Mark and used the rest of the cloth for a bandage. "There, Son. That's the best I can do, but we'll get to the fort soon."

"Thanks, Top." Mark shifted so he could see Speck. "I owe you, Corporal. This is my first bullet, and I sure don't look forward to the next. Wait! Where's the fat man?"

"Oh, him," the rangy Jeb said. "Why, sir, I crammed my bandana down his throat and tied him to that tree yonder. Just didn't strike me like he was s'posed to be runnin' off."

"Draco and his men will be heading south to the Walters' ranch," Allie said, "but it'll be a while before Draco knows what happened here. That won't stop him. He'll have more men."

Mark turned toward the young woman. "Mrs. Shults, if it's any consolation, we gave your husband a decent burial, along with the ranch hands."

"No, no. I'm Anna Shults, their daughter. My folks went to Santa Fe. They're not due back for two days."

"Never occurred to me they wouldn't be at the ranch. I'm glad for your sake your parents weren't there. They will be shaken up when they hear about this. I tell you what, Corporal Speck and Private Dolan will take you home and stay till your folks come back."

Anna cried her thanks and gave Mark a hug. "My folks would thank you, too."

"I'm just glad it worked out."

"Speck, you and Dolan round up those horses and put them in the Shults' corral. And take the Indians' horses. Saddle up our fat friend's mount, too."

"Yes, sir," Dolan said.

"I know it's out of the way, but you need to go by Globe and warn the sheriff of a possible attack by Draco. Do it before or after you go to the Shults. Just be quick. And good luck."

Jeb motioned for the private. "C'mon, Dolan."

"And Jeb," Allie called, "Tell him they can have the rustlers, but we have dibs on the fat man." He turned to Mark. "Son, it will be dawn soon, but I think maybe ye should rest, and we'll take off early. Fat man here can stay attached to that tree for an hour or so."

Mark got little sleep. Stirring, he said, "Top, can you get me to my horse?"

"That I will." Allie helped him hop on one leg.

Mark reached for the saddle horn. "Easy, girl." On the second try, he grimaced. "How can it hurt so much when it's numb?" On the third try, he pulled himself into the saddle. "Did you hear something back there?" He sighed. "Never mind, just ringing in my ears. Any whiskey left, Top, or did you pour it all over me before?"

Allie handed him the bottle. "Here ye are. Not too much now."

A couple of swigs revived him enough to think he could make it to the fort.

"Son, ye don't look too good. Are ye sure you can stay on? I can make a pretty sturdy travois."

"Don't need one. I can ride."

Chapter 31

Allie took hold of the fat man. "Move along, ye fat bastard. Get on that horse so I can tie ye to the saddle."

"C'mon, Lieutenant. You're not gonna take me to the army, are you? Why, that bunch of damn Apaches held me captive. I swear."

"That's a lie if I ever... Jaykers! You're Joe Barker, that Indian agent!"

"Now, Sergeant, I never did anything wrong. Those Indians were—"

"Shut up, you jack-donkey! Just be glad I'm not tying ye face down across the saddle. Staring at road apples on the way to the fort would serve ye well."

After all was ready, Allie and the two men headed north. Late afternoon should bring them to Hellsgate. Primitive beauty covered the desert with its kaleidoscope of shadows formed by the chaparral against the sun. Any other time, Allie would appreciate the beauty. Nobody talked, not even him. He noticed Belle took her lead without Mark's urging. He rode closer to Mark's side and noticed Mark was near unconscious. His leg was bleeding through the bandage.

"That does it. We're stopping." He led the horses to as much shade as a stand of chaparral allowed. He reached for his saddle blanket and spread it by a tree then helped Mark down. He ripped off his bandana and the leather strap from his canteen and re-bandaged Mark's wound.

The prisoner took the opportunity. He dug in his heels, off in a full gallop. His escape came up short when Allie bolted onto Mark's horse and fired a shot in the air. It took only a couple minutes to bring him to a halt. "Ye witless dimdot, how far did ye think ye'd get?"

Allie grabbed the reins and led the prisoner back to where Mark lay. He dismounted and removed the man's rope from the saddle horn. "Ye won't get untied till I say so." He yanked the man from his horse, and he tumbled to the ground.

"Hey! Watch you're doin'."

"Shut up or I'll do it again."

For a safety measure, Allie tied Barker's ankles. He then took his canteen over to Mark. "Here, ye need to drink. You're as hot as a pistol in the sun."

"My wedding day..." Mark drew in a shaky breath. "Where's Amanda?"

"You may not know it, Sergeant," the prisoner needled, "but you might need Joe Barker before we're done."

Allie responded to the comment with a piercing stare. "Lock your mouth," he ordered.

Mark, dazed, said, "Joe Barker?"

"He's a no-count Indian Agent, that's who—"

"Seems I heard that name before." Mark tried to get up.

"Now, Son, just stay put." Allie fished the whiskey from his saddlebag. "Drat it. Empty!"

He threw the small bottle against the ledge behind him.

No sooner had Allie glanced back at the shattered glass, than he heard a soft whir from the nearby rocks. "God in Heaven. I set us up real fine for this one. Don't move, Mark." He turned his head toward the prisoner. "Barker, listen close. We've got us a slight case of rattlesnake over here."

"A rattler? Ha! You saying you want me to rescue you? You forget you tied my hands and feet. What's say we just let that rattler have at it," he howled.

"What's say ye just scrooch yourself over there to that .45 laying by me gear."

The snake began to coil, flicking its forked tongue.

Barker chuckled. "What's to keep me from shootin' you and the soldier there? You got a gun. Why don't you shoot it yourself?"

Allie gave a hard whisper between clenched teeth. "This here rattlesnake is just about hanging onto me left ear. Shoot him now, or ye'll find yourself tied up all alone in 115 degrees worth of sun. And no way to get on a horse!"

Mark managed to get the words out. "What is it, Top?"

"I'll take care of it," Allie whispered. "Our only chance is the Colt."

Barker stared down at his bonds, then at the horses. He inched his way over to Mark's revolver and spied the Bowie. He fumbled with the .45 until he could hold it.

The whir of the rattler became fierce. "C'mon, man," Allie said. "On with it."

With only seconds to think, Barker could use the Bowie and cut through his bonds, but the sergeant would shoot him, snake or not, before he could get on his horse. Twisting into a sitting position, he pointed the muzzle at Allie.

Allie inhaled, sharing the same air with the snake. Then the barrel moved. In the quiet, the shot sounded like a canon. The rattler's head flew off.

"Admirable, Barker. Now, Son, we need to get ye on your horse."

"You owe me," Barker yelled. "I could've killed you!"

"I don't see it that way. Ye did it to save your own skin."

Since that part of his plan had failed, Barker aimed for real at Allie this time and pulled the trigger. The trigger clicked. "Damn!"

"I forgot to tell ye, fat man. Had only one bullet in it." Allie turned his back while he struggled to get Mark to his feet.

Barker snatched the Bowie, gripped it between his knees and freed his wrists, then his ankles. In a flash, he leapt onto his horse. He reached for the reins of the other horses, Springfields still in their boots. "Geee-up!" In a swirl of dust, he dug spur and lowered himself to the horse's mane.

The sergeant scrambled for his gun. He fired, but Barker was already out of range. His laugher echoed behind him.

Allie fired a wasted shot and cursed himself for lack of judgment. At least, he thought, we have one canteen of water, but it has to last. On horseback they could make it. Without a horse, Hellsgate might as well be a hundred miles away.

~~~

Allie put together firewood from the dry branches. "Well, I've eaten it before. Still don't like snake." He prepared it and slid the pieces onto a stick to roast over the fire. Allie lost his appetite when Mark refused to eat.

Transporting Mark on a travois was the only alternative. Two small blessings were his pocketknife and the saddle blanket Mark sat on. Blessings aside, their saddlebags went with their horses. They contained everything, including leather ties. He found saplings in the young stand of trees.

Mark's face had lost its color, and perspiration drenched him.

"Don't ye worry, Son. I'll be quick."

Cutting saplings with a small knife took time. Allie sawed through enough of two skinny trunks so he could break them off with his boot. He tied them together at the top with the leather strap from his canteen and hoped it held. He connected the other pole ends with a cross-strip of a limb and several small branches joined the outer poles. If only he had water to make the strips pliable.

After attaching the blanket to the poles, he pulled it a few feet to see if it held. Carrying weight was something else. At this point, he thought God's assistance would be appreciated.

Allie dragged Mark onto the travois. He looked forward to the sun's going down, but they were a long time from it. The dismal monotony of trudging over the rocky terrain presented a challenge. If a bright moon prevailed, Allie could find his way. *I just hope the only rattlesnake we meet up with is wrapped in me pocket.*

"Top, get gloves."

"They're gone with the horses, Mark."

Allie pulled the travois, dismissing the splinters that gnawed at his hands. The hours all melded into one. Walking. Stopping. Resting. He was aware of the spicy fragrances that floated through the stillness, announcing the cool of evening. He knew he should be taking Mark to safety. But fatigue grabbed him as though his forty-nine years had become ninety. He had to sleep.

Even before dawn covered the moon, Allie awoke. Mark, fevered, breathed heavily. Allie washed his son's face and when all was ready, he reached for the travois. The ground was smooth on this section of the desert, giving hope they could move faster. Mark still slept.

Less than an hour after they renewed their tedious journey, a connecting binding snapped.

With a moan, Mark slipped. Allie set down the travois and rushed to his side. "We'll make it, Son, ye'll see." But he wasn't sure. His faith would carry just so far.

He made repairs with the extra strips and worried—would they hold? There were no nearby trees for him to collect more, and he had already used the leather strap from his canteen. He had no idea of how far he had walked when the nicker of a horse broke the silence. Friend? Indians? Then a voice in the distance.

"Lead on, you so and so. And you best take me right to where you left them."

Allie could see the forms of two men, although the number of horses sounded more like four or five. As they rode closer, he lay on the ground in front of Mark and rested his revolver over his left forearm.

He found himself in their path and had no choice but to call out. "Hold it right where you are." He could make out one rider as Joe Barker. "I know ye, the one on the left. Who's the other?"

"Take it easy, soldier," the second man yelled, by this time, only yards away. "I mean no harm. Does one of these cavalry horses belong to you?"

"Aye, both of them. I mean one of them belongs to the lieutenant here." Allie got up and stepped over to take the reins, still aiming his weapon.

Belle pulled loose and trotted to Mark, poking her soft nose on his shoulder.

"Who are ye, and where'd ye find me prisoner?"

"My name's Aloysius Ezekial Berne, but I'll answer to Zeke. And I reckon you're who I want to find."

"I'm Sergeant McCrae. I'll ask or answer questions later, but if ye'll just help me with me son, I'll be grateful." He went around to Barker. "Ye no-good saddle full of fat, I ought to blow ye off your horse right now. But I'll let the colonel take care of it. Save meself the trouble. For now, don't move a finger."

Zeke looked down at Mark. "Well, I'll be. It's the soldier."

"What do ye mean? Sure, he's a soldier."

"But this one saved my life—more or less. Here, I'll help lift him on his horse. That travois you got there's pretty stressed." Zeke climbed down from his mount and helped lift Mark.

"Say, he sure has a fever. And that leg don't look so good. We needn't waste time." He took Belle's reins and rode alongside Mark to steady him.

Allie rode on the other side. "Son, are ye all right? We're going home."

Mark nodded, saying nothing.

"I do thank ye, Aloysius. And may I say that's a mighty fine name ye have."

Zeke merely grinned. On the way to the Fort, Zeke explained how he had spied the fat man leading the two horses. "I got suspicious when I saw they were cavalry mounts, complete with gear. That big bay over there carried on like crazy, pulling on the reins. Seemed to me she wanted to go back where she came from."

"Aye, she would do that. We can make it easy now. I'm grateful to ye."

"My pure pleasure, Sergeant. And by the way, he had this here Bowie with him."

"Aye, thank ye. Belongs to me son." He turned his attention to Barker. "The army's going to have something less than nice to say to ye. Nothing badder than a Indian agent gone bad."

Chapter 32

When Allie and Zeke rode into Hellsgate, Allie called to a couple privates. "Here, take charge of this man and don't let him out of your sight." They dragged Barker away as his whining polluted the air.

He and Zeke hurried on to the fort hospital where Allie leapt from his horse and ran inside. "Dr. Wilcox. Me son's shot. It's bad. Ye got to help him."

"Bring the lieutenant in." With a speed born of practice, Wilcox cleared his operating table and moved the lamps closer.

Allie and Zeke half-carried Mark inside and laid him on the table. "I know it's serious, Major, but is he going to be all right?" Allie fingered his forage cap.

"Give me a chance to find out. And you might consider getting out of my way." He cut off the rest of Mark's pant leg. Dried blood clung to the makeshift bandage. "Since you're here, Sergeant, bring me some hot water."

Mark grimaced when he removed the dressing and examined the open wound centering his swollen leg, just above the knee. "What did you put on this, sand?"

"Water and a little whiskey. That's all we had."

By this time, three non-coms had followed them inside. "All right," Wilcox said, "all of you. Out of here. I'll take care of him. Sergeant, you don't look so good yourself."

"I'm fine, Major." Reluctant to leave, he headed to his quarters to tell Yvonne.

Her face paled at the news. "I must go to him! Have you told Amanda?

"Not yet, but she may not be that anxious. Him leaving her at the altar like that."

"I'll see about Mark and then find her. But Allie, are you all right? You look so weary."

"Yes, yes, now go, me darlin'. I'll be there soon's I check on me prisoner."

Allie hurried to where he'd left Joe Barker. The two privates still held him in custody.

"Now, boys, this is all a big mistake," the prisoner was saying. "Sergeant McCrae, he—"

"What about the sergeant?" Allie grated. "All right, Barker, you're coming with me." He grabbed the prisoner by the upper arm and didn't loosen his grip until they got to headquarters. Colonel Blair wasn't there.

"Never ye mind, Barker, I'll just rail-hitch ye right here by this horse. 'Course, he might object to the company."

The fat man whined. "This is outright inhumane. Gimme my hat."

"Quitcher belly-aching, or ye won't have a head to put it on." As soon as he spoke, he saw Colonel Blair walking toward them and moved a few steps to meet him. "Sir, the patrol is back. Or, that is, two of us. And this bad news here is Joe Barker. You'll recall him, I expect, sir."

"I certainly do. I've been looking forward to catching up with this scum. Come into my office."

"Sir, the lieutenant's shot. It's bad. Major Wilcox's taking care of him now." Allie had the colonel's full interest.

Blair paused. "I was afraid something like this would happen and hoped I'd be wrong. I'll see him as soon as we finish here."

"Colonel, I got to hand it to this man over here. Without him, we'd never... Aloysius, where are ye? Might ye wait just a minute, Colonel?" Allie raced around the corner of headquarters. There he was, in slumber, leaning against the building. "C'mon now. I want the colonel to know what ye did." He insisted Zeke come with him.

Allie related details of their mission, giving the stranger his due. "And Zeke's being there when we needed him. Well, I can't thank him enough."

"Fine job, McCrae. And I thank you for your help, Mr. Berne. You be sure to have a filling meal or anything else you need before you take your leave."

"Thank you, Colonel. A good meal would be mighty tasty— and some for my horse."

With a slight smile, Blair said, "And I imagine the sergeant here will join you."

"That I will. And, sir, Draco planned on going to the Walter's ranch any day now. That's just it. I don't know the day. But after we did away with his braves, he would've been pretty unhappy when they didn't join him. It'll take him a little time to regroup."

Joe Barker squirmed in his chair. "Colonel Blair," he pleaded, "I didn't kill anybody back there at the Shults' spread—Apaches did it all. You'll go easy on me since I've told you what I know now, won't you?"

"It isn't up to me, Barker." Blair reached across his desk and wagged a finger. "You knew what you were doing, stealing the Apaches' allotment. You have no sympathy from me. If Draco had recognized you under that beard, he would've cut you to pieces."

"It's more than Barker's face full of hair making up a disguise, sir," Allie said. "Looks like he ate most of the beef he stole. I expect he can tell you all about the cattle they rustled from the Shults. But, sir, what about the Walters?"

The colonel lit a cigar from his humidor. Inhaling deeply, he let out a thin plume of smoke. "We'll have a patrol ahead of time at the Walter's ranch. That way we can surprise Draco and his renegades, pure and simple."

"Sir, the lieutenant was sure counting on getting Draco himself."

"I know. He'll just have to let someone else take care of Draco. Right now, take this prisoner to the stockade." The colonel stubbed out his unfinished cigar. "I'm going to see Lieutenant McCrae." He stalked out of his office and headed toward the hospital.

Allie, accompanied by Zeke, again latched onto Barker's arm and dragged him down the front steps.

"McCrae, I'm telling you for the last time, I don't even know what—"

"And I'm telling ye for the last time. You're braiding your own rope with words."

~~~

After the meal Colonel Blair promised him, Zeke said, "Sergeant, I need to be on my way. Had a job for me over at the Walter's spread, if I want it. Truth is, I have an urge to go to California. Just not sure when."

"Don't forget those renegades' plans."

"Yeah, I got that. I reckon I can take care of myself, whatever I decide, Sarge... say, do you have a first name?"

"I do. It's Aloysius. I never met a man with me own name before. And just know from this Irishman, I wish ye luck."

The other man raised a bushy eyebrow. "Don't that beat all? But I'd rather answer to Zeke."

"I know the feeling." Laughing, Allie reached out to shake his new friend's hand.

Zeke turned to leave. Mounting the big roan, he caught a glimpse of a pretty girl in a carriage. "Say, that young woman there. I seen her in town once. Colonel's daughter?"

"His niece, and supposed to be Mark's future wife."

"Well, what do you know. Tell that boy of yours I asked about him. He'll survive. Just you wait."

~~~

Amanda, having planned a venture into Clear Springs, arranged for a couple of townsmen to ride alongside the carriage for the trip back to the fort.

When they arrived, she said, "I can't tell you how much I appreciate your protection, gentlemen. Are you sure I paid you enough?"

They looked at each other and grinned. One answered. "Ma'am, you gave us what we asked. We can't ask for more." They tipped their hats and turned for Clear Springs.

Uhm, chances are I paid them too much, she thought. *But then, what's too much for protection from outlaws? Or, for that matter, from Indians.*

Inside the fort, Amanda noticed her uncle leaving headquarters. She leaned forward.

"Private, would you drive the carriage over to Colonel Blair, please? Uncle John, wait."

The colonel stopped and offered his hand for her to step down from the carriage. "How's my favorite niece?"

"You have another one?" she said, wrinkling her nose. "Now, where are you going in such a rush?"

The colonel paused before speaking. "I didn't want to tell you just yet, but Mark's returned."

"He's back? Well, he probably hasn't even tried to find me." She put out her lower lip as if to pout, but changed her mind. "That shows he doesn't care. He left me at the altar, didn't he?"

"If that's the way you feel. But I'm going to see a wounded officer I happen to respect." In haste, he walked away.

Amanda grabbed her uncle's arm. "An officer? Is it Mark? It is. I know it!" She gathered up her skirts and ran all the way to the hospital, Colonel Blair right with her.

She stormed through the door. "Dr. Wilcox! Where is he? I must see him." She glimpsed Yvonne standing by Mark and rushed to his bedside. "Mrs. McCrae, is he going to be all right?"

Yvonne put her arms around Amanda.

"Please. Tell me!"

"Now then," Dr. Wilcox said, "slow down a little, Miss Blair. A bullet went through the lieutenant's leg. He lost a lot of blood, in spite of the sergeant's care." He changed to a softer tone. "He has an infection. Our next concern is to help him through this fever."

"I know treating a bullet wound is one thing," Amanda said. "Treating an infection is quite another."

"Major," Blair said, "Spare nothing. Is there anything else you need?"

"I've tried it all. Quinine, soda, rhubarb, whatever I had. As long as I have plenty of morphine on hand, he should be free of pain."

Blair moved over to Mark. "Lieutenant?"

Mark would hear or feel nothing, as he had lapsed into a sound sleep.

Amanda straightened her skirt and drew in a breath. "Dr. Wilcox, I need an apron and a cap. I'm taking care of this patient."

Yvonne rested her hand on her son's arm. "I will leave for a while and prepare chicken soup for him—in case he wakes soon and is hungry." She leaned and kissed Amanda's forehead.

Amanda took her self-prescribed duties seriously. The remainder of the day she kept a cold cloth on Mark's head. At night she rested her arm on the side of the bed, in case he regained consciousness while she slept. When she woke, she could tell he'd barely moved.

Dr. Wilcox brought in more blankets and began piling the covers on Mark.

"But I don't understand, Major. He's burning hot already."

"Yes, but my hope is to increase the fever, forcing it to break. It's been done before. We'll have to wait and see."

~~~

The third day after Mark had entered the hospital, Allie and Yvonne returned to see Amanda still sitting at Mark's bedside. Allie thought of how he watched over Yvonne's recovery before they married. *And now Amanda is experiencing the same.*

Dr. Wilcox was putting away a tray of bandages and alcohol.

Allie stood with his arm around Yvonne's waist. "Doctor, we need to know. What are our son's chances?"

"Please say he will be all right," Yvonne pleaded.

"We should know in a day or two, maybe sooner. There's nothing more to do but keep him comfortable." He looked back at Amanda. "That little nurse will help more than I can."

When Yvonne moved over to her, tears at the edge, she said, "Let me stay with him. You must get some rest."

Amanda swept back a wisp of blonde hair. "I can't leave him now, Mrs. McCrae. I must stay."

Allie pulled up a chair for Yvonne and studied his only son. "Ye know, the time has gone by so fast. I recall when Mark's grandfather carried him on his shoulders and told him the ways of the Choctaws." He paused a moment, thinking. "Most important, the judge told him it was a person's heart and not his bloodline that earned him respect. I may need to remind me son. I feel he has not yet got hold of that."

"Yes, Allie, it is close in my memory. Our son loved hearing his grandfather's stories."

Mark still lay in a feverish sleep, broken with episodes of chills. Even with covers, he shivered. When he grew hot, Amanda washed his face with cool water.

"Ye are doing a fine bit of nursing, Amanda. I sure hate to, but I must get to me duties."

Amanda stood. "Please, you go, too, Mrs. McCrae. I will be fine. Besides, I can sleep in the chair."

"All right, my dear, but I will be back first thing in the morning."

That night as Amanda dozed in a chair by his bed, she abruptly awakened, hearing the words, "Wait for me." She sprang from her chair. "Yes, yes, Mark. I did wait. I'm here."

His eyelids wavered then closed.

"Mark, don't close your eyes. Please stay with me." She put her hand on his forehead. "Dr. Wilcox. Come quickly!"

Chapter 33

In short weeks, the first of all the rest of the days Mark had promised Amanda began. To him, the recent past seemed never to have been.

The priest cleared his throat. Amanda gazed at the tall, ruggedly handsome man at her side.

"Do you, Amanda, take this man to be your lawfully wedded husband? Do you promise to love him, honor and obey him, and keep him in sickness and in health, forsaking all others for as long as you both shall live?"

"I do." She kept her eyes shut for a moment.

Mark repeated his vows in a voice everyone could hear. He slid a gold ring on Amanda's finger. Accepting the priest's suggestion to kiss his bride, he prolonged it until the father cleared his throat. Mark was aware of suppressed laugher among the guests.

Embarrassed, he said, "I think it's time to get on with the dancing." They left the chapel, and everyone followed as Mark escorted his bride to the mess room.

The men had removed the tables, except one with refreshments. Even a piano, minus a key or two, was available. Yvonne offered her talents at playing it for the evening.

Several soldiers also provided music—a military orchestra of two fiddles, two Jew's harps, and three harmonicas.

"I haven't danced since the last hop at West Point," Mark said, "but if you think you can stay out from under my feet, I'll sure try."

Amanda moved into his arms. "They didn't play such fast music in New York, so I'll be careful."

As the celebration continued, Jerry Whitfield approached. As if daring Mark to turn him down, he asked, "Mind if I dance with your wife?"

Genially, Mark answered, "No, if my wife doesn't mind, as long as you don't kiss the bride. She's yours for three minutes—no more."

Amanda glanced back at him and smiled as Jerry swept her onto the dance floor.

Mark stood by the punch table, observing the two. He knew Jerry had accepted their marriage. He wasn't worried about him—he just liked watching his bride.

When the music ended, Jerry escorted Amanda back to her husband. With a slight bow, he said, "My thanks to you, Mrs. McCrae, and to you as well, Lieutenant."

With the party well under way, Lafferty brought out his own mouth harp, adding his personal "whee-oo-whee-oo-oo" to the party. A lot of knee slapping transpired. Mark stopped by to thank him for struggling through sugar-icing a cake. Wedding preparations the second time around proved simpler.

Festivities finally drew to a close. Everyone departed after congratulating the couple.

By this time, the sun had sunk behind the mountains that stole its rays.

~~~

Mark opened the door to their quarters. "I don't wish to alarm my new bride, but if you don't want to land on the floor, hold close around my neck."

Before she could reply, he lifted her and carried her over the threshold.

"Oh, Mark, I forgot—your leg!"

"The doctor's wrap is firm. You're not heavy enough to hurt my leg. Besides, I promised the priest I'd protect you."

"We're inside now. Are you going to put me down?"

"Well, if I must."

The light having vanished, Mark lit the lamp. He removed his coat and beamed at his bride.

"Here we are, Mrs. McCrae. I like the sound of that name."

"So do I, Lieutenant McCrae. Mark, I have something for you. Before the wedding we didn't have time. I had asked my cousin in the east to ship it. I used to curl up in this chair to do my lessons at boarding school. And now it's yours for a wedding present. See if you like it."

Mark stretched his tall frame into the big upholstered wing chair. "We just may have to take this back to New York when we go."

"I do believe there's room in it for both of us."

Reaching out, he pulled her onto his knee. "Now, as long as you're here..." Mark removed the single ivory comb holding back her hair and kissed her. She returned his kiss, not passionately, but as an innocent bride.

Mark ran his fingers down her back. "I don't believe I ever noticed so many buttons on a woman's dress before. How do you—"

"Well, I hope you haven't counted buttons on many ladies' dresses. I tell you what. Since I have only a little trouble myself, I'll see what I can do."

Mark smiled and let her go. *I probably could have figured it out.*

Amanda stepped around a screen and removed her wedding dress. The glow from the lamplight cast her shadow through the sheer panels. She slipped into a dainty white nightgown, and taking one more glance in the mirror, brushed through her thick blonde hair. She arranged the folds of soft cloth hanging to her ankles and moved from behind the screen.

"You are the most beautiful creature I've ever seen, Mrs. McCrae. I've dreamed of this moment many times." He gathered up a soft blanket.

Amanda looked dubious, since it was not a cold night.

Mark unfolded it. "Come, stand beside me."

She took her place by him and didn't question.

Mark draped part of it around himself, holding his bride about the waist. He enfolded her with the rest of the cover and gazed into her clear blue eyes. "Now, my love, you belong to this brave and will share my blanket."

He reached for a wildflower from a vase next to the bed and held it over her heart, pressing her close in an ardent embrace. "This is all I have as a present for you, but when we get to New York, I will buy you something very special. Come to bed, my wife," he whispered.

~~~

Morning light drew Amanda from a deep sleep. She nestled against Mark's shoulder, her arm across his chest. She reached for the flower he'd given her the night before and tickled his nose.

He sneezed. "What is this? A woman in my bed?"

"I do appreciate your enthusiasm." Amanda sat up against her pillow. "Is there anything special you'd like for breakfast?"

"Yes," he replied, drawing her toward him.

"You know what I mean," she teased playfully, pretending to push him away.

Reluctant, he released her. "Make my meal a substantial one. If a bit of a girl can do me in, think what a wild brown-eyed Indian girl would do."

"You will never find out!" Amanda gave him a resounding pop on the shoulder, then slipped into her cotton wrapper.

Mark dressed while she prepared eggs and bacon. She had practiced many times and stocked the larder the day before with food their friends brought.

"That coffee smells great." He reached for a cup and had just taken a sip when a noise outside caught his attention. He set down the cup and rushed to the window.

"A patrol's leaving." His brow furrowed. "Whitfield's in command. It has to be Draco." He reached for his gun belt.

Amanda followed. "You can't go with them," she declared, holding on to him. "You're in no condition for a fight. Besides, our train leaves Monday for New York."

"I am in condition, but you're right. I won't leave you again." He continued to watch the patrol shrink in the distance through the gates. "They should have told me."

"I'm sure they didn't tell you because you would have contradicted every reason they gave you for not going. Jerry can take care of Draco and his renegades. That's all you want, isn't it, Mark? To take care of Draco?"

"Yes, that's all." He turned from the window and slid his arm around her. "I'll finish my breakfast now, Mrs. McCrae."

The cheerful morning had taken on a somber cloud.

Chapter 34

Allie showed Rocking Horse into Colonel Blair's office. The door stood ajar. He decided to leave it that way and returned to his desk.

"I sent for you, Horse, and I want the truth, by God! Exactly where did you find that rifle?"

The scout stood, shifting from one foot to the other, bunching his hat into a roll. "Colonel, I was north of gorge when saw wagon of coffins."

"Yes, yes. Go on."

"I stay behind. Then see rifle. Thought no more about wagon and picked up gun. Maybe it fall off wagon. Maybe not. That first time saw wagon."

"The *first* time. Are you saying you saw two wagons?"

"Yes, Colonel. Two wagon. Two days. Second time yesterday afternoon."

Blair called from his desk. "Sergeant, send for Lieutenant McCrae."

Allie moved quickly to the door, "Yes, sir. He's here now." Allie motioned to Mark and whispered, "I don't know whose fur it is, but it's flying."

"Sir, you want to see me?"

"Yes, Lieutenant. I'm more than a little interested in Horse's rifle. What do you know about it? He said something about coffins."

Mark examined the weapon. "Nothing, sir, unless it's the one I saw him cleaning a while back. Fine-looking Winchester, I'll say that. As for coffins, I recall a wagonload of coffins in town, and somehow, it seemed odd."

"Yes, I remember you telling me. I also thought those pine boxes were just that. We still have no reason to believe otherwise, except for where Horse found this rifle. But now, he says 'two wagonloads,'" Blair walked around his desk, sighed and sat in his big leather chair.

"Sir, the first time I knew about Winchesters in Indian hands was when they turned up at the Shults' place."

"The Apaches are always showing up with a few guns of some kind," Blair said. "I never thought much about it, but this is different. What we have here is a repeating Winchester .44-40, the model that's long over-due for this fort."

Blair stood, snatched a cigar from the humidor and slammed down the lid. "You know, maybe those coffins did carry Winchesters. If we're to find who's supplying the Apaches, McCrae, you'd better get on it."

"Yes, sir." He made a hasty exit to give Allie the orders.

"We'll ride soon's I ready the men. He picked up a quill. "I'll have a choice list of who's going before ye know it."

Mark knew the only clue would come from Rocking Horse. As he and the scout departed headquarters, he asked, "You all right, Horse?"

"Yes, Lieutenant." He unrolled his hat, straightened it with his fist and put it on. "Lieutenant, you think me in trouble with colonel? Better I told him about Winchester when I find it. But wanted to keep rifle."

"Don't worry. Right now we've got to see if Draco and his renegades have these rifles, or if he shares them with Victorio. I'm betting only Draco has them."

Mark knew Horse had done his work well for years. Blair and Colonel Hardin always put their trust in the scout. For Horse to have let this pass wasn't his best decision.

~~~

Mark rushed back to Amanda. "Sweetheart, I have to leave—"
Her eyes widened. "Mark McCrae!"

"Now before you say anything, it isn't dangerous. We're just chasing down a wagon. I'll be back tomorrow noon, at the latest."

"A wagon? You're chasing a wagon?"

"It just may have our stolen shipment of rifles. Besides, it's your uncle's orders."

"I guess you have no choice. Then take this kiss with you." She reached up and gave him a kiss he would remember.

"Did I ever tell you, you are hard to resist?"

"No, but if I am, kiss me again."

"I love you, Amanda McCrae. Now I must go."

The patrol was waiting for Mark when he got to the gates. "All right, men. If all goes well, the fifteen of us will be back to

Hellsgate before noon tomorrow. Let's move. Horse, take us to where you found the weapon."

"Past grasslands. North of gorge, Lieutenant." Rocking Horse pointed, squinting into the morning's brassy glare.

As they rode, Mark thought of the number of men under Blair's command. He turned to his father riding beside him. "Top, I hadn't asked you before, but is there any special reason for Blair's command to be smaller than Colonel Hardin's was when I left?"

"Aye. The government continued to send men to Hellsgate. But how many new men have ye noticed since ye got here?"

"Not as many as I think we need."

"We rarely had deserters with Hardin, but that was all ye heard soon after Blair came."

Mark figured that under normal conditions, the older soldiers would have resented a young West Point officer coming in and taking over at Blair's whim. Some probably did. But he felt every mission he went on had to be successful.

"But you know, Top, I've noticed a change in the colonel since he was wounded."

"Maybe having his niece here changed his attitude for the best." Allie winked. "Aye, isn't that what women do?"

Mark answered the comment with a sly smile.

Rocking Horse moved closer. "Lieutenant, up ahead find rifle. Past grove of piñons." Creosote bushes and prickly pear lined the way. The men continued toward the stand of trees. "Here, by saplings. First time I see wagon and find rifle."

"Then we'll go on," Mark said. "It's so dry up here, you can still see partial metal-rimmed tracks about as clear as just made. And I want to know who made them."

"Tracks always lead somewhere," Allie said. "Sooner or later we'll know."

Later came sooner, as Jeb's horse limped up alongside Mark. "Lieutenant, my mount's gone plum lame. I gotta tend to him."

Mark reined to a halt and brushed the dust from his face. "It's near time to call it a day anyway, but not out in the open. We've been at this four hours, plus stopping. That's enough."

Jeb dismounted and led his horse to the shade of a big mesquite. A sharp rock had wedged under his sorrel's shoe. Jeb popped it out and withdrew a can of wax from his saddlebag.

Lighting a lucifer, he melted a small amount and pressed it into the raw area at the shoe. "There. Got it."

"That taking care of it, Jeb?"

"Yes, sir. By mornin'. Leastways, I hope so."

"Men, the horses need a rest, and so do we. From the dryness of it, there's been no rain in a while, but ought to be a stream if we can find it."

Allie grinned. "Molly here's pulling against the reins. Maybe she knows something we don't. C'mon, Lafferty, let's see what she's about." They followed the trail till it split, one fork fading out. But then, Molly's instinct proved right. A quiet stream moved along close to a cliff base.

Allie's voice carried in the stillness. "We found ourselves water. Not much grazing, but there's a little."

Mark didn't expect anything unusual to happen during the night, but he knew better than to make themselves targets from all sides. He rode Belle to the grade and located an area of bare ground. "Perfect." It backed up to a protected cliff overhang, with a long section of dry grass covering the incline. "Horse, take someone with you to get firewood. Get enough. We'll need it when the sun goes down."

After they all settled at the camp area, Lafferty rattled through a couple pans and food preparations. "I know we don't have a cook wagon this trip, boys, but ye can still get ready for a special surprise dee-light. We'll be having 'Old Ned' for supper."

"Ol' who?" Jeb asked. "Oh, Ol' Ned. We've had that afore."

"But tonight I'm making it with a wee bit o' whiskey in the rice." He held up his hands and measured about eighteen inches worth.

"Lieutenant! Over here, sir," a soldier yelled.

Mark hurried toward the voice, about fifteen yards upstream.

"This way, sir. In the grass. I was taking my horse over here to graze when I saw him." He pointed to a man laid out flat on his belly.

"He didn't quite make it to water." Mark stooped to turn him enough for a clear view. He wiped dirt and grass from the man's face. "Why... it's not possible. Clint Webster? Top, we need you!"

The man didn't open his eyes, only groaned.

Allie rushed over and helped carry the man back to the campsite. He offered him a drink, a little at a time. Webster reached for more, but the sergeant held it back. "Hold on now.

Let's see what's wrong with ye." He examined him more closely. "Oh me, not one leg, but both of 'em shot up." Allie let out a whistle. "Would ye just see this."

Webster's eyes pleaded. He managed, "Help me... please."

"Clint? It's Mark McCrae. Who did this to you?"

"McCrae? How did—?"

"Never mind that. What happened?"

"Apaches, some hours ago. They'll be back... for more guns." Webster tried lifting himself up on his elbow but fell.

"He's unconscious, Mark. Hurry with that fire, men!"

They carried the injured man to the camp area where Allie slid a rolled blanket under Webster's head. "Son, did he mean what I think? Sounds like the wagon's close by."

"With a little light still in the sky, maybe we can find it. Jeb, you and Lafferty come with me." For a moment, Mark watched Allie get started with Webster.

"I'll see what I can do for him." Allie removed the blood-dried leather thongs Webster had used for tourniquets, and then cut away his pant legs. "Two bullets bore clean through. Other one's still in ye." He pulled out his knife and seared it on the flame. Ever since Mark's injury, he carried laudanum on patrol—and more whiskey.

"You're doing good, Top. Funny I should care what happens to him. We'll have to look for the wagon without directions." Fortunately, it didn't take long.

Only a few yards from where Webster had lain, Lafferty called out, "Here it is, sir!" He began throwing brush and limbs away, uncovering the box wagon, still three-quarters full of pine coffins. "Lieutenant, a wheel's off. No wonder they left it."

Mark unsheathed his Bowie and pried open one of the boxes, letting the lid fall to the ground. "Winchesters, and lots of them."

"And crates of ammunition," Jeb said.

Mark kicked away some pieces of wood. "Couple broken coffins on the ground. Must've taken as much as they could carry." He paused and turned to Jeb. "Why didn't they kill Webster? Doesn't make sense."

"Well, sir, he probably never thought they'd turn on him. To shoot a man in both legs is a mighty mean thing to do, 'specially if'n you leave him without a horse. He couldn't go nowhere but through death's door."

"I'll have two men fix that wheel and another stand watch. Won't leave the horses picketed far. We can sleep a few hours and hitch the wagon before dawn. We'll be long gone before the Apaches are back."

By the time the men finished repairing the wheel, Allie had removed the bullet from Webster's leg. "It's too early to tell about him living or dying, but I'll get nourishment down him before we leave, when and if he's able."

Mark and Allie dug out their tin plates and headed over to Lafferty's special supper.

"Now then, Son. Tell me who this Clint Webster is. Friend of yours?"

"Not by a long shot. He wanted nothing better than to see me booted out of West Point, or kill me, whichever came first." Mark shook his head and grinned. "If you notice the slant to his nose, you're seeing results of our personal disagreements. The Point kicked him out for his own bad deeds, but I sure don't know how he wound up deserving this."

After supper, Mark glanced once more at their surroundings. "Time to bed down, men. It's been a long day."

"That meal was pretty dang good. Nothin' like eatin' whiskey," Jeb said. He and Allie sat and talked while the sergeant filled his pipe and lit it.

Jeb brought out a tobacco sack. He wrinkled his nose at Allie's pipe and rolled a smoke.

"Top, we'll have the wagon out in the morning. You and Horse can handle that for us?"

"Right ye are. I can see the colonel's face now—us riding in with all these Winchesters. I'll make a wager they're supposed to be ours anyway."

"Webster looks peaceful enough. I'm going to turn in." Mark walked around to the other side of the fire and made a pillow of his saddle, in earshot of his father's conversation.

"Allie, what're you gonna do when that son of yours goes back to New York?" Jeb asked. "You two make a dang good team."

"Guess I haven't let myself think about it. When he told his mother and me about the offer, she had to change upset to joy, for his and Amanda's sake. We just had the one child, ye know, so it's hard to let go of him a second time. 'Course, they can come back if they don't like it. For sure, the colonel's happy about it though."

Jeb stared thoughtfully into the low-burning fire. "He's got a sweet little bride, he has. Reminds me of my wife, blue eyes and all."

"A wife? Ye had a wife? Why, Jeb Speck, in all the years I've known ye, ye never said."

"Yep. Had me a boy, too. Lost 'em both to the cholrey." He paused a moment, then continued, "That's why I joined up. I thought it'd let me forget, but it didn't."

"Jeb, I'm sorry. Only had I known—"

"No, no. That's okay. It's been a long time. My sister said she'd tend after their graves. Always meant to go back but never had the chance."

"Did ye ever have a yen to marry again? Fine upstanding man like yourself?"

"Nah. By the time I ever thought about it, I figured no gal'd take to an ol' codger like me." Jeb turned over, pulling his blanket up to his chin. "Now g'night, an' don't wake me up, less'n she's real pretty."

Allie smiled and soon went to sleep. So did Mark.

Chapter 35

Jeb reached over and jabbed the sergeant on the shoulder.

"What is it?" Allie whispered.

The corporal lowered his voice to a murmur. "Remember that time we was leavin' Jefferson Barracks and thought we heard Indians comin'? Turned out to be buffalo?"

"Aye. Thanks for wakin' me with that little reminder."

"No, no, listen to the ground. It don't sound big, but since there ain't no buffalo up here, reckon we're fixin' to have company."

Mark raised up. "I hear it too."

At the same time, the private on sentry duty ran straight to Mark. "Lieutenant McCrae, I thought if an Apache don't want you to hear him, you won't, but all the same—"

"Wake the men and keep them quiet." Mark tugged on his boots. Rifle in hand, he moved around to Allie and Jeb. "What do you two make of it?"

"Dawn's close enough for an attack," Allie said. "And they'll be after killing us all."

"I'd take a dim view of that." This time Mark was the hunted and didn't like the feeling.

He shifted his attention to the sound but couldn't discern an Indian for the dry grass blowing in the early breeze. Then he saw them, and they were loud. Apaches headed for the stream, yelling and whooping as they drew nearer.

A rifle shot split the air.

Allie fired and dropped an Apache in the water. The horse struggled to regain its footing. "No way to tell how many Indians. They sound like a muster of howling coyotes."

"Dang, it's still kinda dark. But we'll get 'em afore they get us... mebbe."

Mark took aim. He hoped it was the enemy and not a dancing shadow. "Judging from the shots, we're outnumbered, unless it's their Winchesters talking."

Cavalry Springfields barked, black powder whispering from their barrels.

In the shaft of moonlight hovering over the cliff, Lafferty made a clean target when he stood to fire. Down he went with a shriek—the first trooper to fall.

"Now, why did ye go and do that?" Allie yelled. He scored a direct hit, plugging the Apache who shot his friend right between the eyes.

"Top, I'm going for rifles and ammunition." Mark berated himself for not passing out rifles sooner, but he never dreamed the Indians would come before dawn.

"Boy, be careful. If they see ye..."

Mark lowered himself to a near crawl and made for the wagon. He reached into the one open coffin, fumbling until he dragged out six or seven rifles. One clattered to the ground, and he froze. Nobody noticed with all the shooting coming from the semi-darkness. He grabbed a small box of ammunition and would come back for more.

Two braves raced across the stream. A peal of rifle fire struck one and knocked the other off his horse right before a third rode over him.

"I never heard so much whoopin' from a small bunch of Indians. If I dinna know better, I'd think they had their bellies full of pinther juice. Maybe they do." A bullet ripped through the top of Allie's cap. He snatched it off and howled, "Why I'll—"

"Top, watch it!" The next shot again barely missed the sergeant's head. "Here! Take this rifle."

Quickly loading the sleek new Winchester, Allie let go a full volley. "Begorrah! This is some kind of weapon!"

"Jeb, pass these rifles out and get some more ammunition."

Then, silence.

Wait! "Hold your fire, men" Mark ordered. "They're withdrawing."

Horse rose to his knees. "Why we not leave now, Sergeant?"

Allie motioned to him. "Stay down! If we pull out now, we'll be easy targets."

"While they're doing whatever it is they're doing," Mark said, "we've got business of our own. "Four of you men come with me." He led them to the wagon. They struggled to roll it to the picketed animals. "Hitch 'em up and be quick!"

A soldier ran toward them. "Lieutenant! The Apaches, they've set fire to the grass. What's our next move, sir? They're gonna box us in."

Already engulfing the dry grass, flames spread toward the campsite. "Get some help and. see everyone has a Winchester. Then carry all the cartridge boxes you can and spread the ammunition the length of the campsite. On the double."

"By dang," Jeb snapped, "if'n they came back to get this stuff, I guess we can be right gracious about lettin' 'em have it."

"With wind blowing from the east," Mark said, "they'll think the smoke'll block us in before the fire runs out of grass."

As three of the soldiers spread the ammunition, Mark added the remaining boxes near the exit point where their trail took a slight curve. He watched Apaches line up on the far side of the stream. "Fire will reach the ammo in minutes. Be ready!"

He and the men scrambled and found two downed troopers, plus Clint Webster. Not sure if they were alive or dead, they loaded them in the wagon between the coffins. "Come on, Top."

"Not until I find Lafferty!" The sergeant began searching near where his friend fell.

"Lafferty, where are ye?" he asked in a hoarse whisper. "Answer me, ye hardheaded mick!"

Mark hesitated but knew they couldn't, or wouldn't, leave him. "Did you hear that, Top?"

"Aye." Allie followed a faint sound to where his friend lay.

"Don't leave us now, Lafferty. Hold on, ye hear?"

Allie ran back toward Mark. "Son, he's hurt bad."

"Are you sure he's alive? Our time's running out."

"Yes, yes. He's still breathin', but I don't know for how long. Ye got to come."

Mark swung down from his horse. The two of them managed to carry the Irishman to the wagon, and with help, lowered him into an empty coffin.

"Lafferty, if ye wake up in there, don't worry. It's only temporary."

It was close to daylight, but the first rays had not yet appeared over the eastern mountain.

"Get ready, men. A year's worth of ammunition's planted back there. We go as soon as the show starts. If there's enough left of them to follow us, we have all the rifle support we need."

The fire had cleared the grasses, leaving nothing but smoke. Apaches charged for the campsite right when the ammunition erupted like booming thunder, exactly as Mark planned.

"Move out!"

Allie whipped the horses to a full gallop. The scout sat beside him, rifle ready. Troopers rode behind, leading the extra mounts. Mark and Jeb stayed close to the wagon.

The soldiers flung themselves forward on their horses and headed to Hellsgate as the trail fled behind them.

Chapter 36

Mark stood by Clint Webster's cot in the fort hospital where Dr. Wilcox had taken preliminary care of him.

"He's awake now, Lieutenant. He's doing pretty well, considering."

Mark looked down at the wounded man. "Clint, I'm glad you're better. I still don't—"

"You have to understand, Mark, my father was... is, a proud man." Webster turned on the hospital cot, trying unsuccessfully to shift his legs. "For generations my ancestors were military— the Revolution, 1812, War between the States. And now look at me, McCrae."

"I can see you took a detour."

"When I didn't prove myself at the Academy, it was more than my father could take, having his son kicked out of West Point. He returned my letters. I couldn't go home."

"I hope you had a good reason for supplying guns to the Apaches."

"It wasn't my first choice, but the chance for gunrunning came up, and I needed a bank account from somewhere. I wanted to show my father I could make it without his help."

Reflecting on the events of the last two days, Mark wondered why he was even having this conversation.

Clint stared, as if into nothing. "And instead, you saved my life. What do you think they'll do to me?"

"I don't have an answer. I hope we didn't save your life only to have you lose it."

"I'll be lucky to keep both my legs. For now, I'll just lie on this cot, waiting for whatever happens next. I'm sorry, Mark, for everything."

"I'm sorry, too, Clint."

~~~

"Rider in!" the sentry yelled. The gates of the fort swung open.

The trooper rushed through. "Where's Lieutenant McCrae? I've got to see him." Taking the signal from the sentry, Private

Dolan galloped straight to headquarters. "Lieutenant McCrae!" At the sound of the commotion, Mark and Allie sprang to the porch.

The harried private, panic in his eyes, climbed from his horse, gasping. "The patrol, sir. They wiped us out! Everybody—"

"For God's sake," the colonel blurted, coming from his office. "What is it?"

"Sir, we didn't have a chance." The private gulped water from his canteen, soaking his shirt. "We were ambushed. Draco and his men was waitin' for us about six miles this side of the Walters' place. When they finished with us, I s'pose they went on to the Walters.

"Lieutenant Whitfield," Mark said. "Is he—"

"That's just it, Lieutenant. They slaughtered everybody, except me an' him. Only reason Draco let me go was so's I could bring you a message. I don't know why me, it just was."

Mark grabbed his arm. "What's the message, Dolan?"

"Sir, I'm tryin'. He said tell you he'd kill Lieutenant Whitfield unless you fight him." The private swayed, catching onto the porch railing.

"Fight him? When? And where?"

"Colonel, can I sit down? I'm plum—"

"Yes, yes. Sit down." Colonel Blair shoved a chair under him.

"Draco said to meet him in two days at the Treaty Rocks. His exact words were, 'Saber against lance until death.' If you win, Lieutenant Whitfield goes free. And if you don't, well, he dies, right along with you. That's all he said, sir."

"What about the rest of the men. No one left alive?" the colonel asked.

"No, sir, all of 'em dead. It was awful. All those men..."

Mark took no time in responding, "That's it, I'm going, and Dolan, I'm glad you're safe."

"Then you're not going alone," Allie said.

~~~

Mark hadn't seen Amanda yet, and now he had to face telling her he was leaving again.

She turned pale when he told her of the massacre. "But why can't soldiers rescue Jerry?"

"Because if they tried, Draco would slit his throat before they even got close." He placed his hands on her shoulders. "You understand, Amanda. I have to go."

Tears brimming, she turned from him. "It's nothing but a duel, Mark. It's barbaric. But yes, you have to go." She reached up and kissed him. "I love you."

"And I love you. But now, I best be sure my saber is in top shape." Taking the weapon from the corner of the room, he headed to the fort blacksmith.

Angus McDuff stood a head taller than Mark. His well-muscled arms stretched the sleeves of his faded blue shirt. The red glow of the iron heated the room, and sweat poured like a river down the smithy's back.

Mark told him of his upcoming encounter. "What I need is a keen edge on the business side of my weapon. I'd like you to check it out."

The big Scotsman complied. "Hand 'er over, Lieutenant. You know what the men think of these things. It's all in knowing how to use it. From what I hear, you do. That's the difference." McDuff took the saber and studied it. "But this is heavier, Lieutenant."

"My personal weapon, Angus, not regular issue."

"I'm glad to hear that, with you getting ready to plow into maybe a ten-foot lance. The blade's in perfect shape, but that's not what I'm concerned about."

Suddenly anxious, Mark leaned over to have a look. "Why? What's wrong?"

"A keen edge won't be much help when the grip is loose. Look, I'll show you." He held it toward Mark and pointed to a weak spot right at the cross guard.

"But I didn't see that. Didn't feel it either."

"Well, you'd sure notice once you got to flailing it around. Probably come loose. I'll weld it, that is, if you don't mind a little patch-job. Won't take long."

"By all means."

"Like I said, the blade's fine. I'll just give it a little buffing." When finished, he handed it back to Mark.

Mark touched his fingers to the edge. "You know, I think I can shave with this."

The big Celt laughed. "Hold on a minute." He began searching for something and finally came up with a book tucked away in a wooden chest. "Ah, here it is. I knew it was here someplace.

He turned to a page, showing the map of Scotland. He brought out a dried four-leaf clover and handed it to Mark.

"Lieutenant, I've had this a while. Your father thinks lucky clovers come only from Ireland."

"I do thank you, McDuff. If I come back from this one, your lucky charm worked, dried or not.

"My best goes with you, laddie."

~~~

Mark noticed Amanda remained quiet through supper. They had already talked of their new life at West Point and of the cottage they would have to themselves. If the apple trees were plentiful, as Mark had said, she would bake many *takon chito* pies for him. He had taught her a few Choctaw words. He also told her of the swimming hole off the Hudson, and of furry squirrels chasing each other around the tree trunks. All this they had anticipated.

Tears filled her eyes as she stood. "I understand, Mark. I only wish we had already left for New York."

"If they still want me, we can be a little late." Mark held her close, not wanting to let go.

"Sweetheart, you're shaking. It'll be all right."

"I know you have to leave, but I'm afraid. Afraid for us."

"I don't fear death, Amanda. Only life without you."

During the night, Mark drifted in and out of sleep. He pictured Draco's lance—different from the white man's. He would make it from a long *sotol* stalk and possibly with a bayonet for a blade. If not metal, mountain mahogany—filed to a sharpened point—either just as deadly.

Mark knew his own expertise with a saber. *After all, I learned it at West Point, and they want me back for what they taught me.* In a burst of imagination, he settled on one specific strategy. He would have at least a fifty-fifty chance.

At first light, Mark prepared to depart. He soothed Amanda's worry with a kiss. Her anxious face reflected her troubled mind.

"Remember my love, a saber is as reliable as the man using it."

Amanda released her grip on him. "How much more can I take? Come back to me, Mark."

~~~

After saying goodbye to Amanda, Mark saddled his horse. He thought of his words to her the night before. *If there's any way at all, m'love, I'll return.*

Allie joined his son. Worry marred his features, dulled his blue eyes. "I guess we're ready. "One thing I have to tell ye, though. I went by to see Lafferty. It seems like we're keeping our cook after all. He insulted me right off, so I know he's going to make it."

"That's great news, Top. Another tough Irishman."

"Ye know, Son, I'm not sure it's right not to tell your mother what you're up to."

"Maybe so, Top, but I'll take odds on winning this fight, and she would've worried all for nothing."

The two soldiers rode out, not knowing if either or both would return from the Treaty Rocks. As the sentry closed the gates, a voice startled Mark. "Lieutenant McCrae?"

Mark and Allie drew to a halt.

To the left, a lone rider sat atop a big roan. By reflex, Mark put his hand on his revolver.

Taking one look at the man, he said, "Zeke Berne, is that you?"

When Zeke rode close, Mark stretched over to shake the cowboy's hand.

"It's me all right, boy. I wanted to see for myself that you'd pulled out of it. Now I see you did, I'll be on my way."

"I thought ye might've gone on to the Walters' place, but was sure hoping ye hadn't, Aloy—I mean Zeke," Allie said."

"Fact was, I did. After the ambush. Them Apaches must have lost a few of their own. Big posse from Globe ran into them, but they were too late to help the soldiers. What few Apaches was left retreated outta there."

"Where you off to, Zeke?" Mark asked.

"I seen me a place once... Sonoma Valley. That's where I'll be headin', if I can get there in one piece. 'Course, I'm in one piece right now because of you, Lieutenant. Thanks again."

After saying goodbye, Zeke turned his horse—this time for California.

"Aloysius Ezekial. Aye, a mighty fine name."

Chapter 37

Mark and Allie picked up the gait to a fast walk toward the Treaty Rocks. "Ye know, Son, Draco's put you through a lot, but this time, it's going to be close up."

Mark looked over at his father as if he hadn't thought of the comparison. "It's not that I'm scared, but I'm sure as hell a little bit nervous."

He told Allie his plan necessitating their early arrival. Stopping twice to rest the horses, they continued until familiar landmarks came into view. In a couple hours, the rising field of boulders loomed before them. Mark dismounted, and walking slowly, he defined a space he hoped would soon be a death arena for Draco.

"This layout seems about right. The grade should work, but I need one more thing." He found what he wanted—a flat-topped stone wedged between two larger round ones. Allie helped him carry it to the lower part of the boulder field, where Mark twisted it into the ground. "That should be perfect."

"From your plan I'd say it's the stone ye need. I'd draw a line in the dirt far enough away, so when ye see the line, ye'll know where the stone is without actually seeing it."

"Right. I knew there was cause for bringing your Irish self along." Mark made a narrow line about eight feet long in the sand. He made it a bit crooked, so if Draco noticed it at all, he might think a snake was responsible.

The stage set, Mark gazed out onto the plains that seemed larger because of the vast silence. Two riders, one leading the other's horse, came into view from the north.

"See... over the ridge there. I believe we have company."

First came the giant Draco, then Jerry Whitfield, hands tied behind him. Three more Apaches followed, keeping their distance.

"Would ye look at that, Son? Sure and begorrah. The sonuvabitch looks to be seven feet tall."

"Thanks for pointing that out, Top."

Allie reached over and clasped Mark on the shoulder. "Get this donnybrook over as soon as you can."

"My plan exactly."

As Jerry came closer, he didn't need to speak. Mark could see the desperation in his eyes.

The big Apache dropped the reins of Whitfield's horse and rode to where the McCraes stood. Dismounting, he leaned upon the red and blue lance as if it were indestructible. "You not so smart, McCrae. You missed lookout at my camp. We showed your army good."

"So that's how you knew to ambush our patrol. Very heroic, Draco." *The sentry must've been the noise I heard back when I got shot.* "But what about the men you brought? This fight is only for us."

"Draco does not bring. They come watch. What does other bluecoat do here?"

"He is my father and will take my body to the fort if you're lucky enough to down me."

The Apache drew back his shoulders. "McCrae, you ride ghost pony by time sun set. If you good enough kill Draco, leave where I fall. Choctaw soldier not defeat this warrior. We begin."

Mark placed himself within the starting area he had chosen. *Point—saber!* It seemed a puny weapon beside the ten-foot lance. He sidestepped toward the center of the clearing.

Draco followed as if on a tether. He held his lance close, the last two feet of it tucked behind his elbow.

Mark reached the line in the dirt, ready to put his plan into action.

The Apache continued gesturing with his weapon as he moved to the next boulder.

This isn't working. He's moving too far away.

Draco turned, his eyes holding a fixed glow of fire. He thrust the lance.

Mark leapt aside. The deadly blow barely missed. He badgered the giant into his planned arena then moved down the slope. *Where's the line? I don't see it!* Taking another step back, Mark slipped on the very stone he put there earlier. Pain exploded down his leg. He forced it away and scrambled to his feet, moving sideways.

Draco charged, waving his lance in a circular motion.

Like a whirling dust devil, Mark exaggerated cuts in the air. *Keep watching the saber, Draco, not me.*

On the opposite side of the buried stone, Mark exposed his left side for a split second. The Apache took the bait and made the expected lunge.

Mark stepped away as the lance overshot the stone. It wedged into the large boulder just above.

Confusion flashed across Draco's face, but he was too slow.

Mark slammed his saber downward onto the shaft. The stone made a perfect fulcrum. The wood cracked.

Draco shrieked and wrenched the lance from its place.

Mark anticipated the next thrust. For a second, he imagined the hoped-for split growing wider as it approached Draco's hand.

The Apache lifted his weapon, eyes wild with fury.

Mark resumed the frenzied slashes and brought the saber across the weakened lance. He said a silent prayer for Angus McDuff. His weapon struck the knot of the sinewy thong.

When Draco raised his lance, all he had was a shaft with the pointed head dangling almost free from the end. His startled expression made it obvious he never expected the bluecoat to be so clever. He swung the shaft at Mark, striking him across the side of the head.

The saber flew from Mark's hand. He fell against the boulders.

The Apache lunged. With both hands, he pressed the lance across Mark's throat.

Every nerve string in Mark's body responded. One strong leg wasn't enough to push the Apache away. No time for indecisions. He'd try. Drawing his knees up, he kicked out with all the power he could muster, propelling Draco back.

Dragging himself upright, Mark grabbed his saber. He managed a roundhouse swing. His blade struck with a sickening thud.

Three fingers dropped to the sand, blood gushing from Draco's slashed knuckles. The Apache drew back, pain scrawled over his face. He made no sound. He glanced down at his hand and his eyes widened. Then, desperate, he reached for the lance with his other hand. He aimed the splintered shaft at Mark. It missed by inches.

Still several feet from his rival, Mark made ready to move in with a final strike of the saber. His head throbbed.

Even the sighing wind had stopped.

Breathless, Mark said, "I should have killed you at the gorge. Now your warriors can tell your people how the great Draco met his end at the hands of a half-blood."

While scrambling backward, the Apache tore a leather thong from his leggings and tried to twist it around his bleeding hand. "Your bluecoats will not win."

"Perhaps they will."

"You have Draco trapped. Show your strength now." As strong as he was, the Apache seemed to weaken, waiting for the deathblow.

The time had come—the chance Mark had waited for. He hesitated. From the other side of the rocks, Jerry called out. "Kill him, or let me have the pleasure."

Draco quickly turned his back and reached for a knife from his leggings.

"Face me, Draco!"

"You not kill this warrior." He spun around and took aim.

Jerry shouted, "Watch out, Mark!"

In one movement, Mark dropped his saber and drew his Bowie. He flung the razor-sharp weapon at his foe. The blade disappeared deep into Draco's chest. The Apache's throw went wild as he cried out, his death song curdling in his throat. His face contorting in disbelief, he pitched forward onto the rocks.

Exhausted, Mark stared down at the Apache but only for a moment. His encounter now finished with Draco, he walked over to Lieutenant Whitfield and untied his ropes. He gripped Jerry's hand. "Thanks, friend. I owe you."

"You've already paid it."

"Are ye all right, Son?" Allie rushed over to him. "That's a lump growing on your head there."

Mark touched it. "Doesn't hurt a bit. I'll live."

Allie pointed toward Draco's three companions. "We best leave. They will take care of him and will not speak his name again."

"Well, I guess this is what we came for," Mark said. He glanced a last time at the Apache. "Have we further business here?"

"Perhaps a little," Jerry dismounted and walked over to the fallen Indian, rolling him over with his booted foot. He withdrew the Bowie knife and wiped it clean. "You may be needing this." He handed it to Mark.

"Maybe, but I hope not."

With an Irish grin, Allie said, "I meself can't think of a reason, but ye never know when something might turn up." He reached over and clasped his arms around Mark. "Remember, Son, a man has a choice. He is either good or evil, no matter his heritage."

Allie's words gave him a certain peace he'd been longing for. Breathing a grateful sigh, Mark mounted his horse. He thought that, after the dust and blood settled, perhaps there would be no more killing with the Apaches. Without Draco, the attacks on settlers like the Shults and Walters might cease. He wondered if Victorio would find his pleasant valley where the grass is green and the game plentiful. Somehow, he doubted it.

"Prepare to move out!" Mark mounted his horse and booted his saber. With Allie by his side, the three men turned toward Hellsgate.

As they approached the fort, Mark could think only of long blonde hair and blue eyes.

www.ingramcontent.com/pod-product-compliance
Lightning Source LLC
Chambersburg PA
CBHW071307250626
47159CB00004B/1335